About the Author

Grace Heathers uses her fiction to peek through the curtains of suburban homes and expose the dark secrets inside.

When not writing, Grace devours psychological thrillers and mysteries by her favourite authors - and major inspirations - Patricia Cornwell, Nicci French and Lee Child, amongst others. She also enjoys travelling, watching crime boxsets and taking long walks in nature, during which she plots the next macabre twists her stories will take.

She lives in Staffordshire with her husband, son and two cats. She can be reached at GraceHeathers.com

An Inconvenience is the first in the Edith Rose Brown series. The second, A Mind Without a Voice, is coming soon.

AN INCONVENIENCE

GRACE HEATHERS

First edition March 2024
Paperback ISBN 978-1-0686679-0-9
Hardback ISBN 978-1-0686679-1-6

Thank you to my amazing husband and beautiful son for helping me see a brighter side of life and giving me the confidence to be myself.

Thank you also to the fantastic editor Nicky Lovick for your patience, humour, and guidance.

The worst thing is the helplessness,
when you have no control, and that pit is in your stomach, and
sickness in your throat.

Each knock back,
each defamation,
each time you can't speak out and say,
'NO'.

And you just want to scream until there's nothing left.

But you can't.

You just take it and smile and hold back the tears,
because any retaliation, even eye contact,
triggers more, and you don't want more.

So, you're quiet, and compliant, and accept:

this is your lot.

No one will ever know the beauty inside you,
because all they can see is the ugliness he's left behind.

No one can see you; no one can hear you.
Invisible.
That's all,
a shadow,
a whisper.

An inconvenience.

Chapter 1

'Mr James, can you think of any reason, even if it seems trivial, why your wife would be catching that train?'

Liam shook his head slowly.

'Has she any relatives or friends she would be visiting?' The officer waited.

'No,' he answered quietly. 'I've told you, I think she's been taken, or something's happened to her. I can feel it.' He put his head in his hands.

'That is a line of enquiry we're taking seriously, Mr James, but we do need to explore all avenues.'

Liam nodded.

'Could there have been an appointment you may not have known about? Or, do you have any birthdays or anniversaries coming up? Could she have been on her way to buy something to surprise you? Or organise?'

This was the fourth time in three days he'd been asked the same questions, over and over again. Liam was sitting on his sofa opposite the officer in an armchair. *How many more times will she ask?* he thought to himself. There was no one; Liam couldn't think of anyone, or anything, and he'd kept telling them that. 'No, no one. Nothing.' He stood up, frustrated with how long it was taking them.

The police had been with him nearly two hours this time, asking the same questions over and over.

Did they have any problems in their relationships, any arguments, no matter how minor?

What were the names of Hannah's close friends?

Did she get on with all of your friends?

How often did she go to the gym? Did she have any friends there, or maybe instructors she spoke of?

What was her daily routine? Where did she shop? Did they eat out? Where did they go?

They went on and on; he kept telling them, then he told them again. 'I got up. Hannah was half-asleep so I took a coffee up to her, gave her a kiss and left for work at 6:30am, as I do every day, and that was the last time I saw her. This is ridiculous, I can't give you anymore. I don't know anything else.' He sighed.

He'd repeated his story over and over. He hadn't heard from her all day, which was unusual. She always texted him when she got to work, less than a mile from home at a cafe in Lichfield. She always FaceTimed him at lunch and chatted to him on her breaks when he was free. Liam would ring her on his way home to let her know if he was stuck in traffic, and she'd always time dinner so they could eat together. When he hadn't heard from her after a couple of hours, he sent her a text:

love you, guess you're busy, have a great day x

By lunchtime she hadn't called him, as she normally did, so Liam rang her – no answer, and he'd started to worry. He'd rung her work about 2:30pm and spoken to Jane, her boss. That's when he learned she hadn't even been to work. When Liam couldn't get hold of her, he'd driven home from central Birmingham where he worked.

At home he'd checked their CCTV and saw Hannah leaving the house at 7:06am. That didn't make sense because her shift didn't start until 9:00am, and it only took her fifteen minutes to walk to work. Why had she left so early?

The police had checked the location tracker they both had on their phones; it was turned off. They tried Find My iPhone – no luck. There had been no calls or texts to Liam since she'd left that morning and Hannah's phone, it seemed, was switched off. None of her bank cards had been used. Liam told the police he'd checked them immediately, and the accounts; no withdrawals, no transfers, no unusual pending transactions. Apart from the clothes Hannah was seen wearing on CCTV, nothing else of hers was gone.

Liam couldn't give them any more information than he already had. He'd told them everything he could. They were still none the wiser, and Hannah was no closer to being home.

Chapter 2

Initially, a young PC, Adam Sturges had interviewed him, but Liam had broken down and started crying uncontrollably. Adam said he'd felt out of his depth, so he'd asked his officer in charge, Detective Chief Inspector Rachel Taylor, if she could step in. Rachel was already annoyed she'd been allocated Adam. The response to the apprenticeship scheme had been mostly negative from the rest of the force, particularly those like her who felt the newbies would inevitably get fast-tracked over and above those with years of experience. And now, here she was looking after Adam because someone higher up the chain had apparently spotted his potential. She hadn't seen any potential though. *If you want something done right, do it yourself.*

Since then, DCI Taylor had spent hours with Liam trying to understand more about Hannah, about them as a couple, to try and get some inkling of what had happened. Although Liam had reported his wife missing, he was immediately a suspect – the spouse always is – but his behaviour, his consistency and his desperation since the first call to 999, suggested he wasn't responsible for Hannah's disappearance; he seemed genuinely distraught.

His eyes were raw-red and sore-looking, and when he wasn't crying he'd stare into space, shaking his head. He certainly gave the impression that he couldn't believe Hannah was gone, but both protocol and experience had taught Rachel to treat Liam as prime suspect. Rachel assessed him as he answered her questions, watching him move through the spectrum of emotions, looking for any hint that he knew more than he was letting on; that things hadn't been as rosy as he'd said and Hannah had just left him, or, worse, he'd done something to her.

Three days had passed now and there was still no word or clue about Hannah's whereabouts. At first, they'd assumed she was a leaver or had just got caught up or delayed somewhere. They told Liam to be patient, see if she turned up. He wasn't happy. They'd advised him it was unusual to investigate so early on for a missing adult. Nine times out of ten they turn up within a few hours. It was only Liam's insistence that she'd been taken that made them look deeper. It was clear from what Liam had said that this was out of character for her and there was no obvious reason for Hannah to leave. *But why had she left early that day?* It niggled away at her. Also, the CCTV evidence from the station had been recovered the previous day by Adam as part of the investigation and he'd noticed the red rucksack, which Rachel begrudgingly gave him credit for. Hannah didn't have it when she left the house, so she'd picked it up on her way to the station, somewhere. Adam had gone to the cafe where Hannah worked, but the owner had said that even though Hannah had an alarm fob, she didn't have any way of knowing if she'd used it that morning; the alarm was old and didn't keep history. Adam had told her they'd be back in touch if they needed more information and Rachel had decided she'd lead that interview too – after she'd spoken to Liam yet again.

Liam had painted them a picture of Hannah's life; it seemed she was a home-bird. She didn't go out much, was a bit reclusive even, Liam had suggested. He'd said he'd tried to encourage her to get out more and meet people, but she liked her own space and was very happy. Apart from working at the Cathedral View Cafe in Lichfield, she didn't go anywhere else unless Liam suggested it and went with her.

'We have a great life together,' he'd said. 'We have loads of holidays, we plan for the future, talk about our retirement and, yes, like any couple we have our ups and downs, but I can't think of anything recently that could have caused a problem.'

'What sort of plans?'

'Well, where to start?' Liam paused and smiled, unexpectedly.

'Hannah was researching resorts for our next holiday. She'd been saying for ages that she wanted to go to Sri Lanka, maybe go to an elephant sanctuary. Oh and, of course, the big one; we're planning to have a baby.' Liam choked as he said it, his eyes filled again.

Rachel nodded, feeling a glimmer of compassion.

'I know you think she's left me, but she hasn't. You don't plan to have a baby if you're unhappy, do you?' He looked at Rachel, eyes hollow with grief.

Rachel knew people had babies in all sorts of circumstance and it wasn't always an indication of a happy life.

'And we're planning an extension for when the baby comes,' Liam carried on. 'Hannah wanted the house finished first, then start a family.

Everything she did centred around us; having a baby, a new chapter in our lives. She said she'd finish work so she could focus all her energy on bringing up our family. Not that she needed to work; I provide enough.'

Rachel nodded and added to her notes. 'Thank you.'

Chapter 3

Liam couldn't think straight, he was tired, emotional and angry. He'd been asked the same questions over and over again and the days and sleepless nights were merging into one another. The first officer they'd sent seemed useless, he looked about twelve, but this one, Rachel, seemed to have more about her and her questions made him think back to when he'd first met Hannah: on the last day of his old job five years ago; the turning point in his life.

He was out with his team at JoJo's in Brindley Place, celebrating his promotion. The team was all-male, fuelled by testosterone, working their way round the available, and often unavailable, women in the office. He was moving on and up in the company, and his team knew it was good for them; it paved the way for their own promotions. Keeping in with the boss and sucking up was the culture in Liam's team. They pandered to his demands and laughed at his jokes, and although most of them thought he was a knob, he wasn't someone they'd challenge. Liam knew this, but he didn't care – the atmosphere he'd instilled was one that he'd grown up in; work hard, play hard. He hadn't been given an easy ride so why should anyone else? It earned him, and them, big bonuses, those that didn't fit went elsewhere.

They'd been drinking in JoJo's for five hours solid, since 6pm, and were at varying levels of drunkenness. Liam stood up, swaying slightly, to get more drinks, flashing his cash and new-promotion generosity.

And there she was.

Hannah had her back to him, behind the bar serving some loser who was pissed out of his head. The place was busy and loud, the music blaring with the usual Friday night after work drinkers. Liam pushed through the throng, sidling in next to her customer, hoping to jump the queue. As she worked, filling glasses from the optics, Liam checked out the long blonde hair skimming a bare waist where her crop top ended. He followed the curve of her spine down to her hips as she turned round and caught him looking at her bum. 'Can I help you?' She smiled.

Caught red-handed.

He looked up, startled, and was struck by her turquoise eyes. He couldn't remember anyone with such beautiful eyes, and the body to go with it. She was much younger than him, he thought. Early twenties, maybe; younger even.

Although Liam knew he wasn't too shabby-looking, he was older at thirty-five. A confirmed bachelor with a string of exes, he was carrying a bit of weight from too many nights out and trying to live like a nineteen-year-old. He was tanned, but showing the signs of too much UVA from his sunbed addiction, and the first strands of grey were poking through his dark-blond, surfer-style hair.

'So, what can I get for you?'

Liam was so taken with her eyes – it was as though they could see right into his soul – that his usual banter failed him. Normally he'd have come back with some quip and a cheeky hope that they'd be shagging later on, but not tonight. 'Six Jägerbombs, please,' he asked politely.

Liam went back to his team with the round to the usual looks of horror and screwed-up faces, but they all downed them with the standard ritual of 'never again' and 'oh, that was gross'. As his colleagues' football banter got back underway, Liam kept looking over at the girl who'd just served him, but she didn't look up. He liked a challenge.

The night wore on until the early hours, moving from bar to bar. More shots and tales, until the group were blocked from entering one venue for being too drunk, and they gradually dispersed into taxis and by foot.

Liam staggered back to his apartment alone. He had a bachelor's apartment overlooking the canal; one-bedroom, open-plan kitchen–diner, lounge, like so many apartments in the city. It served his lifestyle. It was low maintenance, with laminate floors, and, apart from the odd piece of Ikea, it was pretty spartan. It was largely somewhere for Liam to crash and store his designer wardrobe.

Sunday mornings were Liam's quietest time of the week. He'd get up late, walk down to get breakfast at one of the cafes on the canal. Then he'd spend a good part of the day either watching sport sprawled on his sofa in front of his sixty-inch TV, or reading the news on his iPad with a black coffee on his balcony amongst his dead plants;

blossoming only when his mother first put them there. He'd nurse his weekly hangover as canal life drifted past. Often, he'd see the previous night's revellers hobbling along the paths, leaving apartments. Half-dressed girls doing the walk of shame, still in their short skirts, high heels and make-up halfway down their faces. Their hair no longer pristine, and clearly having had more than a good night's sleep. *Slags,* he'd think, ignoring that often it would be his apartment they might be sneaking out of.

The apartment had seen its fair share of one-night stands, and occasionally longer affairs that either fizzled out, or ended with insults and fireworks, slammed doors, and broken plates.

He'd already decided to look for a new apartment now he'd had his big promotion to director, and he was expecting his life to change. But, at that moment, when he met Hannah for the first time, he didn't realise just how much.

Chapter 4

Relieved at getting back behind the bar after clearing tables, Hannah had had enough of being chatted up and having her bum felt, and here was one more middle-aged jerk thinking he was god's gift. Smile, Hannah, two more hours of this crap and you can go home, she thought to herself, at least you're on the safe side of the bar now.

'So, what can I get for you?' she asked, expecting the usual replies of 'how about you on my face', or 'your legs round my waist'. It never failed to surprise her how unoriginal men could be. Instead, tonight, she just got, 'Six Jägerbombs, please.' Which was a relief. She was tired of having to come up with witty comebacks; setting boundaries but not upsetting the knobheads was company policy.

Hannah served his drinks and sent him on his way. 'Next!' she shouted across the bustling bar as another contender for Drunk of the Year pushed his credit card forward, grabbing her attention.

'Alwight, dawling,' he slobbered and grinned.

Oh joy, she thought and smiled at him.

Hannah's job was a means to an end. At twenty-one, she'd done her stint of travelling before uni, and now she was trying to finish her studies in Art and Design without too much debt. She worked four evening shifts a week in JoJo's and had just managed to get two mornings at Rosie's Cafe on the canal, although she'd be knackered from them, what with bar work the night before, and studying every other second she had spare. She was hoping to build up her shifts between lectures and studying, and at some point she was also trying to fit in the uni life that she'd heard so much about but had so far failed to find.

She enjoyed her studies, but was struggling to fit in with the cliques and unwritten rules. Still, life was busy and unlikely to change anytime soon as she worked, studied and slept.

Hannah's shift ended long before Liam's group finished drinking, and she got a lift back to her grotty shared house. She was just looking forward to a cup of tea and bed – no doubt her other housemates Emily, Sam and Lorna, would still be up; drinking and bitching like they always did. All she wanted was sleep; real, uninterrupted sleep before her early shift at Rosie's started.

Chapter 5

Listening to Liam talk about their plans for the future and starting a family, Rachel drifted for moment. At forty-four, she felt she'd missed the boat. She'd always wanted a family, but it just hadn't happened for her and Jay, her long-term boyfriend; sadly now her ex.

She pushed the thought out of her head and asked Liam, 'Do you know what Hannah wanted to do before you met?'

'What do you mean?' he asked.

'Well, you mentioned she was at uni. What was she doing there, and what did she want to do afterwards?' Rachel asked, thinking that Hannah must have had the ambition to do something before they met. Maybe that's what spurred her to leave; if she had.

'Erm…' Liam thought for a moment. 'Something to do with art, I think. She didn't stick at it for long. To be honest, I'm not really sure.'

'OK, thank you,' Rachel paused again, the cogs in her brain whirring. 'So, do you know why she left? Were there any problems with anyone she knew at uni? Or you mentioned previously that she'd worked in bars and cafes in Birmingham, do you remember any issues back then?'

'No, I don't know why she left. I guess she didn't enjoy it, she never really said.' He shrugged. 'How is this helping? You should be out looking for her,' he added.

'We are, Mr James, but this all helps. I know it doesn't feel like it, but it does.'

Question after question gleaned no new information. Rachel was getting frustrated herself; she nearly always had something to go on, but this case was troubling her. Liam's insistence that she'd been taken didn't ring true; the evidence just didn't stack up to that. On CCTV they could see Hannah get on the train, sit briefly, then stand and move out of sight of the camera. They couldn't see her inside the carriage, or where she got off along the route. Did she meet someone? Did she get off on her own? Had something happened to her recently at work, or on her way to work? Had someone approached her? Was she threatened? *Was* she taken?

The clues Rachel had were: Hannah leaving earlier than normal, not going to work, her getting on the train, and having the rucksack by the time she got to station. CCTV showed she was definitely on her own when she left the house and when she got to the station. With the evidence she had, the strongest possibility was that Hannah had left Liam; it seemed the most logical explanation. Trying to dig deeper with her questioning with Liam was difficult; he seemed very fragile. He was heartbroken, distraught and exhausted; not a good combination when you want to say, 'I think she left you.' To suggest that Hannah may have just upped sticks and gone without so much as a goodbye. It was something he'd probably never imagined, or entertained for a split second. He seemed very much in love and believed Hannah to be so as well. Statistically though, Rachel knew most women die at the hands of someone they know, often their partner. Had Liam found out she was leaving and then killed her? Rachel had been watching him closely for anything that gave him up. But there was nothing.

If Hannah hadn't left him, where was she? She'd obviously left the house herself and got on the train. Was she being coerced? And, if so, for what reason? Had she been kidnapped? Liam seemed fairly well off, but certainly not rich enough by any stretch of the imagination to motivate a ransom demand. Plus, there was no ransom request.

Was Hannah being blackmailed, or Liam? Had either of them got involved in something they shouldn't? Had something in either of their pasts caught up with them? Rachel's experience had taught her never to rule anything out; some people are just a couple of bad decisions away from getting themselves into serious shit.

'Mr James?' Rachel paused. Liam lifted his head slightly to hear the next question.

'If we assume Hannah hasn't chosen to leave, and has potentially been taken, we'd need to assume that there's a reason she's been taken.'

'This is what I keep saying, I'm sure she's been taken, I don't know how many times I have to say it.' His annoyance with Rachel was clear.

'I understand that, but is there anyone you can think of that may bear a grudge or may be unhappy for some reason? Friends, work acquaintances, family, any workmen that have been at the house recently?'

Liam interrupted. 'No, we get on with everyone, unless there's someone at the cafe that I don't know about; a customer, maybe, but I genuinely can't think of anyone. No one comes to mind. This is ridiculous; where is she?' He started crying again.

'OK, thank you.'

She wanted to dig deeper with her next line of questioning, but he needed to calm down.

'Let's have a break for five minutes, shall we? I'll make us a cup of tea,' Rachel said.

Liam nodded as she stood.

What if we're all invisible,

living our own private hell,

waiting to be rescued.

But no one will come.

We have to rescue ourselves.

Chapter 6

Eight of the ten tickets were booked, two left to do and the ferry crossings to book. That should be more than enough to throw him off her scent. The first ticket would be the only one she used.

Hannah had been planning for months. She'd researched where the trains and stations had cameras and what areas to avoid. She'd get on, change in the toilet, and get off two stops later. She knew which buses she'd get that were going in a completely different direction to the train tickets she'd booked online. Then she'd catch another two trains, paid for in cash. She'd saved for twelve months, £2,620.50 in the account Liam didn't know about. Her trip to the Inverness refuge on trains and buses would take about eleven hours and cost £163.40, and she also had to factor in her decoy tickets which cost £208.20. It aggrieved her to waste so much of her measly savings, but it was a necessary evil. Overall, her escape plan would cost £371.60.

£371.60 to freedom.

All made possible through the technology Liam had tried to control her with, but now it was her way out. Hannah's boss, Jane, had tried in vain to get Lichfield to move with the times; she'd installed a laptop and advertised as an Internet cafe. It made little difference to her clientele, who were mostly retired and came in for traditional cafe brunches, lunches and afternoon tea, or office workers who wanted a quick break from technology. The laptop sat idle most of the time; it was only Hannah who really used it before her shift started. It was the least risky time, twenty minutes here and there. Twenty minutes that Liam didn't know about.

She always had to let Liam know where she was; not that she needed to as he had every tracker app possible installed on her phone. She couldn't use the internet after work and stay longer pretending to do overtime; he'd have expected to see more money in her wages and would have questioned her relentlessly. She had to FaceTime him at lunch so he knew where she was, and to make sure she wasn't with anyone, so she couldn't use the internet then. She couldn't Google on her phone; Liam checked her history every night, and he was the only one allowed to clear it. She was only to use her phone to speak to Liam, or text him, but he could read her texts on his iPad anyway, having linked it to Hannah's phone, so nothing was private. Nothing.

Hannah had needed time to plan, so she told him the cafe was struggling and that she was worried she'd lose her job; there was talk of reducing the team. That was a lie, of course, and a big part of her tactics to be able to get the time she needed to use the internet and plan her escape. She suggested to Liam if she went in a bit earlier and showed willing, it might buy her some brownie points with Jane. She knew he'd like that; he wanted her to stay in the job, he had more control over her there. He knew where it was, knew he could turn up at any time once it was open, it was close to home and it had good Wi-Fi, so he could see where Hannah was on his tracking apps. Jane was older, happily married, and he liked that; she was a low threat.

Hannah knew he watched her, checked on her. He made sure of that. She wasn't allowed to have friends outside of the selected few couples that Liam deemed to be safe or who benefited him at work. These so-called friends were so absorbed with themselves that they didn't see what was going on right in front of them. Or, if they did notice, they wouldn't say anything.

Liam was that guy – charismatic, charming, made you feel like a million dollars. He dazzled people and manipulated friendships for his own needs. Hannah was seen as the beautiful, supportive wife who adored her husband. The couple had been put on a pedestal, no doubt the envy of many. Hannah remembered, after a couple they knew announced their divorce, one of their other friends, Nicky, said, 'If you and Liam ever split up, I'd lose my faith in love. You're perfect.' That's what men like Liam created: illusion, and Hannah supported and perpetuated the illusion. If she didn't, she'd pay for it.

If only they knew.

She booked the ferry ticket, the last one she needed to do, and she welled up as she did it, thinking about the enormity of her undertaking and the risks ahead. How had she let it get so bad that she was running, and had to go to these lengths?

Hannah thought back to when it first started, on a Saturday in May. They'd been together about three months, nearly five years ago. Five horrific years of manipulation, coercion, and violence. In hindsight, the day they met was the worst thing that had happened to her, the day that had brought her to where she was now; trying to escape and fearing for her life.

Liam had been into Rosie's a few times and they'd chatted. He was funny, charming, and quite good-looking in an older, rugged kind of way. He wasn't pushy and took his time getting to know her; a real gentleman, she'd thought.

Liam eventually asked her out, talking her into Sunday lunch after her shift at Rosie's.

After that it was a classic whirlwind romance, and she'd started stopping at his most nights as it was more convenient, being close to work. He'd pay for her taxis to get to uni, wined and dined her, and it wasn't long before she was swept away. Hannah had never been treated so well. Liam was funny, intelligent, caring, and soon she wanted to be with him all the time.

He talked her into moving in. 'Just temporarily,' he said, 'it'll save money, and it's practical.' She gave up her room at the shared house and he paid off the rent she owed; it was a relief not having to see her housemates each day. He'd walk her back from the bar after work, laughing and chatting, so she felt safer. Then they'd make love. Hannah's life became entwined with Liam's. They'd been together just three months, but it felt like three years. They were a couple, they were in love, they were a team, and they were unbreakable.

Three months in and Hannah tried to talk Liam into going with her to her friend Jason's twenty-first birthday. He'd said he didn't want to go because he'd feel out of place. Hannah was disappointed, but she could see his point and eventually decided not to go herself. It was on a night that Liam ended up being away from home with work – he'd had to go up to Leeds. Hannah still wanted to go to the party, but she stayed in; she didn't feel right going without him. As he said, they were a couple, and couples do things together.

A week passed and suddenly Liam asked if she'd gone anyway. It was completely out of the blue, and Hannah sensed he was agitated.

'No, you know I didn't,' Hannah replied.

'Look, you can tell me if you did,' Liam answered, sharply.

'I didn't go,' she said, a little shocked that he didn't believe her the first time.

'I won't be angry.' He got more agitated; his speech quick, his voice slightly raised.

'Honestly, I didn't go, why would I lie about it?' Hannah felt herself get defensive; she'd never seen Liam like this before. Had something happened that day to upset him, that made him question her loyalty and love? This wasn't like him at all; not her Liam.

The questioning went on and on, and it didn't matter what Hannah said, he just kept asking her, over and over. 'Look, if you went, I won't be angry, I don't want you to feel you have to lie to me.' Each time he got angrier and louder. It was their first serious argument, and it frightened Hannah. Was she about to lose him, to lose what they had?

She wasn't lying though, why should she? Plus, she wouldn't have gone without him; surely he knew that?

Question after question, and Hannah just kept saying, 'No, I didn't go.' She tried to reassure him that she didn't want to go without him. 'We're a team, we're a couple, we do things together.' She repeated the words he always said to her, but he just carried on and on, questioning her relentlessly.

By now Hannah was crying, and she thought to herself this is it, he's going to dump me, he doesn't trust me. She was exhausted by the argument and after an hour had gone by her eyes were raw with crying and Liam's questions eventually fizzled out.

She thought that was the end of it. It was only the start.

Chapter 7

She checked through the tickets, marked them off against her notes, checked and double-checked. Her mind was distracted, still on that first argument. She needed to focus; she checked again. Everything was booked and in order. One more step to freedom, she thought. If only she'd gotten away from him that first time.

I've wasted years, I can't waste anymore, she thought back to that night again.

The argument had seemed to be over. Liam made a mug of coffee, sat down and leant in to cuddle her, kissing the top of her head. Hannah was reluctant; he was accusing her of going out without him…but was he, really? He was just asking her, wasn't he? She'd become defensive, it was her, not him. She tentatively cuddled him back.

'We're OK, aren't we?' he asked as he held her tighter.

'Of course we are,' Hannah replied quietly, but still wondering where this had come from.

'Let's go and get some food,' Liam said brightly, as though they hadn't been arguing for the best part of an hour.

In an instant he'd changed back to the caring, loving man she knew; she was relieved the argument was over and agreed to go out. She showered and freshened up, covering her puffy eyes and red nose with makeup until she looked good enough to venture outside. She didn't want anyone to see she'd been crying; what if they bumped into someone they knew? She didn't want anyone to think there was anything wrong.

They left the apartment just before 3pm and she kept thinking about the argument as they walked along the canal towpath. Why had he been so concerned? What had she done to make him feel like that? What could she do to make him happier? She tightened her grip on his hand and leant into him. *He must know how much I love him*, she thought to herself; disappointed that maybe he didn't.

They walked down to Brindley Place and it was bustling. One of the food festivals was on with stall after stall of Indian, Caribbean, Mexican, Italian, Chinese, anywhere Hannah could think of was there; the aromas of spices from around the world filled the air around them. They knew where they were headed, however, and what they wanted to eat, but they didn't want to miss out and agreed to get a selection of artisan cheese and chutneys on the way back home.

Hannah loved this time of year. May was always such a hopeful month. It often had beautiful weather and the city centre would start to liven up. Lots of outdoor events, music, food markets with deli stands or craft stalls started to appear on random days, bringing people from all walks of life into the outdoor space. On weekdays it was mostly business, with people rushing to and from work and meetings; laptop bags, tablets, and phones in hand. The occasional tourist would wander around, the sound of excited school kids on trips to the Sea Life Centre or shows at the NIA. In the evenings and at weekends, though, it changed and morphed into the wider city linked by the canals and an easy walk up from the Mailbox, where Hannah loved to eat and drink, but couldn't afford to shop.

They sat outside in the fresh spring air at their favourite bar next to the canal bridge; it always had a good tapas selection. They picked far too much as usual, mixed feta and olives, pork belly bites, caramelised onion hummus, chilli prawns, salt and pepper calamari and halloumi fries. They shared a bottle of their favourite New Zealand Sauvignon Blanc; crisp, citrusy, and clean. The afternoon was relaxing, chilled, and unplanned – Hannah's favourite kind of day. They talked and laughed and as they finished their tapas and ordered another bottle of wine, Liam apologised for earlier.

'I was just worried, I don't know what I was thinking,' he said. 'I had a girlfriend who went off with someone at a party we were at, but I know you're not like that.'

Hannah snuggled up to him and enveloped herself into his chest and arms. He'd been hurt before; she understood now. 'Of course, I'm not like that,' she said softly. 'I'll always love you, I'd never hurt you.'

They gradually got drunker and the argument became a distant memory. The afternoon drifted into the evening with newbies arriving for the start of their night. After the third bottle of wine the sun started to go down and the evening chill set in. They stumbled back to the apartment, too late to buy the cheese – the stall now closed. They got home and collapsed on the sofa. Hannah felt queasy from too much wine; the room was spinning, she had the giggles, and was laughing at everything Liam said. She could see Liam sitting up, swaying, looking at her – or she was swaying? She wasn't sure which. She was still laughing when Liam asked, 'Did you go to the party?'

'Oh, you're so funny,' she giggled.

He asked again, 'Did you go to the party?' More sternly.

Hannah wasn't really sure what he was saying – something about going to a party. She loved parties, and they hadn't been to many. 'Yeah, yeah,' she said, thinking they were going to go back out somewhere.

'I knew it,' Liam snarled as he stood up and slammed his hand across the back of Hannah's head.

The force of it jarred her neck and she fell off the sofa onto her knees, slipping over and landing on her shoulder.

'I fucking knew it, you lying bitch!' he spat.

Hannah put her hand to the back of her head, aware of the thud and the pain, but confused about what was happening.

'I knew you were lying, I knew I couldn't trust you,' Liam hissed.

Hannah was too drunk and dazed to stand up, so she curled into a ball. She could feel Liam pulling her under her armpits, trying to lift her up. She looked up at him with tears streaming down her face; she was in shock, suddenly sobered, but really confused. 'I thought you meant we were going to a party now,' she cried. 'I'm sorry, I didn't go. I wouldn't go without you. I thought we were going to a party now,' she whimpered. She heard the front door slam as he left the apartment.

Hannah, still on the floor, was rigid, curled in a ball and sobbing. She was crying so much she couldn't catch her breath. She didn't know what had just happened; why it had happened. She didn't know who Liam was anymore, what he was. After a few minutes she uncurled and pulled herself up onto the sofa. The back of her head had a heaviness to it, her elbow and shoulder ached, and her right knee stung. She sat on the sofa, hugging her legs with her arms. She wanted to press Reset to remove the last few minutes, the whole day, go back to the way they had been when they first woke up that morning and everything was perfect; as it should be. Those few minutes had burst her bubble – her future with Liam, gone. She was dazed, drunk, exhausted, and frightened.

Hannah didn't know what time he got back, but he was next to her when she woke up Sunday morning. She showered and left for her morning shift at Rosie's without waking him. Her colleagues could see that she was quieter than usual, but assumed she was hungover. They joked with her about a heavy night, and she smiled at them. The back of her head throbbed all morning, her other injuries less so.

Hannah replayed the previous day's events over and over and questioned herself all morning as she worked. She'd drunk so much she didn't trust her memory; none of it made sense. She couldn't understand him being angry; it was out of character, and obviously he would be upset if he thought she'd lied to him, but she hadn't.

At the end of her shift, she walked slowly back to the apartment and thought it through again. Her hangover had subsided, and it became clearer, so clear she realised Liam wasn't who she thought he was. If what she thought happened had happened, she needed to get out now. She needed to pack her bags and leave. She'd been living a lie the last three months; she was heartbroken, but knew she needed to leave. Liam had lost her trust. He'd changed so quickly, and who was to say it wouldn't happen again.

Liam would be at the gym when she got back, so she needed to be quick. She'd get what she could, go to her parents, and ask her dad to help get the rest of her belongings back. She put the key in the door and realised Liam was in – there was music; an old Louis Armstrong song, 'What a Wonderful World'.

Shit, she thought to herself. In that moment she decided to leave straight away. She could get everything with her dad another day; she needed to just go now and not look back. She was just pulling the key out of the lock as quietly as she could when the door opened.

'Hello, pisshead, how are you feeling today?' Liam smiled and laughed. He pulled her into his arms gently kissing her forehead. 'How's your head? You took quite a bang when you fell off the sofa.'

Hannah was shocked. 'What do you mean?' She couldn't believe he was lying.

'Don't you remember? We got back and you fell off the sofa, pissed, and banged your head,' Liam said with such confidence.

Is that what really happened? No. He'd hit her, he'd definitely hit her, she tried to replay the night.

'Want a coffee?' he asked, taking her bag and guiding her towards the sofa. He put the kettle on and started telling her about some old bloke in the apartment across the canal. Hannah didn't listen as he spoke, but she smiled, nodded and pretended. Liam talked like it was any other day, as though nothing had happened. Whilst he was speaking, she kept trying to make sense of it. She had been drunk – maybe she had fallen off the sofa? If he had done what she thought, he'd act differently now, wouldn't he? He'd never done anything like that before. He couldn't have done it.

Liam put a film on, one of the ones Hannah had wanted to watch for a couple of weeks and pulled her in for a cuddle. The titles rolled, and they settled into the sofa. The afternoon drifted into evening, they ordered a Chinese and things just went back to normal.

That was the first time.

It wasn't the last.

Chapter 8

'Mr James. Liam.' Rachel paused, putting her cup of tea down on the coffee table, before asking her next question. Liam was understandably upset, and she needed to tread carefully. 'You mentioned you and Hannah had your ups and downs. Can you tell me a little more about that, please?' She watched his reaction.

'What?' Liam said, startled, and sat upright.

'It's just a routine question. I'm sorry we have to ask it, but we have to explore every avenue,' Rachel explained calmly.

'I don't know, you know, just stuff.' Liam relaxed. 'Stupid things, like who emptied the dishwasher last or, oh I don't know, whether we agreed on wallpaper.' He took a deep breath and sighed. 'We just get on, we always have. I know it sounds corny, but we're soulmates. Even when we argue it only lasts a few minutes. I don't think we've ever had what people would call a serious argument. If there's something wrong, we just talk about it; we agreed that at the start. Any problems, talk about it. That's how we've always been.' He sighed again and slumped back into his armchair. 'Look, can we finish this tomorrow? I can't think now, I'm exhausted.'

'Yes, of course, that's fine, I'll ring you in the morning if that's OK to check what time you want to carry on.'

How can you love me if you hate me so much?

Chapter 9

Hannah logged off, put her notepad back in her locker, and took a deep sigh of relief as she shut the door. Then she thought about Liam and nausea washed over her – what if he found out? Now she'd actually booked the tickets there was something for him to see, to pick at. What if she let it slip, innocently said something that pricked his curiosity, his anger?

That anger that controlled her. The fear of doing something wrong and paying the consequences. That's how all of this had started; she was too scared, too naive, too alone to be able to stand up for herself. When she'd tried in the early days, the consequences had been dire. After the first time he'd hit her, variations of that first incident replayed over and over again. They could go for weeks without an argument and then from nowhere Hannah would innocently fall into a trap. It was a roller coaster of happiness and bliss, and then despair and hopelessness. It was always her own fault; she would be stupid and say something to antagonise him. She was such an idiot. She'd be talking about something and Liam would question her. It could be something innocent, such as relaying a joke she'd heard at work and he'd start.

'Why are you messing around with them? You're there to work, they're not your friends.'

Once he'd started that was it – it would spiral and get worse. Sometimes violently, but mostly he was verbally and emotionally abusive; the damage *fear* did to her mentally was sometimes greater than being hit itself. Fear of the potential violence, and fear of what would happen next; fear that paralysed her ambitions.

She'd wanted to leave, but where could she go? Liam had systematically isolated her over time. She had no money, no friends, no confidence, no self-esteem. She hardly spoke to her parents and family anymore, and if she did, Liam was always there; always watching, always coaching her. How to be, how to act, what to say, what not to say. He'd alienated her from everyone, and who would believe her? He was the life and soul of the party; they wouldn't believe he was capable of doing what he'd done.

They'd blame her. They'd say she was lying, selfish, greedy. He gave her everything – what more did she want? She had no proof of his behaviour. She couldn't tell him she didn't love him anymore, that she wanted to leave. That wasn't an option – it would never end well. She knew that.

Sometimes she would argue back, and shout, 'Is there anything you like about me?' You moan about everything. I'm not good enough for you, so why do you want me?'

But he did, and he wouldn't let her go. He seemed to always be there, always checking, always questioning, losing his temper if she put a foot wrong.

As time went on, she learnt his triggers and played it safe, avoiding arguments. Anything for an easy life, she'd tell herself. But that meant her whole existence became meaningless. She'd lost the ambition to do anything. What was the point when you were rubbish at everything? She didn't want to go out and just went where she was told – the gym, the supermarket – but always with him. In the early days she carried on working at Rosie's, increased her shifts, but left the bar and then uni; he wouldn't allow it. When she'd tried to argue back, he always had an answer: 'You don't need to work, I earn more than enough for both of us,' he'd said. 'You don't need to go to uni, if you don't need to work.'

It wasn't just about the money or a career, she enjoyed it. She enjoyed being independent, meeting people, having something to do, to say, to talk about. He took it away, he took everything away.

Rosie's became her only outlet, the only time she saw other people without him. She got quieter and quieter as the months went on. She'd dream about a different life but that was stupid; without Liam she had nothing. She *was* nothing.

Knowing you were worthless was probably the hardest thing. Knowing that, no matter what you do, you would never be good enough. Liam made sure she knew that every day, always telling her how lucky she was that he stayed with her. Not many people would put up with her behaviour, but he did because he loved her. She was lucky because she had him, he told her constantly, and reassured her he'd never leave her.

Every day she tried to be better; cooking, cleaning, shopping, how she dressed, how she behaved, what she ate. She could always improve – no matter how hard she tried, she'd always have room for improvement.

She no longer had anything to say; nothing of interest that anyone would listen to. Often, if they were out with Liam's work colleagues, she'd always do her best, she'd try to be charming and funny, but he'd always tell her, 'You're boring them, Hannah, they're not interested.' It got harder and harder to think of anything to say. How do you speak if no one wants to hear you?

Often, he'd interrupt her when she started to talk; he knew she was going to say something useless, so he'd talk over her, and say something interesting or funny.

That was fine though. He was there to shine, not her.

Chapter 10

As Rachel pulled up outside Hannah's parents' house, she thought about the interview with Liam. She'd watched him and his reactions throughout and although he did seem genuinely distraught, something at the back of her mind was niggling at her. After her interview with Liam, she'd talked about it with Emma, her best, the previous evening whilst they were looking at the forensics on another case. 'Sometimes, things are too good to be true,' Emma had said.

Was this one of those times? Had Hannah left because she'd just had enough? Had she left, as many partners do, never to be seen again because they can't deal with the mess of a divorce, and leaving is the quick route out? Had she met someone, someone in the cafe perhaps, at the gym, or whilst out shopping? It happens, and it happens a lot. Couples rarely look as they really are, and, in Rachel's experience, there was no such thing as perfect.

Rachel approached the house, a neat semi-detached with hanging baskets in full bloom of reds and pinks, and a paved driveway for two cars. She was aware of a woman she assumed was Hannah's mother, Pat Chattaway, standing in the window watching her approach. Before she had chance to knock, the door opened and she was greeted by Hannah's father, Terry, who guided her into the open-plan kitchen diner, offering her tea and coffee as she sat at the dining table. She could see the likeness of Hannah in both of them. They were both shorter than average, Hannah had her father's eyes, unusually bright-blue almost green, and her mother's nose and blond hair. They were nervous, expectant; waiting for bad news, maybe. Parents were usually impatient, they'd want answers she couldn't give and promises she couldn't make. Although she'd had to wait for them to get back from their holiday, in Cornwall, before she could speak to them; she found it a little surprising. Maybe it meant this had happened before and Hannah disappearing wasn't anything new. Rachel thought this was a good starting point after explaining that Hannah was still missing, and she was trying to gather more information to help find her.

'Has Hannah ever left home previously, either whilst she's been with Liam or when she lived with you?' she asked.

Terry took the lead, quite abruptly Rachel thought, and loud. 'Not that we know of, but that girl's got it sorted; she's got a good husband who provides, so there's no reason why she'd leave.'

Pat smiled at Rachel.

'She doesn't have to work, she has lots of holidays and a good roof over her head,' he added loudly.

'And do you know if she's happy?' Rachel asked, knowing it was highly unlikely that Terry was even bothered by that; she wondered if he ever even thought about his wife Pat's happiness.

'Of course she's happy,' Terry exclaimed. Rachel felt he was quite aggressive with his response. Pat smiled again, bowing her head, and Rachel had to stop herself from shaking hers in disbelief.

'We were worried when she told us she was going to university to do painting, for god's sake.' He rolled his eyes. 'She's not going to make any money at that, is she? So, when she met Liam, we were, great, she's sorted, and we don't need to worry anymore.'

'Mrs Chattaway, do you speak to your daughter very often?' Rachel asked.

'Erm,' she started.

Terry interrupted: 'Often enough.'

'I'm sorry, Mr Chattaway, but can you let your wife answer, please?'

'I don't like your tone,' he snapped back.

'It's OK, Terry.' She squeezed his hand and he visibly relaxed as he sat back into the dining chair. 'We're just very worried. And, yes, we do speak. Probably not as often as I'd like, but they've got busy lives and I don't like to interfere.'

Pat was much calmer and gentler in her manner than her husband. Rachel imagined she often played peacekeeper between him and others.

'Thank you. And how often would you say it is, once a week, every two weeks?'

'Oh, just you know,' Pat looked a little embarrassed. 'Usually at Christmas and sometimes for birthdays.'

Rachel was quite taken back and felt a little sad for them as a family. She couldn't imagine not seeing her parents and her brother

Ian as often as she did, or at least talking to them, which was usually every couple of days, even if it was just a quick hello.

'So, when was the last time you spoke to Hannah or saw her?' Rachel asked.

'Erm, now let me see,' Pat put her finger to her mouth as she thought.

Terry sat next to her, his impatience growing as he fidgeted in the chair, huffing loudly, not even trying to cover it up.

'It would be, erm, March for her birthday,' Pat finally said.

'So, three months ago,' Rachel stated. She was surprised by the length of time, but not all families are close, she knew that from her work.

'Last March, I mean, last year.' Pat smiled awkwardly.

Rachel didn't react, just nodded, updating her notes.

'And can you remember how she seemed?' It felt like a pointless question given the length of time, but she needed to ask.

'Fine, she was fine,' Terry interrupted. 'Look, do you have any idea where she is?' Terry demand impatiently.

'That's what we're trying to establish. I do have more questions,' Rachel said, although she felt they'd be pointless given their seemingly non-existent relationship with their daughter and evident impatience to get back to their own lives.

'Ask away then,' Terry answered, shrugging his shoulders.

'How would you describe Hannah and Liam's relationship?' Rachel asked.

'Normal,' Terry answered, 'she cooks and cleans, he goes to work. Normal.'

'Terry,' Pat said quietly, 'she's only trying to help.' She smiled at Rachel again and added, 'They seemed very happy from what we could see; they do have a lovely lifestyle but they always seemed so busy, always away on holidays, or at parties. We have invited them to a lot of things and the family have too, but they were always busy, so you know…' She sighed and Rachel started to feel sorry for Pat; maybe she did want a closer relationship with her daughter.

'What was Hannah like before she went to uni?' she asked.

'Headstrong,' Pat answered immediately and smiled, as though she was proud of her.

'Yeah, ain't that the truth.' Terry shook his head.

Pat shot him a look and carried on. 'She was headstrong, independent and focused. She wanted to run her own business in art and design; she was very talented, you know, but you don't plan for falling in love, do you?'

'Good grief,' Terry interjected, 'Pat, I know you have this rosy glow of how the world should be, but it's really not like that. She met Liam. And let's face it, he was loaded and she was sorted; her painting was just a hobby and as for independent and focused…' He shook his head. 'I don't know where you're getting that from.'

'Well, it's my opinion,' she snapped back, the tension visible across her face. Rachel got the impression Pat was used to biting her tongue.

After that she just got one-word answers from both of them.

'Do you know if Hannah had any friends?'

'No.'

'Do you know why she'd be catching the train?'

'No.'

'Do you think she left Liam?'

'No.'

Rachel felt like asking, *Do you care?* She answered for them in her head. *Hell, no!*

She left them and headed back to Liam's house for the meeting time they'd agreed that morning. After that she'd go to the cafe; hopefully people she worked with daily knew a little more about Hannah than her parents.

As she drove, she rang her parents' house.

'Hey, Mom, just thinking about you,' she said when her mum answered.

'Hiya, I thought you were working today?' she answered.

'I am, I'm just in the car between shouts, and thought I'd give you a call. How's Dad's foot doing?' she asked, hoping her dad's blister he'd got from walking nine miles on the coastal path from Torquay to Brixham the previous week had improved.

'Honestly, I'm starting to wish they'd amputate it, and his head whilst they're at it,' she laughed.

'That bad?' Rachel laughed.

'You'd think he'd run a marathon!'

'It was a long way though, Mom. I mean, you're no spring chickens.' Rachel laughed again.

'Oi, madam, you can go off people, you know!'

'Sorry.' Rachel giggled.

'Sorry, love, I need to go, I can see Gill walking up the drive, love you.'

'OK, bye, love you loads, love to grumpy too,' Rachel said as her mom ended the call to see her weekly Costa coffee, partner in crime.

She continued on to Liam's house.

Liam hadn't mentioned much specifically about family and friends over the hours she'd spent with him. Although she'd asked, he seemed to skim over it, and she needed more background. She felt her questions were getting clumsy. Although routine, it was clearly upsetting Liam, but she had nothing to go on. Having spoken to Hannah's parents that morning, she wanted to try and understand what Liam's view of their relationship was; did Hannah get on with them, talk to them? She'd heard her parents' side, now she wanted it corroborated.

Page by page I watched my life burn.
Dropping one by one.
I helped,
I showed you,
I agreed.
And then we tore each page from my diary,
from before we met.
Lit the corner.
Watched it burn.
I was sad,
but you didn't know that.
You told me it was the right thing to do.
A fresh start.

I didn't realise I needed a fresh start.

Chapter 11

Hannah walked slower than usual through the alleyways back to her house, taking in her last couple of days of Lichfield. It should have been a beautiful place to live, but for her it was a prison. She never got to enjoy all that the cathedral city had to offer; she felt as though she was always on the outside looking in. Watching everyone else enjoy the annual events; the food festival, the proms in the park, the Bower and the cathedral Christmas lights. She'd listen to her customers talking about their plans, when they were meeting, and then afterwards, reminiscing about what a great time they'd had. Jane would always have at least three outdoor food stalls a year when events were on, and Hannah looked forward to working at each one; excited by the interaction they gave her with new people. They made her feel part of something special, a bit more of the community and reminded her of happier times before she met Liam; a life that seemed so distant – but was now within reach again.

Liam wanted her to forget her life before him, as though it had only started at twenty-one. He hated the thought that she'd ever had friends, boyfriends and holidays without him, even fun without him. He did his best to delete her memories, to delete anything that she felt was interesting about her. As soon as she'd start to reminisce about her previous life he'd shut her down. 'Not interested, Hannah, I don't really need to know that,' or, 'Why are you telling me this?' So, she'd stop and talk about what they were going to do together instead, pretending he hadn't hurt her feelings.

Not long after the first incident, Hannah got home from Rosie's and found Liam sitting on the sofa with her diary next to him.

He's been through my things.

Since the age of eleven, her grandma had always bought her a new diary at Christmas, ready for the new year. She wasn't religious about filling it in, but every so often she did, recording special memories and occasions. Her old diaries were still at her mum and dad's house, but Liam had this year's next to him, his hand on top of it.

Hannah tried to think if there was anything in there that he'd be unhappy about. She hadn't written much in this year's; she'd stopped when she moved in with Liam, only writing about their first couple of

46

dates. Then she remembered her first entry on New Year's Day. It was about the previous night's party with her old school friends Liz, Elaine, Cathryn, Yvonne and Lisa. They'd got together over Christmas whilst they were all home from uni and pre-planned their New Year's Eve party. They'd all got blind drunk and, as the clock turned twelve, she'd snogged a lad called Greg from a group they'd been chatting and dancing with. She'd met up once with Greg afterwards a few days later for a coffee, but, in the cold light of day and without a good dose of alcohol, she realised he wasn't for her and they didn't see each other again.

Hannah knew by the look on Liam's face that he'd read it. There was no point arguing with him about privacy or it being normal for a girl her age; that would only fuel his anger.

'We should burn this,' he said, holding it up in his hand. He wasn't angry or shouting, he just stated it matter-of-factly.

'But it's got our first date in,' Hannah replied. She didn't want to burn it – it was hers. Even though it didn't have much in it this year, her diary was precious to her; they were all precious.

'We don't need a diary to remind us of that, Hannah, don't be stupid. And I don't want to know about you and your slaggy friends and what you did before we met – you're too easily led by people like that.'

'They're not slags,' she said quietly.

'Seriously, you expect me to believe that? You've been hiding this from me.' He stood up, facing her, waving her diary in front of her face. Hannah stepped back and bowed her head. She could see where this was heading, and there was no point fighting back.

Later that evening they walked along the canal to where it left the buzz of the city; the towpaths overgrown in the shadows under the bridges. Hannah walked in silence, Liam talking. 'It's for the best, Hannah, it will help you rid yourself of that life, people like that.'

She didn't respond.

Liam had taken a box of matches out of his pocket and stopped under one of the bridges. Hannah tore the first page out, her New Year's Eve party, and Liam lit the corner. She held it until it burnt nearly down to her fingers, then dropped it in the canal. Liam took the diary from her, turned to the next page with writing on and gave it back. She tore the page, he lit it, it burnt and she dropped it. The little charred remains of her diary floated on the top of the water – a few measly bits of paper that meant so much to her. When they'd burnt each page, they walked back home. Hannah held her empty diary in her hand close to her chest; the only writing left was her name inside the front page.

When they got back, Liam took her phone and blocked all her contacts except her family, and then deactivated any social media pages she had. Two days later, he bought her a new phone with a new number, only adding his own and her parents' numbers in.

'There you go, a fresh start,' he said, handing her the phone.

Chapter 12

Deleting her life and her contacts was just the start of him controlling everything, but sometimes Hannah would fight back. Sometimes she'd be brave. Sometimes.

About a year after they'd been together, Hannah wanted to see her parents and the rest of her family; they had a funeral to attend. She needed to be there for them, for her. She needed to say goodbye to her cousin Carl, gone at twenty-five; cancer, too young, too soon.

Liam didn't want to go; he didn't know them, he'd said. 'You've hardly seen him since we've been together, that's not real family!' he'd yelled at her.

It was his fault she never saw Carl anymore; every family event, after the first two, they hadn't attended. Always finding excuses: away, work, too busy, other events, made up most of them. Liam didn't want her with anyone who could influence her and he'd do his damnedest to keep her away from others; especially Carl.

Carl was three years older than Hannah and when she was little she followed him around like a shadow, always copying and trying to get in on whatever he was doing; football, cricket, Xbox. When she was eleven, she'd started at his school and he'd made it known, any problems and he was there; he was her protector. He'd given her previous boyfriends the onceover, grilled them jokingly about their intentions, checked them out, made sure they were OK for her; or not. Maybe that's where she'd gone wrong with Liam; she'd got too involved, too quickly. Carl wasn't at uni to guide and protect her, she stood alone; maybe she felt Liam filled that gap.

In the early days when she started going out with Liam, after their first meeting, Carl had dropped the odd comment, 'Going for the old geezers, are you now, cuz?' and, 'I'm starting to forget what you look like.' He joked about it at first, but, as Hannah made more and more excuses not to see or talk to him, he got serious; even turning up once as she left class.

'Can we go for a coffee? I'm worried about you,' he'd said.

Hannah could see Liam waiting for her in the car park.

'I have to go, some of us have got work,' she'd lied. 'I'll message you, honest, I've just been mega busy, love you still.' She'd smiled.

'Just make sure you do, or I'll have to keep stalking you.' He joked, but Hannah knew he was worried.

She'd felt guilty when she left him. Maybe if Liam wasn't watching she'd have been braver, had the courage to say something, maybe that one conversation, the one that didn't happen, it could have made all the difference. But she'd shut him out.

That was the last time she'd seen him.

When she found out Carl was ill, Liam wouldn't let her visit him. 'It's for his own good, you don't look well yourself. I think you're coming down with something, you should stay away from sick people, you could kill him with your germs.'

She ignored the torrent of excuses coming from him. Hannah knew it was nothing to do with that, he didn't want her anywhere near Carl, her family; reaching out to them in a moment of *unsupervised* conversation.

And then…it was too late.

Three weeks after hearing Carl was ill, her mum rang. She'd volunteered to call round the family, keep everyone informed about her godson; Carl was her younger sister, Mary's son.

'Oh, Han,' she said, when Hannah answered the phone.

'What? What's wrong?' Hannah could hear the sadness in her voice, her stomach turned over, fearing the worst, tears already welling.

'It's Carl.' She couldn't speak, couldn't explain, she didn't need to, Hannah knew.

'Oh, Mom…no.'

Three weeks, that's all, and he was gone.

Hannah was devastated. She was angry at Liam for not letting her go and see him, to tell him she was sorry, that she was there for him, and now she was determined to go to the funeral. She knew he'd be awkward about her going, and make life difficult, but surely he wouldn't stop her going completely. If Liam didn't want to go, she'd go on her own. She checked the train times to Four Oaks in Sutton Coldfield and she'd agreed to meet her parents at theirs first. Then they'd drive to Streetly Crematorium together. She'd kept quiet about it all week, avoiding the inevitable argument.

The morning of the funeral she'd got up, showered, and started to quietly get ready. She'd put her make-up on, just a bit; she didn't want to antagonise him anymore that she already had. She'd just put a black shift dress on and he flung the bedroom door open.

'You shouldn't go without me!' he screamed at her. 'There's nothing you can do, he's dead, what's the point?' His face was red, the veins in his neck and forehead bulging. 'Get that fucking dress off.' He grabbed the front of her dress at the neck, pushing her backwards onto the bed, then turned and slammed the door as he left the room.

'He's my family and I'm going with or without you,' Hannah cried, trying to pull the door back open. She couldn't. Liam held the handle on the other side; she was trapped.

'Let me out, you psycho!' she screamed at him.

The door opened and he stormed into the room.

She fell backwards onto the floor and Liam bent over her, pounding her ribs with his fists. She rolled into a ball, protecting as much of her body as she could.

'I'll show you a fucking psycho if you want!' He kicked her in the small of her back.

She winced and cried out in pain. 'I'm sorry, I'm sorry,' she sobbed.

'Now look what you've made me do,' he hissed at her as he left the room, slamming the door, leaving her on the floor.

Eventually, Hannah uncurled herself and sat on the bed. Her body stung where he'd hit her, the back of her eyes were heavy with the pressure of crying. She felt the neck of her dress, it was torn; her collar bone sore and scratched where he'd grabbed it. She looked at her watch; she was too late for her train. Her head was spinning, panic set in and regret overwhelmed her for letting Carl down; she couldn't miss his funeral. She looked at her watch again; if she could get out soon, she'd get a taxi straight there and make it in time. As she sat there, she thought to herself; it's been twelve months and it's getting worse. I have to get out. This isn't right.

She'd had enough. He'd already stopped her seeing Carl before he died – she was going to his funeral and he wouldn't stop her. She decided at that moment that she wasn't coming back. Things had gone too far now. Her need to leave pushed all the questions of where she'd go, what she'd do and what people would say to the back of her head.

She could hear the TV and knew Liam was sitting on the sofa watching football as if nothing had happened. As far as he was concerned, the conversation was over. Hannah undressed and put her jeans and a jumper on. If Liam thought she'd accepted she wasn't going, maybe his guard would be down and she could get out. Her body was grazed and stinging, but she was used to the pain now; she just got on with it as though nothing had happened. She walked out of the bedroom and into the bathroom, locking the door quietly behind her. She stood looking at herself in the mirror, distraught with grief for her cousin and for herself. Tears streamed down her cheeks, her eyes were raw; the makeup she'd put on earlier, gone. She composed herself, washed her face, took a deep breath and walked out of the bathroom. Her shoes were in the hallway next to the front door, the pot with the keys in next to it. She walked into the kitchen, spotting Liam sprawled on the lounge in the open-plan space, out of the corner of her eye. She put the kettle on and quietly started making a cup of tea and coffee, pretending to get on with the day. It was standard routine: fight, punch, cry, carry on as though nothing happened. It would never be talked about again; erased. Whilst the kettle was boiling, she walked back into the hall, put her shoes on and went to grab the keys. They were gone.

'Shit,' she said quietly to herself, her stomach turning over. She looked back through to Liam on the sofa and could see the keys next to him on the coffee table. He didn't look at her, he just stared straight ahead at the TV.

She took her shoes off quietly and went back into the kitchen, finished making the drinks and sat in the armchair in silence, waiting for Liam to get up and leave the room, or fall asleep.

It was 11:05am and the funeral had already started. Hannah felt her anger boiling as she held back her tears; something she was used to doing. She now just wanted to call her mum and tell her everything. Liam had already taken her phone off her earlier in the morning; she could see it on the sideboard flashing in silence each time a call or text from her mum came through.

If she could get the phone and go back into the bathroom, she could call her mum or at least text her and ask for help. Hannah stood and started tidying up, staying out of Liam's way. She went back into the hall and into a cupboard to get a new cleaning cloth. She walked towards the sideboard to clean it, so she could see her phone. She had three missed calls off her mum and two texts. She picked the phone up as she sprayed cleaner and put it in her back pocket.

Liam stood up. 'I'll have that,' he said sternly, holding his hand out. Hannah gave it to him, and he put it down next to him on the sofa.

'Sit down,' he said, 'you're doing my fucking head in today.'

Hannah complied and sat back in the armchair, staring into space whilst the morning turned into afternoon. Liam watched football, then cricket. She made him some lunch; she didn't eat. She felt sick and knew she wouldn't be able to swallow.

After four hours, whilst her parents and family were at Carl's funeral where she should have been, her phone came back to life as new missed calls and texts appeared.

Liam glanced down to it and looked at Hannah. He picked it up and read the texts from her mum. Then passed her the phone and watched as she read it.

10:42am: Are you OK, we need to leave, Mom xx

10:50am: We're leaving now, meet you there? Mom xx

11:08am: Where are you?

11:11am: It's starting, space at the back when you get here x

3:15pm: Hannah, ring me please, urgently, Mom.

3:18pm: Are you OK? Ring me xx

3:20pm: Can you ring me please.

She clicked on the call history.

3:00pm: missed call

3:01pm: missed call and voicemail.

Liam leant over and pressed Play on the voicemail, they both listened.

Hannah, are you OK? I can't believe you missed Carl's funeral, can you ring me as soon as you get this please.

Hannah handed the phone back to Liam with her head down. He didn't take it; instead, he told her what to write.

3:22pm: Sorry Mom, I've been projectile vomiting, food poisoning I think. I've been in bed all day, feel really bad.

Liam checked it first, let her send it and then took the phone off her.

After she sent the text Hannah gave up fighting. She sat in the armchair quiet, distant, thinking. Over the past months Hannah had become adept at lying to everyone else, always making excuses, always what Liam wanted, not what she wanted.

This isn't right, I need to leave, I can't stay, I'm better than this.

She just needed to get out of the apartment. Tell her parents everything, tell them what he was really like.

Hannah's eyes were raw and she couldn't speak, her throat was so sore from sobbing.

'Come and sit with me,' Liam said.

Hannah got up and sat next to him, and he hugged her. 'We're OK, aren't we?' His usual indication they were done; he'd *forgiven* her, they could put it behind them. He also knew that she'd missed the funeral and the threat had passed.

Four hours later, they were watching a film. Liam paused the TV and stood up, finally leaving the room to go to the toilet. Hannah was beginning to think he'd never go; she'd made him four coffees.

This was her chance.

Hannah put her shoes on, grabbed her phone and the keys as quietly as she could and moved to the door. She heard the toilet flush as she opened the front door. She got out onto the communal landing and ran as fast as could; It was too late, her head yanked back as Liam grabbed her hair. She fell backwards, stumbling, trying to grab her hair with her hands to stop him pulling a chunk out. She grabbed his hands instead, and he pulled her backwards and upwards, her feet trying to find the floor, tripping over herself as he shoved her back into the apartment and threw her onto the sofa. He sat down next to her, pressed Play and the film resumed.

'You start crying to anyone and I will kill you. You do not betray me again,' he whispered in her ear. 'You will behave, you will show me respect and you will not defy me.'

Hannah didn't speak for the rest of the night, sitting in silence, terrified.

They went to bed when the film finished, and Liam leant over to kiss her. She was hoping that was all, but unfortunately not. He pulled her hands behind her back, pushed her onto her front and thrust himself into her as hard as he could. This wasn't love, it was rage.

'Don't defy me again,' he said as he finished. Hannah just lay there, still on her front. She had no tears left; she just lay there for hours awake, exhausted, frozen, thinking.

Chapter 13

The next morning, Hannah woke to soft music playing, the smell of fresh coffee and Liam singing along to 'What a Wonderful World'. She knew what that meant.

He entered the room. 'Hello, beautiful, I've made you breakfast.' He brought a tray in with croissants, coffee, and a rose. Hannah associated flowers and nice food with the aftermath. The thought of it made her feel sick; she knew what it represented, it always happened, every time. The ritual, the apology.

This was the worst though. He'd never threatened to kill her before. The rape she was used to, she just submitted now; it was easier than fighting. She no longer belonged to herself, her thoughts, her dreams, her breath. She belonged to him. She was his.

Her job was to love him, to show what a solid couple they were, to prove what a brilliant and loving man he was. She was nothing more than a fake watch, an adornment, an accessory, and a cheap one at that.

Liam excitedly set out their day. Breakfast, a walk to the shops so he could buy her something sexy to wear, come back, get changed and lunch at the Italian round the corner. She hated that place. The apology meal. The place where he'd put her on a pedestal, and she could eat what she wanted, anything. She'd pay for it later though; everything was a trap. So, she'd order a salad starter, drink sparkling water, have the lowest calorie thing on the menu. No dessert – she was full, she'd say. She wouldn't fall into the trap; she would give him no excuse.

Whilst Liam had been asleep the previous night, she'd thought about how she could escape. He worked so close to the apartment she couldn't risk leaving during the day. He'd check on her regularly, and she was sure he'd put cameras in the apartment. Too often he commented on her day, what time she got up, what she'd watched on TV, when she showered or dressed. It was comments few and far between, but it was enough to say 'I'm watching you'. She was trapped even when he wasn't there. The apartment had become a prison. She no longer worked, or went to uni, she had no friends. Her family were more and more distant, and no doubt her missing Carl's funeral, well, would that be the last straw? Would her family relationships be tarnished for ever more? The sadness she felt in her heart was

56

overwhelming. She desperately wanted to talk to her mum, tell her she was sorry, tell them all she was sorry. But when would that ever happen? When would she get the chance?

Every part of her life was under scrutiny.

At that moment, in the dead of night she accepted that this was her life. She realised to survive she had to comply with everything he wanted – she would have to make her life bearable. He only hit her if she did something wrong, so from now on she wouldn't do anything wrong. She would listen, she would do as she was told, she would give him no reason to be angry. It was her own fault for the arguments, it was always something she did wrong; she needed to do better.

From that day Hannah 'behaved' and did everything for him – every meal was perfect, she always looked good, she worked harder at the gym, the house was spotless, she greeted him every evening with a kiss, a cup of tea, his dinner ready. He was clearly happy, now she was the perfect wife; all his efforts had paid off.

Hannah was empty. She stopped thinking about herself, and everything she did was for him; she existed only for him.

I'm sorry I'm so useless.
I'm sorry I'm so fat.
I'm sorry I'm so ugly.

I'm sorry I'm not good enough for you.

Chapter 14

It was the day before her escape, her last shift at the cafe. Liam allowing her to start work again when they moved to Lichfield had opened up the opportunity to get away. She'd miss working there. She'd miss Jane, and she also regretted that Jane would be short of staff until a replacement was found, but she had to go.

Hannah placed her change of clothes in her rucksack and put it in her locker ready for the next day. The next time she opened it would be her last, as she made her break for freedom. She couldn't believe she was so close to leaving him; five years of hell nearly at an end. Over the past few months, she constantly doubted she could do it. She was terrified of leaving, but more terrified of staying. Every day she was scared that he'd catch her out and find out what she was doing.

The thought of him finding out made her shake to her core. It was now standard daily practice for him to question her every day, relentlessly. Who'd been into the cafe, who she'd spoken to, what she'd had for lunch. She always showed him on FaceTime that she was alone, because she had to eat with him watching, but he'd check and question her to make sure she hadn't been snacking. He'd make sure they'd go to the gym regularly; he was looking after her health and thinking about her, he'd say. He'd often say how good some other woman looked, that they obviously worked harder than her. She needed to believe in herself more he'd say, she could do anything and look amazing if she put the effort in.

Hannah tried hard to please him, to look good, but she was fat and ugly, and she didn't try hard enough. She asked if she could go on her own once without him so she could work harder. She really just wanted time to herself.

She wished she hadn't asked – that was a huge argument.

Why did she want to go on her own? Who was she meeting? Why did she want to go without him? He was so hurt and angry. 'Do you realise how much you've hurt my feelings? You're just selfish,' he'd yelled at her.

It spiralled and Hannah knew what was coming. He checked her phone, messages, her browser history. She'd been looking at a holiday she thought would be good for them, and that just made it worse.

'Why are you looking at that? Who are you going with?' he shouted as he pushed her hard and she'd tripped backwards over the corner of the rug. As she landed on the floor, her head hit the wall with a thud. She put her hand backwards onto the windowsill, and the first thing it touched was a glass Caithness paperweight. They'd bought it at a weekend away in Fort William in Scotland. She grabbed it, and as he was storming towards her she randomly threw it at him. It made contact with his elbow, and it just exploded. There was blood everywhere. Hannah immediately regretted it. It stopped him in his tracks though.

Hannah shot up and ran over to him. 'I'm sorry, I'm sorry, it was an accident, I'm so sorry, I didn't mean it,' she panicked, waiting for the first blow. It didn't come.

Liam was quiet as Hannah cleaned up his elbow. It was a tiny cut but deep; it stopped bleeding eventually.

'I just wanted to book us a weekend away,' Hannah said quietly, 'because I love you so much. I want time for us on our own.'

They had dinner in an uncomfortable silence, watched a film and went to bed.

The next morning, Liam brought her breakfast in bed with flowers he'd bought that morning. 'Love you,' he said brightly. 'I've ordered a treadmill for you.'

Hannah felt a darkness fall over her. She'd already given up uni for him, work, and now she'd be more trapped. She regretted leaving uni. It had kept her sane before, seeing other people, their lives, the fun they were having. It was Hannah's link to reality.

She didn't need uni, he said, he'd provide, why did she need a degree? She'd probably fail anyway, it was a waste of time. Why did she want to spend time with the people there as well? They weren't friends, they were just acquaintances. She thought back to the day they'd agreed she wasn't going to uni, or, more to the point, that he'd agreed, and she did as she was told. Now it was happening with the gym. She'd never see another soul, she thought to herself.

'I've ordered it so you can exercise when I'm not here,' he said, smiling. 'And, no more secrets. You don't need to look at holidays without me, we should pick things like that together.' Another rule added to the ever-growing list.

She smiled back and said, 'Thank you.'

Five years on, and Hannah had learnt the 'rules' the hard way. They weren't written down, but it was clear her life was guided by Liam's screwed-up perception of the world. Often, she didn't realise a rule existed until she'd broken it.

- No drinking alcohol or caffeine.
- No eating cakes, fat, sausages, bacon, bread, red meat, sugar; basically anything that tasted nice.
- No talking to men – don't look at them. At work, 'Just do your job. If you give off the wrong signals you'll get chatted up. You're so naive you don't even realise, so don't encourage them.'
- Don't dress like a slag. No high heels, short skirts, tight clothes, low tops. 'I know how men's brains work, don't encourage them.'
- No social media. 'Why do you want to talk to people you don't know?'
- No talking about us. It's private, it not anyone's business, you don't share anything about us. 'Got it?'
- No lying. 'I'll know.'
- We do everything together, why does anyone else need to be involved?
- No friends unless they passed the criteria: happily married, his 'considered safe' list. Hannah never really knew how they made the safe list, but it was a short one. She felt as though they had lots of acquaintances, but she never felt she had a friend, someone she could talk to, someone who cared. 'People are always out for themselves, Hannah, they don't care about you, they're not friends.'
- No going out with anyone, including her parents. 'They're trying to split us up, they don't want you to be happy. If you want to see them, we'll go together, that's what families do.'
- The house must be tidy, always, that means no messy hobbies. 'It doesn't matter if you can clean up after, you'll never get it spotless.' Hannah loved to paint and sew, Liam hated it, and it just became harder to do because Liam would moan before,

during and after. He took the joy out it; he took the joy out of everything.

Her life now was void of happiness apart from her garden. Moving to Lichfield gave her an outside space, a place of solitude, something that was her own. Something she could focus on and be proud of; it was the one solace she had, the time she felt was hers. She loved her garden, she could tend to it from dawn till dusk. Planting, pruning, watching new life unfold day by day. She'd hung various bird feeders when they first moved in and watched an array of different species feed on them daily. She'd bought a bird book and took time identifying the various little visitors she had; little families of sparrows, thrush, blue tits, nuthatch and a cute little robin couple. She started to recognise the same birds visiting, along with a cheeky squirrel who'd hang upside down with his fat white belly bulging whilst he tried to steal the bird food. Everything else that she did, apart from working at the cafe in Lichfield, she did with Liam. Everything she did with him, he critiqued. For her own good of course, always trying to make her better, to improve her. 'You could be anything, achieve anything, you just have to believe in yourself more,' he'd say. So, he helped by pointing out everything she did wrong. Twice a week, they did circuits together at the gym. All the way round he'd tell her to try harder, to do it differently. 'Look how's she's doing it, she's got better technique. If you try harder, you can have a figure like hers.'

It got to the point, usually about three hours before circuits, where she'd get an excruciating pain in her stomach. It would bloat, cramp, and she'd be doubled up in pain. She'd try to tell Liam that she couldn't go.

'You're letting me down again, you do this every week.'

'You're lazy.'

'No wonder you're fat.'

'This is our thing, we should do it together.'

It wasn't, it was like everything else. It was his thing, not hers. She'd still go, and she'd feel like she'd pass out with the pain. This went on for months until she said she had to go to the doctor. He went with her, of course. The doctor came up with IBS. Irritable Bowel

Syndrome, basically the name for something they can't attribute to anything in particular.

'It could be related to food, anxiety, lifestyle,' the doctor suggested. Hannah knew it was anxiety and stress; she knew exactly what triggered it.

Liam focused on her lifestyle and food after that, even more than before. She was now teetotal, and her diet consisted of chicken, fish, vegetables and salad, no dressings, or sauces unless she made them herself. She was already skinny, not by Liam's standards but by anyone else who had a set of eyes in their head. Hannah couldn't see she was too thin – being told she was fat and ugly every day made her think she was.

'No one else will want you looking like that,' he'd say. And he was right; who'd want her looking like that, fat, ugly? She was rubbish at pretty much everything, and she was lucky that he stayed with her.

Hannah hadn't always thought like that though. Before she was brainwashed into believing she was nothing but a shadow. Before, when she had freedom of thought. Before she had to be truthful with everything because to be caught out, well, she wouldn't be caught out.

She never lied to him.

Chapter 15

In the morning briefing, at the station, Rachel had given her update to the rest of the team. She felt her words disappear, drifting over the heads of her colleagues; her update absorbed by the newly painted white walls of the station. She clocked one of her colleagues, Parker, take a sneaky look at his watch; eager to get out to do his job, or eager to get home? Either way he wasn't listening. Unlike Adam who was sat upright, engaged, eagerly taking notes. *That won't last*, she thought to herself.

'Parker,' John said sharply as he stood up.

'Boss,' he said sheepishly, assuming the same upright position as Adam. The new, cheap plastic chair creaking as he did; they reminded her of the ones she had in primary school, only bigger.

John repeated for the third time how busy the contact centre were compared to normal. He'd been in the monthly leadership team meeting the day before; pressure was coming from the top to perform better and quicker.

'Eighteen percent higher than this time last year. That's eighteen percent, folks. So, I appreciate you're all working your butts off and we all know that the heat always seems to bring out the *crazy* in people, but we need to close quicker and move onto the next incident. Gone are the days when we had the luxury of time to ponder. I need speed.'

Yes, boss, they'd all said.

Rachel sat in Liam's front room opposite him for the fourth day of questioning, thinking about what John had said; she needed to move this along, but it was dragging.

'Mr James, I know we've already spoken about Hannah's family, but I'd like to get a bit more of an in-depth picture of her relationship with her parents. Maybe any things they did together, with or without you?' Rachel pressed gently.

'To be honest, I'm not really sure what more I can add. They never really seemed that close,' Liam started. He sighed as he sat back into his chair. Rachel waited a few seconds to see if he added more, but he said nothing.

'How often does Hannah see them?' she asked.

Liam sat forward and shrugged. 'I dunno, maybe twice a year.' He paused and thought for a moment. Rachel waited patiently and let the silence between them expand, then he continued, 'They usually drop in on her birthday and at Christmas. They're not really close as I've said.'

'Do they talk on the phone much?' Rachel felt she wasn't getting anywhere. Liam was either being evasive or the lack of contact between Hannah and her parents was just how it was.

'Not really,' he shrugged. Rachel got the sense he'd had enough.

'Do you know if they had any particular fallings out over anything?' She tried to dig a little deeper.

'Maybe, I don't know,' Liam shook his head. 'I know Hannah was upset that she wasn't invited to her cousin's funeral, and after that they didn't speak much. I was often saying to invite them over for a meal or for Sunday dinner. I offered to cook a Mother's Day meal last year and Hannah just said, "what's the point?" I don't think they showed her any love growing up. It was a real shame.'

Do you really not see this?

Do you really think this OK?
Why don't you say something?

All I need is for someone to hold out their hand,
to say 'it's not right.'

Hold out your hand and I'll take it.

Please…

Just hold out your hand.

Chapter 16

Their wedding had been guided by the ever-evolving set of rules she had to obey. It was 5th August, just over two years after they met. Hannah invited thirty-eight people to the wedding; all relatives, Carl's family noticeably absent. By then there were no old friends left; she'd lost touch when Liam 'digitally' cut her off and it just became easier to not have friends. Her friends had tried to get in touch, usually through her parents, but she'd made up so many excuses of why they couldn't go to weddings, holidays, nights out and christenings, the invites eventually dried up.

The rest of the guests, 179 of them, were Liam's relatives, work colleagues, random people off the street it felt. Hannah remembered looking around the room at the reception thinking, *I don't know who any of you are.*

Liam was in his element, working the room, connecting people, high-fives, and hearty pats on the back. It felt more like a business network event at times. Then Liam would take centre stage, regaling stories of how amazing he was; often at Hannah's expense. Hannah also 'worked' the room, but she felt like a shadow, drifting in and out of other people's conversations, sitting on the fringes. Anything that involved her was superficial. 'Oh, wow you look beautiful, have you had a nice day?'…'This has been a brilliant day, one of the best weddings I've been to'…'When we got married, we did…blah, blah, blah, blah'. Throughout the whole day, Hannah didn't have one conversation that had any depth. This incredible, amazing, generous wedding was as shallow as her marriage was going to be.

Liam had allowed her to drink one glass of champagne for the toast. Hannah didn't finish it – what was the point? What was there to celebrate, plus she'd only have to pay for it later. She raised her glass and took the traditional sip and put it down. The bubbles bursting on her lips, the sip so small it had dissipated before it reached the back of throat. She watched Liam get drunk on cider, wine, champagne, shorts, and shots. Hopefully he'd be too pissed to consummate their wedding later on, she thought.

She looked around the room at the 'wedding cast' Liam had invited. Work colleagues, clients, and suppliers, nearly all men apart from two;

the token female execs in the company. The 'cast' was meant to show his popularity. Half of them were probably hoping for a promotion, a bonus, a pay rise, some deal or kickback. Rent-a-crowd, she thought. If he wasn't the boss, would they be there? Their beleaguered wives and girlfriends were shadows like Hannah. *The Invisible Army*. How many of them wanted to shout in that moment, 'Just shut the fuck up will you, you stupid dick!' Hannah imagined them all standing up at that point and shouting it out loud together. She felt a moment of joy at the thought and then an overwhelming sadness passed over her, rooting itself in her heart.

When did she give in? she thought, when did she stop fighting? How was she here marrying this man she hated? Why didn't she just say, 'No', when she was asked earlier that day by a stranger? All she wanted was for someone to rescue her, to ask her how she was, did she need help, is this what you want?

When it happened though, when that stranger asked her, 'Do you take this man to be your lawful wedded husband?' Hannah had replied, 'I do.'

He'd already asked the congregation, 'If any person present knows of any lawful impediment to this marriage, he or she should declare it now.'

No one stood up and shouted, 'No, he treats her like shit, she deserves better.' Instead, when he'd asked there was a hushed silence, broken only by a couple of giggles.

Hannah had looked at her parents. *Mom...Dad...anyone?* She made direct eye contact with Liam's mother Edith, did she know what her son was really like? Edith broke the gaze, and Hannah knew she was on her own; she'd always be on her own. No matter what he did, no matter what they saw, she was always on her own. Standing up and shouting it out at a wedding was unthinkable; every bride and groom's worst nightmare. Not Hannah's though. If someone stood up and shouted it out, it would have rippled through the church, and one after another would have stood up,

'No, she deserves more.'

'No, he's a monster.'

'No.'

'No.'

'No.'

They'd have had the bravery to stop the wedding and save her, wouldn't they?

But why would they when she knew she'd perpetuated the façade of their perfect life. So no one stood up, and there were no ripples; the wedding had continued.

And now, how could she say, 'No' when asked if she took Liam to be her lawful wedded husband, when she knew no one would stand with her and rescue her. They'd have all had their day ruined, Liam would have been humiliated, everyone would be angry with her for wasting their day.

At the reception Hannah carried on with her smiling and laughing, floating around her pretend perfect day, with her pretend friends. The night ended with Hannah thankfully alone in bed in the honeymoon suite and Liam in the hotel bar with his 'friends', loud and rowdy until about 4am. His friends had banged on the door loudly, she'd opened it and they dumped him on the bed, face down. Apologising for ruining their wedding night. Apology not required, Hannah thought.

Hannah and Liam left for honeymoon three days later on a two-week Caribbean cruise.

They often went away for long weekends and holidays and they'd been to the most amazing places. They both loved travelling and that became Hannah's escape. When they were away mostly it was OK. She pretended she was someone else, in a different life. They were more on display, eating out, sunbathing, walking, sightseeing, so the opportunities for arguing were less. They always argued in private and outwardly they were just seen as an in-love couple.

Their honeymoon was no different.

Hannah read books she'd bought at the airport as she lay by the pool. She imagined if this was her real life she'd order cocktails and have tapas, relax, laugh and make friends with other travellers. In reality, she drank water and lived on the abundance of 'fresh healthy food' Liam had pointed out to her on the immense all-you-can-eat buffets. No puddings for me then, she thought.

Liam would paint a picture to other guests that suggested they were richer than they were, talked about cars they didn't have, places they hadn't been. He embellished everything he said. Everyone loved

Hannah; she was 'so attentive' and 'such a good listener', Hannah realised it was easy to pretend, plus everyone else just wanted to talk about themselves. So, she could act a bit dumb, not say very much, not know anything and not have an opinion. She'd smile and laugh and make Liam look good. She'd gaze at him adoringly, squeeze his hand, he'd brush her hair away from her face, kiss her forehead. They'd put on a display that others would be envious of, but so shallow that they didn't even notice it was all fake.

On the third day of their honeymoon, Hannah looked over the side of the ship whilst they watched the sunset. It was beautiful, the night was perfect, and there was a warmth so calming from the sun with the breeze washing over her. She imagined climbing over the railings, falling into the abyss of freedom. She saw the sea as a stepping stone into another world; somewhere safe and quiet. She could just float away. A tear trickled down her cheek. Liam was standing behind her with his arms wrapped round her waist holding her tight, his head nuzzled into her neck just below her ear.

'Isn't this perfect?' he whispered.

'It is,' Hannah said quietly, knowing she'd never get away from him.

She should have married someone who loved her for being her, who wanted children with her, who wanted to grow old with her. Liam made it clear she wasn't allowed to have children. The first and only time she'd broached the subject, Liam point-blank said, 'No, we're not having children, I don't want you getting fat.'

Although she suspected it was more to do with him wanting her full attention; not sharing her with anyone else. She remembered feeling as though she'd been punched in the stomach, angry that Liam selfishly kept her in a relationship, always on his terms. After that, every three months, she begrudgingly had her contraceptive injection; did as she was told.

That dream, like so many others, had drifted away. She should have been an artist by now, selling her paintings and sculptures, maybe teaching a little. She didn't want to be rich, just earn enough for to live, and to love what she was doing. She didn't dream of huge houses or expensive cars; the things that motivated Liam. She wanted to be self-contained, with a family, two or three children.

Before she met Liam she'd ventured into jewellery design as part of her uni course, and she'd started selling some at craft fairs and online. He never knew about it though; she'd have felt silly telling him in the early days. He was this big hot shot director and she made trinkets; that's how he'd have seen it. So, she didn't tell him that she had it, or that she had a bank account for the business, and over time she forgot about the £53.46 that was left in it. When she started saving up to leave him, she'd kept her tips in her locker until Jane asked her to help with the banking. It was the same bank she'd used before so she started paying them into her old account. She didn't bank all her tips though – she still took a little home each week, just enough to throw Liam off. Every time she added a few pounds to her account, here and there, was a step closer to her new life.

From that day on her honeymoon, when she thought the only way out was to throw herself overboard, to today, when she was ready to leave, she'd changed a lot.

Sometimes there was no warning

but mostly she could tell.

It wasn't always just before it happened.

Sometimes they'd be out,
and she'd see his jaw clench,
and the bone and muscle would
tighten and stretch through his skin.

His Adam's apple would move.

Ever so slightly,

and she knew from that moment,
there was no going back.

Chapter 17

Looking back, she could see how brainwashed she'd become, believing her life was as she'd chosen it to be. Avoiding conflict with Liam meant they could go for weeks without an argument, and things would be wonderful. Liam would be funny, caring, supportive. They'd go for days out, eat at restaurants. Healthy food, of course, and no drinking; Hannah by now pretending to herself that these were her choices. They'd go for long walks, or bike rides, visit cities and towns, stroll along rivers, or stare at paintings in galleries. Hannah would think that their bad times were behind them, and they were OK. Things would be good from now on. She would forgive and forget his previous behaviour, because this was the Liam she loved.

In the bad times she would say to herself, *If it happens again, I'm leaving* or, *if it's like this next month, or next year, I'm leaving,* but then he'd be nice and caring and she'd be pulled into a false sense of security. Things would be perfect again. If she did as she was told, things were good. So, it was up to her to make sure everything was OK. If she didn't wind him up, it would be good all the time. But sometimes she was stupid, she'd forget to be good, and she'd ruin things; it was always her own fault.

One day on a sunny August bank holiday, they'd had a beautiful day in Stratford-upon-Avon. Visiting the butterfly farm, having a picnic by the river and walking through the town. He'd held her hand as they walked and occasionally stopped to kiss her; she lived for the days he was like this, when all was perfect in her world. The sun was shining and Stratford was at its best, with families and couples walking, playing, eating. There were street entertainers, re-enactments, craft and food stalls. They walked along the river, past the weirs and under the willow trees, the dappled sunlight across their path. It really was the perfect summer's day.

Nothing bad had happened for a few months and Hannah had let her guard down, just a fraction. It would always be like this now. He trusted her now; she never put a foot wrong. When he trusted her, things were good; they were as they should be. She felt as long as she maintained his trust and didn't let him down, they'd be OK. They'd be happy together. They'd grow old together, they'd be normal. That was all Hannah wanted; to be a normal couple.

They left Stratford just after 5pm, leaving their summer's day behind. On the way back, they decided to stop at a canal-side pub for a meal. They'd driven past it a couple of times before and had commented on how lovely it must be; being on the canal, sitting outside eating, like how they used to when they first met, and on a day like today it seemed the perfect end to their trip.

As they pulled into the car park, Hannah spotted her old friend from school, Alex. She hadn't seen him for years. She'd met him on her first day at primary school and had been in most of the same classes until she left sixth form thirteen years later. Alex lived just round the corner from Hannah growing up and they walked back from school every day in a big group. She had so many happy memories with him, always a friend and never a boyfriend, just a brilliant mate. When they left school, he went to Cardiff University as she went off travelling, staying in touch for a few years. But since Hannah had met Liam, she hadn't spoken to him – for at least two years.

She was so happy to see him, she forgot herself and shouted, 'Alex!' across the car park, waving to get his attention. 'Liam, it's Alex from school. Oh my god, that must be his wife!' she said excitedly.

Alex was helping a woman about Hannah's age into a car, she was clearly heavily pregnant. He turned and immediately recognised Hannah. He spoke briefly to the woman and she got back out. By now, Hannah had run across the car park and was standing in front of him.

'Oh wow, Hannah, long time no see.' He leant in and kissed her on the cheek and gave her a hug. 'This is my wife, Jess, and in there's Jack.' He pointed to her very pregnant stomach. They chatted briefly and she turned to introduce Liam, but he was still standing by their car across the car park. She looked over to him, his face stern, and she realised her mistake. *How can you be so stupid, Hannah*, she thought to herself; she'd ruined their perfect day.

'Oh, it was so lovely to see you, Alex, good luck with everything. I better go.' And she made a hasty retreat.

Alex looked a bit dumbfounded and said, 'Oh, OK, keep in touch. I'll give you my number again.'

But it was too late; Hannah was already back by Liam.

They stood there for a few moments in silence whilst Alex and Jess got back into the car and they both waved them off as they left.

'Who the fuck was that? Is that how you act with everyone?' Liam spat under his breath.

A family walked past into the pub and Hannah and Liam were silent. When they were out of earshot, Hannah responded, 'Alex and I were at school together, he's like a brother.' She was calm, but as she spoke she felt herself shrink back, tears started to well, her voice shaky as her confidence abandoned her; she knew any meagre attempts to trivialise it would be pointless.

'Have you slept with him?'

'Of course not.' Hannah felt angry that she had to defend herself. Her stomach tightened.

'Do you kiss everyone like that?' He was getting louder.

'Like what? It was just a peck on the cheek. His wife was there, for god's sake.'

'Oh, and what would you have done if she wasn't there?' he said sarcastically. 'I saw him feeling you up.'

'You're being ridiculous, it was a hug,' Hannah said, thinking to herself that she needed to stop arguing back with him – her evening was already mapped out. She tried to compose her face, but she couldn't stop her lips trembling as she tried to hold in the tears; to no avail.

'I'm being ridiculous? Seriously, I'm not the one fucking kissing other people, or fucking them for all I know.'

Hannah felt her head spinning and she saw Liam compose himself, his jaw clenched.

'Get …in…the…car,' he hissed.

Hannah got in the car, Liam slammed her door shut and stormed round to his side. Her heart was racing. Should she carry on arguing, or defending herself? Would it make it worse? Would it make any difference to the outcome? No. She had to stop arguing, it was making things even worse.

Liam was silent for the rest of the drive back to Birmingham.

Hannah looked out of the window, tears flowing silently down her cheeks. She dared not look at Liam; he'd see her crying and start shouting again. Maybe he would calm down by the time they got back; the red mist would have dispersed. Maybe. He'd think it through and realise it was innocent. That she loved him and only him, and she wasn't leaving him or having an affair.

The silence was oppressive. An hour later they were at home, pulling into the underground car park of their apartment block. Hannah's heart was pounding and her breathing short. Maybe he'd calmed down.

Hannah put her key in the door, and, as she stepped inside, Liam grabbed the back of her neck and pushed her hard against the wall, bashing her cheek. He hissed into her ear, 'Never do that again. You need to show me some respect and appreciate what you have.' He lifted her skirt, pulling her pants down with his other hand still holding the back of her neck.

Later, much later, she could hear Louis singing, 'What a Wonderful World'.

At night, when he was asleep
and she was in her peaceful place,
when the time was hers,
she'd lie.

Daring not to move or breathe
as tears trickled down her face.
She didn't want to wake him,
she didn't want him to see her cry,
because then,

he'd punish her.

So, she chose her time
to let the anger and the pain out.

He wouldn't know though,
and then she'd fall asleep,
in peace.

Chapter 18

As time went on, Hannah became more and more introverted. By the time they moved to Lichfield, she couldn't really remember who she was before. What her ambitions were; what she'd ever wanted for herself. Everything she did was guided by Liam's wants and needs. She loved working at the Cathedral View Cafe; it was her escape. She knew Liam only let her go to work because it stopped her doing anything else; he had control over her there, but she still felt it was her happy place. She could interact and talk to the customers; obviously within the rules and boundaries, but it was still her escape.

The only truly private space she had was her own thoughts. She'd daydream all the time about a different life.

Serving the lemon tea ladies that came in every Thursday at 2pm, Hannah thought about their last, expensive holiday to New Zealand. They were standing watching the mud pools in Rotorua bubbling away at boiling point, the pressure mounting, throwing the mud up high into the air and making big dollopy, untidy splats as it landed back on itself. There was no one around and she'd imagined pushing Liam in; the perfect murder. He'd have been sucked in, boiled alive as punishment for his vile bullying behaviour, and she'd have carried on living. Later that evening she'd overheard a family talking, one of them clearly a firefighter and he talked how people killed themselves in the pools. Their bodies bobbing back to the top. *Oh well, maybe not the perfect murder then.* As she fantasied, she'd over-poured the tea and spilled it all over the table, having to apologise to the ladies.

Her thoughts got darker over time and Hannah realised that, deep down, she'd known for a long time that her life wasn't right. Listening to her colleagues moaning about life and embracing the good showed her that things could be different. She'd forgotten what normal should be, what was acceptable and not acceptable. What they moaned about was insignificant; the dishes, the housework, snoring husbands. She did wonder, though, if – like her – they hid their real lives. Maybe what they said bore no resemblance to reality. Maybe people all walked around lying about everything, to appear normal and happy. Maybe they were all invisible. All caught up in their own version of hell. What if everything was fake? And they were all carrying on;

acting their parts. No one ever knowing what goes on behind closed doors, no one ever knowing what's behind the smiles, the laughs, the tears.

Hannah knew only too well what it was like to be in a room full of people and to feel completely alone. What if everyone felt like that? Wanting to be rescued, wanting another life, fearful every day. What if the reality for everyone was too much to bear? So, they all pretend. All smile when they really want to scream. Show concern when they really want to shut down; to stop, to walk away.

Hannah felt her life was merely trying to get from day to day without incident. Trying to get to bedtime. She always felt safest at night, when she was in bed, under the covers, and Liam asleep. In those moments, before she fell asleep, she was at peace.

Chapter 19

'OK, thank you,' the stupid officer said. She was doing his head in now. Why couldn't she just fuck off and leave him alone?

'What about other members of her family? Were there any historic problems if she wasn't invited to her cousin's funeral?'

She's like a bloody pitbull, Liam thought to himself.

He was getting frustrated now – there were too many questions. He hadn't anticipated so many about her family. He hated her family. Always there. Always poking their noses in. He had to put his foot down when it was her cousin's funeral; that was too much. Why should he have to spend the day with a bunch of people he didn't know? He had better things to do with his time.

'She didn't really mention them, to be honest.' Liam looked at Rachel to try and gauge what she was thinking. She made him nervous. He didn't know what she was going to ask next. 'There weren't that many at our wedding, I know that much, but they all seemed nice enough to me,' Liam lied again.

Hannah had asked for more people to be at the wedding, but she'd included people from school, the cafe, the bar, uni – they weren't friends, they were just people she knew by chance. He didn't know them, and he didn't want to waste good money on food and drink for them. They'd have proper friends there, people he liked who he wanted to spend time with. Hannah talked about her so-called family all the time when they met. Blah blah blah, he'd thought to himself. *Who gives a fuck, they're in the past*. He didn't know why Hannah had to keep going on about them, rubbing it in about how *wonderful* her family were; it was an unwelcome reminder of how dysfunctional his own were. He avoided them, so why would he spend time with hers. He'd told her: she didn't need them now. They were a family, they didn't need anyone else. He let her keep in touch with her parents, he'd even put their phone numbers in her contact list in her new phone; what more did she need?

'What about school or uni friends? Was there anyone specific she mentioned she didn't like?'

Why the fuck is she asking that again, how many times?

'Like I said,' Liam said sharply. He could feel himself getting angry, so he took a deep breath and composed himself. 'Like I said, Hannah could be a bit of a recluse at times, she liked her own space,' he answered, but the officer just sat waiting for him to say something else. The silence was long and uncomfortable.

'I'm really sorry but I feel quite ill, can we have a break?' he asked, feigning exhaustion.

'Of course, Mr James,' Rachel said.

Good, now fuck off.

Learning to lie.

Learning you have a choice.

Learning you are worth something.

Learning, this is your life.

Not his.

Never his.

Yours.

Chapter 20

Hannah always liked the lady who came in every Wednesday at 3pm; rain or shine. She'd been there the first day Hannah started her new job in Lichfield; not long after they moved into their house. She always spoke to Hannah, asked how she was, whether she had plans for the weekend, what she'd have to eat later. To most customers, Hannah was invisible. She liked that though; she could blend into the background. Occasionally she'd get a chatty one who would ask awkward questions, asking about her husband, what he was like, did they have children, and then *why not*? The more questions, the more lies she had to tell, and the more lies she had to remember. This lady was different. Judith always asked questions that were easy to answer. Hannah didn't have to lie, and it made her feel valued and relaxed. She didn't ask questions just to make conversation; she genuinely wanted to know how she was.

Once, when Hannah was tidying her table, Judith put her hand gently on top of hers and said, 'Choice, my dear, it's the most important tool you have. Use it wisely.'

Hannah felt as though Judith knew her, she could see into her soul and understand her.

Judith ran a local domestic abuse charity. Jane told her all about it; the terrible story of Judith fleeing in the middle of the night with only the clothes on her back and two toddlers. She'd broken free, made a new life for herself and her children, and gone on to set up the charity almost thirty years before.

One day, when Judith was leaving, she gave Hannah a leaflet and said, 'If you ever need to talk, I'm here. Just read this and leave it at work, don't take it home.'

Hannah looked at the leaflet – it was from Judith's charity. She wasn't a victim, though, Judith must have misunderstood something she'd said; she was happily married.

'I'm fine, thank you,' Hannah said sharply; embarrassed at Judith's presumption.

Judith put a hand on her shoulder as she left.

Hannah put the leaflet in her pocket. She didn't need it; there were people in much worse situations than her. She would put it in the bin.

She had a good home, a loving husband, and they did everything together; they were a team. How dare she think Hannah was in that situation, nothing was further from the truth.

Hannah cleared the table and went to the toilet. She sat on the toilet, opened the leaflet and read the bullet points:

- Does your partner call you names or put you down in front of others?
- Do they isolate you from family and friends?
- Do they withhold money?
- Have there been any sexual assaults?
- Do they make threats towards you?
- Are they tracking you?
- Do they destroy your personal property or sentimental items?
- Do they criticize everything you do – from your appearance to how you act?
- Do you feel like you're constantly making excuses for their behaviour?

Hannah didn't see herself as a victim, but she mentally ticked every box. She read the list again slowly. Each bullet point made her angry, brought the memories flooding back, a reality check she didn't want to hear; she wondered when she'd started to believe her own lies. Carefully, she folded the leaflet up, and put it back in her pocket.

For the next hour of her shift, all she thought about was the leaflet and What if? *What if I could leave? What if I'm strong enough? What if today is the most important day of my life?* She thought back to a book she'd been given by her friend Elaine for her eighteenth birthday, when she was thinking about uni. Hannah was full of self-doubt; her dad was telling her to get a job in admin and she wanted to paint. He was constantly telling her she would never amount to anything, and her friend was telling her to believe in herself, to do it, to be ambitious, be unfettered by the restrictions her father placed her. Elaine had riled her up when they were out.

'I'm on a mission with you, Hannah Chattabox, I want you to be the best you can be, how you want to be,' she said. Elaine had drunkenly held Hannah's face in her hands. 'Promise me you'll read it tomorrow,' she demanded.

'Yes, yes, yes, I will honest,' Hannah had said, as she grabbed her hand, dragging Elaine onto the dancefloor.

The evening after her birthday, post hangover, Hannah had sat curled up in an armchair with a coffee and the book. *Beliefs and how to change them...for good!* by Tony Burgess and Julie French. It was short, and punchy and had lots of practical exercises in. Hannah read it cover to cover and did all the exercises in one go; she decided that evening she was going to uni, and that was that. Her mum had smiled when she told them, her dad was less enthusiastic.

Hannah had often thought about the book during the time she was with Liam, but the thoughts were fleeting as she resigned herself to a life of *servitude*.

She thought back to the exercises as she worked – serving, distant, smiling, nodding.

What if I can do this? she asked herself, over and over.

What if I can do this?

What if I can do this?

What if I can do this?

She dropped the 'what if' as the book instructed.

I can do this.

I can do this.

I can do this.

Suddenly, she felt a lightness and an unfamiliar feeling, an old feeling she'd lost over her years with Liam. *Ambition.* Ideas and thoughts flooded her head; filling a space that had lain infertile for years. She went to the toilet with her notepad and tore the first few sheets of orders out, leaving bare pages. Bare pages waiting to be filled. She sat on the toilet lid and scribbled, capturing everything she could. She hadn't felt so motivated, so sure, so alive in years. She couldn't help smiling as she wrote. Eventually, she looked at her watch; she needed to get back to work. She put the notepad in her locker and went back to serving the last few customers before close.

But she also worried all afternoon, on her way home, whilst she was cooking Liam's favourite dinner, and when she got her regular call from him driving back from Birmingham to make sure it would be on the table.

He'd soon be home.

He'd soon be questioning her.

He'd soon find out.

She heard the front door open and her heart raced; it was beating so hard it hurt as her chest tightened. As he walked in her hands were shaking so much, she dropped a plate of food on the floor. It smashed, leaving a pile of chicken, pasta and vegetables mixed in with the broken china.

'You idiot, what did you do that for?' Liam shouted. 'Fucking useless, clean that up. Where's mine?' He pushed past her to the dinner table, sat down and started to eat.

Hannah cleared the food and bits of plate from the floor; she wouldn't be eating anything tonight. As she was tidying up Liam asked his usual questions but was so distracted by her ineptitude that he glossed over what she was saying, as he dropped out snide comments.

When they went to bed, Hannah felt quite pleased with herself. She hadn't told Liam about her conversation with Judith; she'd kept it to herself, she'd actually lied.

It was the first of many lies, and it became the most important thing she'd learn to do.

That night, Hannah lay in bed, thinking. She thought about what had happened since she met Liam. She thought about the leaflet. She didn't want to admit it, but she knew she was a victim of domestic abuse and violence; she was ashamed.

She lay there as she did most nights, with a jumble of thoughts, but tonight was different. Her thoughts had been written down earlier that day, they had form and motivation, a direction.

Hannah had a moment of pure clarity. *I can do this.*

She knew at that moment, at 3am in the morning, that she wanted to leave, that she would leave, and she needed to plan how to leave. She'd thought about it so many times over the years, but always made excuses for his behaviour; consoling herself that she'd leave next time. This time was different. *I can do this.*

The next time Judith came in, Hannah immediately went to serve her.

'Are you OK, my dear?' Judith asked with her warm smile and tender eyes.

'Can I talk to you?' Hannah asked tentatively.

Over the next few weeks Judith came in more frequently and Hannah had quiet conversations with her as she served and tidied up around her each day. Judith gave her back her confidence and Hannah started to realise she did have a choice, and that she would use it wisely.

Life with Liam remained the same, but Hannah felt her strength returning. After her usual FaceTime lunch with Liam, she ate a chocolate biscuit. It tasted divine; it tasted of freedom, it tasted of her future. She felt so pleased with herself for eating it, for not feeling guilty, for knowing it was her choice to eat it, that she had another. She didn't tell Liam when he asked what she'd eaten that day; that was a turning point.

There was no way she'd ever be able to divorce Liam. She'd never forgotten what he'd said about killing her. She knew he meant it, divorce wasn't an option; she realised now, more than ever, how much the threat of violence controlled her. Just because he had hadn't hit her for a while didn't mean he wouldn't. He controlled everything, he would never let go of that control. She had to leave, and he could never know where she'd gone.

Chapter 21

Leaving took planning. It took time to get the money together, and to come up with a plan to make sure he never found her. Her plan needed to be fool proof. She had to think like him, and think what would he notice about her? What changes would he see? What would give her up?

She'd already learnt to lie to him, a little more each day. But slipping up about eating a biscuit would have very different consequences to slipping up about her escape plan. She knew how to pretend to others, to lie and smile as she crumbled with fear inside. This was a skill she needed to hone, to lie to him more and more, without guilt, without fear of retribution. Otherwise, he would know.

Knowing she would leave gave Hannah an inner power that made it easier to plan and to lie. She had the end in sight. A life free of fear and violence. A life with a future, with hope, laughter, and love.

Survival skills were what Hannah had learnt in the time she was with Liam. Every time she complied with his wishes and didn't fight back and bowed to his orders, was another day without violence. She felt she controlled his violence, and if she controlled his violence, she thought that meant she controlled him.

She knew how far to go in an argument and, when they did argue, she wasn't compliant all the time. She'd argue back, usually defending herself when he accused her of eating things she hadn't, or speaking to people she shouldn't, or her weight, or if she bought food that wasn't good for them, or how much exercise she hadn't had. It was always about what she should or shouldn't do, never about him. She could never turn the tables and ask him.

So, Hannah knew how to argue, what to say, what not to say, when to stop; it controlled the violence. She didn't see until now that his violence had controlled her and all she was doing was complying more and more; it gave him the power, not her. Now though, she knew that she needed to harness her newfound confidence if she wanted to escape. She needed to take her power back if she was going to survive.

She aided Liam in constructing the lie, the facade, the veneer. The outside view was a beautiful couple, in love, blessed; a source of envy to others. In reality, it was covered by an ugly scab, and if anyone had bothered to pick at it, it wouldn't have taken long to see the truth.

No one ever did though.

As Hannah thought about her new life and what she would do, she started to realise that she had to employ the same methods that had managed his violence; she had to survive. She had to think ahead. She had to be smarter. She had to make sure there was no way of him finding her. She knew he would be relentless in his search for her, so she had to leave enough to throw him off, but she needed to make sure the police, if they were involved, knew she'd left, and that she didn't want to be found. The last thing she wanted was a long drawn-out investigation trying to find her and then Liam discovering where she was. So, she'd instructed Judith, if Liam had reported her as missing, she should inform the police after she'd gone; once she knew she was safe at the refuge. They would know then that it was her choice to leave and for them not to follow. She also asked Judith if she'd visit her parents, explain she was safe, that she was sorry for leaving, and that at some point, not now, but at some point, she'd be in touch.

As Hannah regained her confidence, and her self-esteem grew, she could now see Liam for who he was, and she'd stopped making excuses for his behaviour. He was someone she once thought was good-looking and kind, but she now only saw the ugly inside him. She saw him for what he was: a narcissist, a bully, a pathetic egotistical misogynist. Everything he did revolved around him; what he thought, what he wanted. He had no concern for anyone else, or good thoughts about anyone else. His entire existence was about him and him alone. Hannah needed to play on that until she was ready to leave and everything was in place for her to escape.

At times she had to stop herself from saying what she really thought. When she wanted to tell him what she was doing and that she could see him now, and knew what he was, and he was pathetic, and she was leaving. But she had to play the long game and stop herself. One slip and he would beat the living daylights out of her. And, if he went too far, it would be the last.

Sometimes,
When you can only go forward,
no matter how scary,
you have to go.

You have to be strong and realise,
this is it.

Your way out.

Your only way out.

Chapter 22

Today was the day. She'd gotten up at 5:45am as she always did to cook Liam's breakfast and make his sandwiches. It was light outside; the sun was already casting its warmth across the garden. She waited for the kettle to boil and the grill to warm up as she watched the morning birds dancing around the garden. Short sprints of flight from one branch to the next; busying themselves and singing the new day in. The lily pad she'd put in her pond a couple of years before and thought had died had sprouted new leaves. A single flower was almost ready to bloom, and although the overriding thought in her head was to leave, she still felt a pang of sadness knowing she wouldn't see the lily open in all its glory. Still, she felt like the lily, waiting to flourish, open, and be free.

Hannah made the coffee and took it up to Liam in bed, as she did every day, and returned to the kitchen to cook his bacon, poached eggs, beans, mushrooms, and tomatoes. He always got up at 6:00am, showered, ate, and left by 6:30am; today was no different. It took every ounce of her soul to remain calm and normal, and not give anything away. He gave her a kiss, a peck on the lips as he left; the last one she'd ever have to endure.

Hannah watched him pull away and knew it would be the last time she'd see him, the last time she'd be in his shadow and fear his presence. Although she couldn't wait, a panic set over her and a fear of failure. What if she couldn't cope on her own? For five years she'd not been allowed to make decisions, to make choices, to have any opinions. She'd hadn't paid bills for years, applied for credit, a mortgage. She couldn't even remember what she liked eating before she met him. She felt as though she was hitting the Reset button; back to factory settings, and had to start again. To start learning how to be an adult, how to live, how to have fun and how to enjoy herself. How to make choices, how to make decisions. The freedom to make the wrong decision.

The thought was fleeting, and, as soon as he was out of view, she was back up the stairs, to quickly shower and dress. Her stomach was turning over, and she felt too nauseous to eat. She'd get something later she thought to herself, something she really wanted. No judgement, no snide comments; maybe a pain au chocolat and a latte. She relished the thought.

She left the house just after 7am, earlier than usual to ensure she caught her first train on time and her connections ran smoothly. She also wanted leave the house before Liam arrived at work and checked the CCTV; she knew he watched it when she left each day, so she had a small window to get out of the house and on the train before he realised she was gone. If he'd seen her leave, he may have tried to ring her, or worse, driven back to Lichfield. She ran to the cafe once she was out of sight of the home CCTV and let herself in. She disabled the alarm, opened her locker, and grabbed her rucksack; it contained a change of clothes, her notepad and a phone that Judith had given her. She reset the alarm, locked up and ran to the train station to get the 7:44am into Birmingham New Street. Although, that was the first ticket destination, she wouldn't be getting off there.

The wait for the train was excruciating. She was fifteen minutes early and it felt like an eternity. It was already hot and going to be another scorcher of a day. An older woman, in her fifties maybe, sat on a bench, cooling herself with a Spanish fan. It reminded Hannah of one her grandma had given her when she was a toddler: black and lacy with red bits and silver sequins; she'd felt so proud, so grown up when she got it. A few office workers, male and female, stood around her; most on their own but a couple of them, women, chatting about the previous evening and then bitching about someone called Jodie who wasn't pulling her weight, and apparently wore heels far too high for an *office environment*. Hannah tried to blend in with her fellow travellers, but fidgeted; stepping back and forth trying to see who else was there. Making sure Liam wasn't. She stood at the far end of the station, away from the steps leading up to the platform, and slightly out of view of any new arrivals walking up. The space around her was filling up and she felt claustrophobic, unused to her environment. Every time she saw the top of someone's head emerge up the steps she stepped back further and leant forward, peering along the platform to get a glimpse, just in case it was Liam. She wouldn't feel safe until she was on the train and headed towards her first stop.

If it was him, she'd decided she was going to make a scene and call for help. She looked around at the other people on the platform –

would they help? By now they were a mixture of loud school children, students, office workers, and two burly men in yellow high vis jackets. If she made a scene, she'd have to scream and kick, attract the attention of them, or the driver maybe. As she thought it through, she could hear the train in the distance hum along the electrified rail as it got closer. A few more people ran up the steps, but now Hannah couldn't see them properly. There were too many of them. Her travel companions moved toward the train, as it came to a standstill in front of her. The train doors beeped and slid open, a few passengers disembarked, and the space around her emptied as people boarded in a hustle of bodies. But, Hannah held back whilst she watched the other passengers board. Liam definitely wasn't there. She felt an overwhelming sense of relief, and the tears started to well; she could feel a lump in her throat closing her airway. She swallowed and took a long deep breath to calm her nerves.

I can do this.

She stepped forward out of the shadows and looked around before she got on. The last time she'd ever be in Lichfield. The last time she'd wake up fearing what Liam would say or do. The last time she would have to defend her actions.

She stepped onto the train and sat down in the quiet section with four other passengers, including the lady with the fan, all sitting separately, going about their day. She wondered what she looked like to them – could they tell it was a huge, life-changing day for her, or was she invisible as always? She texted Judith on her new phone.

I'm actually doing this, I'll text you tonight, so you know I'm safe, and I'll let you know to tell the police in a few days. Thank you so much for everything, you're a beautiful, amazing, selfless lady x

A gentle beep indicated the doors were closing, and the train slowly pulled away. As it did, Hannah felt a wave of relief run over her so strong it made her dizzy. She'd done it – she was finally on her way. Her mind was racing, in trepidation for the day that followed, for the life that followed; for the life she'd left behind. She hadn't even been on a train on her own in years and it felt overwhelming. Suddenly, she realised she'd forgotten herself already. She quickly got up, went to the toilet, and changed her top and trainers. Both now green, she put her red trainers, red rucksack, and blue hoody inside a bag for life.

Minutes later, she was waiting at the doors to get off at Blake Street station, hood up and her blond hair tucked out of sight. She had to exit, walk a few minutes up to the main road and catch the first bus into Four Oaks, the next bus to Tamworth train station, then by train to Crewe, then onto Inverness. She kept checking her watch; she hadn't had to plan catching even one train for such a long time, let alone trying to time everything together with buses thrown into the mix. What if she missed one, and it all fell apart and she was stranded? Don't be silly Hannah, you can do this, she told herself. It's just a train, people catch them every day.

Her breathing was fast, her arms shaking and she felt faint. She took some long, deep breaths as the train slowed. *Calm down, Hannah, you've got this.*

Her escape had taken so much planning and lying and constantly fearing she'd be caught. But she'd done it, she'd left, and by the end of the day she'd be safe in Inverness. She expected to be there for a short time before getting a job, her own place, and a life she dreamed of. A life she deserved. Nothing fancy, just free and safe; that's what had kept her going these last few months.

The train came to a jolting stop and the doors beeped. Hannah pressed the button for them to open. She looked down and checked her watch again; fifteen minutes for the bus and two hours before the train. Everything on time, going to plan. Hannah couldn't help but smile to herself, she felt giddy with excitement. Scared, yes, but excited; it was actually happening.

She stepped down onto the platform and ran down the steps into the car park, to get to the road. As she hit the last step she stopped in her tracks as she stared directly into Liam's eyes, less than two feet away. He stood next to a car – not his – with the passenger door open.

'Get in,' he said, almost in a whisper, without taking his stare off her.

Chapter 23

Judith sat in her office going through her case files of the women and children passing through her doors. She thought about Hannah and although she no doubt had a difficult day ahead, train and bus jumping, and a long journey to Inverness, she'd taken that all important step. She was finally free to make her own choices. She could choose her lunch on the train. She could choose to stop off if she wanted to en route. She could choose to sit next to whoever she wanted. Choose to talk to whoever she wanted. She could laugh and not worry about what Liam would say, or ask, or do.

She'd woken at 6am and worried all morning that something would go wrong until she'd received a text from Hannah earlier in the day.

I'm actually doing this, I'll text you tonight, so you know I'm safe, and I'll let you know to tell the police in a few days. Thank you so much for everything, you're a beautiful, amazing, selfless lady x

When Hannah was safe and well away from Lichfield, and, if Liam had reported Hannah as missing, as Hannah suspected he would, Judith would let the police know, in confidence that Hannah had left. There was no crime to investigate; she didn't want to press charges against Liam. She just wanted to leave, and she didn't want him to know where she was. Hannah would go to a local police station in Inverness and let them know to corroborate the story. It would be a week at the most. Once Judith had received a text from Hannah, she would speak to the officer in charge, so no further time was wasted. She also needed to visit Hannah's parents, to explain why she'd left and not told them; that would be a difficult conversation. Although Hannah had said that she did want to contact them in the future; maybe when she was stronger, more confident.

Judith had helped thousands over the years. She was well known by the police as a trusted partner and confidante. Her selfless acts had no doubt saved lives, helped rebuild lives, and offered people a place of safety and sanity at the worst point in their lives. She'd offered Hannah the same but she'd resisted, constantly saying that Liam would find her, she couldn't just leave, she wanted to do it her way, get away as far as she could. Judith told her the charity would support her through any prosecution if she wanted Liam arrested. And they'd help her sort her finances, where she'd live. They both knew though that prosecution would be difficult. There was no evidence. Her side would be seen as hearsay, speculation, fabrication. Liam would twist every instance and Hannah would be left likely in a worse situation.

Even if Liam was charged, and Hannah was believed, he'd either get a slap on the wrist and any prison term would likely be short, and he'd surely go after her when he was out. Reluctantly, Judith had to agree that Hannah's plan was sensible. It was the least risky, and she would be safe at the refuge in Inverness whilst she started to rebuild her life. It was her best chance of safety. As long as Liam had no idea where she was, she was safe.

Run now, you idiot.

RUN !!!

Chapter 24

Hannah felt the blood in her face drain away as she steadied herself on the car door. Bile surged up within her. She had no thought of running, screaming, shouting; the fear was all-consuming, paralysing. Hannah got in the car without looking at Liam, head bowed. No words could form.

She waited for the punch, expectant that it would be any second, and she braced herself for the impact. It didn't come.

In silence he took her bag, looked through it and found her phone. She looked up as he switched it off and put it in his breast pocket. Then he took out her notepad and waved it in her face. Hannah turned away from him as it skimmed her cheek.

'Idiot!' he spat, shaking his head as he threw it in her lap.

Hannah gasped as she looked down at the notepad with everything in it, her meticulous plans; he knew everything.

Liam placed her bag on the back seat, returning to put Hannah's seat belt on. As he leant over her to fasten it, the familiarity of his smell and his clothes suffocated her; she could barely breathe. Her chest tightened and searing pain spread from the front of her shoulder through to her back, and her brain started to kick back to life. It was telling her to scream, to fight, to get out, run, get help. But her body betrayed her. She felt paralysed, unable to move her arms and legs. Her body was shaking internally, but outwardly she was rigid with fear.

Liam shut the door, returned to the driver's side, and got in in silence. He didn't look at Hannah, and although she wasn't looking at him directly, she could sense that he was looking straight ahead.

She waited for the impact from his fist; it still didn't come.

Scream goddamn you, scream, you fucking idiot, this is your only chance, you have to do it now.

She looked around as other travellers walked past the car. Only moments before she was the same as them; her day planned, her future more certain. She willed every atom of her body to scream, she tried to force her lungs to obey and scream like she'd never done before, but nothing came. Her breathing was laboured and heavy; she couldn't catch her breath to make the slightest sound.

Fucking scream, you idiot, you're worth more than this. Scream, fight, kick him.

The last traveller disappeared from view. *It has to be now.*

Suddenly, a wave of energy took over, compelling her to move. Without thinking she released her belt, her hand grabbing the door to open it, but it was too late; Liam's left arm slammed across her chest, pushing her back down.

'No,' he said firmly, without any emotion.

Hannah tried to push forward, but he turned towards her, as his right hand came up below her chin, grabbing her jaw. His finger pressed hard into her skin, his face pushed up against hers.

'I said, fucking no!'

Hannah sank back into the seat as he reinserted her belt. Her last ounce of will dissipated along with the hope that she would ever be free of him. An intense coldness settled throughout her body, as hopelessness shrouded her; she wasn't strong enough, she'd never be strong enough.

Liam started the car just as another turned into the car park, stopping briefly in front of them, the passenger, a teenage lad in school uniform, got out. The driver, a woman, waved her apology for blocking them. Liam nodded back; calm, detached. More people arrived for the next train; he waited patiently for them to move from his path.

Hannah waited also; it would be soon – the punch. Perhaps when they were back home where no one could see, where no one would care. Her neighbours had no doubt heard the shouting and screaming. As much as Liam wanted to keep that side of him hidden from the rest of the world, when they were home, when he couldn't control himself, the anger in the house would often spill out, but no one ever said anything. They'd nod awkward hellos, avoid eye contact; surely they must know what he's like, surely they'd have heard and talked about it. But no one ever rang the police, knocked on the door when she was alone, asked if she was OK.

Too much trouble.

Don't get involved.

Not my problem.

Liam pulled away, indicating, checking the road; perfectly in control. As he did, his elbow flew up and smashed into Hannah's face, hitting her cheekbone and the side of her nose. She felt the crack as her head flew back, jarring her neck, and the heat of the pain spread across the side of her face.

Chapter 25

He could hold his anger in no longer. He wanted to beat the lying bitch to a pulp in that instant; but he had better plans for her, an elbow to the face was just foreplay. She was going to learn respect and would do as she was told. Any stupidity he'd shown in the past to trust her and let her think for herself was now revoked. He'd shown too much leniency; she would learn what it is to be a wife.

It was her own fault she was in this situation, and she was going to learn the hard way. She may have been planning, but so had he, and she would pay for her treachery. Involving other people in their lives, being brainwashed, and siding with women like Judith wouldn't happen again. Now she was back where she belonged, she wouldn't be allowed such freedoms anymore. He'd been far too soft with her, against his better judgement, and now that would change. She would be treated as she deserved. She had her punishment coming, and then she would start learning again how to be a good and loyal wife, not the conniving, evil slag bitch she'd turned into.

Liam thought back to that first day when he'd seen Hannah; her turquoise eyes had bewitched him. That's what she'd done: bewitched him. He never saw how much she lied and manipulated him back then; this was all her fault. After that first night he'd seen her, he'd been back to the bar every evening and watched her work. She had a coolness about her, with an innocence that still showed through. It was a potent combination.

Two weeks had passed, and he went to Rosie's for breakfast one Sunday morning. And there she was. She looked different without makeup and dressed in the cafe uniform; dark-blue jeans, pink short-sleeved shirt with Rosie's logo, a single dark-pink rose embroidered on the breast pocket. She looked beautiful, her blond hair tied back into a low bun that tucked into the nape of her neck, wisps of hair framing her face, accentuating her eyes.

Liam wanted to say something when she asked him for his order. *Act casual,* he thought. He ordered his usual without plucking up the courage to say anything else. When she brought his coffee over, he stumbled out a sentence. Clearly she thought he was an idiot and brushed him off. One of the other girls brought his breakfast out and Hannah didn't look at him again.

He continued to go to the cafe and chatted. Just small things, breaking the ice, until after a few weeks they'd speak, and she'd laugh at his daft jokes. As they became more comfortable around each other, their conversations became more natural until he eventually asked her out. He'd fallen in love the first time he saw her, but, for Hannah, it had taken longer. He treated her like a princess; he'd never been so pulled in by anyone, no one had come close.

He'd meet her after work, look after her, protect her, make sure she wasn't being hit on by idiots in the bar. He wanted her to move in as soon as she could and he made it easy for her by paying for everything. She gradually stayed over more and more until it became the norm and she moved in fully. She could save her money, not get into debt.

She still had some immature tendencies; wanting to go out with her so-called friends, but he pointed out they weren't real friends.

They didn't know her like he did.

They didn't love her like he did.

They wouldn't look out for her like he did.

She didn't have a wide circle of friends at uni, but the ones she had gradually moved on and Liam and Hannah settled into coupledom. He preferred it like that – he had Hannah all to himself.

They argued occasionally when she tested him and pushed him. He knew she lied about different things; what she'd eaten, who she'd spoken to, who she sat next to. She was worse when she drank, so he'd gradually cut down her drinking. She'd started to put weight on too, so they went on a health drive, going to the gym instead of the bars. Eating healthy food in, rather than going out.

They were a team; they did everything together.

He looked out for her and could see when people were trying to get in the way or trying to get one over on her. He'd tell her how naive she was, but that he'd protect her; no one else loved her like he did, no one else really had her best interests at heart.

On one of the few visits from her parents, her mum had wanted them to go out for a so-called 'girls' lunch. When they arrived, Liam greeted them. He'd bought flowers for Hannah's mum and said he'd booked a private chef for the evening who would cook in the apartment. There was no need for them to go out to a busy restaurant; they could be spoiled at home.

Hannah constantly pushed the boundaries and it drove Liam up the wall. Over the years though, she'd settled down, she stayed in and they did everything together. He helped her shop for clothes too, not many men would do that, he'd tell her. He helped pick out things that suited her. She needed to mature though; she was in a couple, not single, so her clothes should reflect that. She'd be lost without his guidance. She wasn't very good with money, so he looked after everything, paid for everything, sorted the bills. If Hannah wanted anything she'd only to ask, she could have whatever she wanted; within reason.

Sometimes arguments got out of hand. She was like a child, trying to get her own way. Liam didn't like losing his temper, but she knew which buttons to press and she had to learn to show him more respect the way he showed her respect. If it wasn't for Hannah's immature behaviour, they wouldn't argue. It took time for her to grow up, but, over the years, he'd helped her, supported her, moulded her. He loved her, he would have gone to the ends of the earth for her, to protect her.

So, for her to do what she'd done was a betrayal he could never forgive. She had everything and she'd ruined it. He looked across at her as he drove, Hannah's head was slumped forward, a bruise emerging on her cheek, a trickle of blood below her nose. It was her own fault, what else did she expect?

Chapter 26

'Hello, Mrs Jenkins, is it?' Rachel asked Jane.

'Er, yes, it is, Jane. I'm the owner here.'

Rachel could see she was very nervous. 'Is it OK if I ask you a few questions about Hannah James?' Rachel asked, hoping today's interviews would shed some light on Hannah's disappearance and she could get the case closer to being solved. Her boss had already texted her twice for an update and asked if she could pick up another case; one of her colleagues, Ross, had called in sick – again. She had offered Adam to go back to the station but John refused and said *he needed to see things through as part of his training*; Rachel had begrudgingly accepted to carry on babysitting him.

'Of course, please take a seat. I'll just let the girls know to carry on without me.'

Rachel and Adam sat and waited. She looked around the cafe. She'd never been in before, but it seemed nice enough, clean and tidy, and the menu looked pretty good too. Jane came back.

'Can I get you anything?' she asked.

'No, it's fine thank you.' Rachel smiled and indicated for her to sit. Adam shook his head.

'Oh, OK.' Jane sat down. She was upright, rigid, her hands clasped on top of the wooden table waiting for Rachel to speak.

Jane answered all the questions; Hannah's routine, her duties, working hours, favourite customers, any problems, any observations.

'Hannah was a lovely girl, a favourite with the customers. She was brilliant at her job, quiet and shy but always smiling.' Jane paused and slowly shook her head. 'I don't understand where she could be. You work with someone every day, but I realise I don't actually know that much about her. She was a great listener, always there for the girls when they wanted to have a rant about something. She never moaned about anything herself, though. She was reliable, never sick, always punctual, did everything asked of her, and more. She was, is, I'm sorry, the perfect employee.' Jane's voice was shaking, and she was clearly getting upset as the gravity of the situation started to dawn on her.

'What was her relationship like with her husband?' Rachel asked, curious to know if Hannah talked about Liam at work.

'Oh I don't know, to be honest. She always seemed happy, never complained about him, not like the rest of us, whinging about our other halves,' she laughed as she relaxed a little. 'He came in to see her sometimes,' she said brightly, 'she always looked pleased to see him.' She smiled as though remembering Liam in the cafe.

'He was lovely, very attentive.' She smiled again. 'Oh, and he brought her flowers sometimes. He'd also turn up as she was finishing her shift, have a coffee half an hour before we closed, and he'd take her off to dinner. I wish my husband did that occasionally,' she thought out loud. 'To be honest, she had the perfect life. I know she didn't need to work, but she liked being here, with us, with the customers, you know. I think it got her out of the house,' Jane finished.

'Does Hannah have a locker or keep any personal items here?' Rachel asked.

'Oh, yes, yes she does, a locker, erm, I've got a master key somewhere if you just hold on a sec.' Jane hurried off to find the key.

She returned, and Rachel and Adam followed her through to a small cloakroom with three tall lockers and piles of cardboard boxes with polystyrene takeaway tubs inside.

'Sorry, excuse the mess.' Jane looked embarrassed as she opened one of the lockers.

'It's OK,' Rachel smiled. 'I'm OK from here.' She indicated for Jane to leave her.

There wasn't much inside the locker; a black cardigan hung up, a pair of slip-on ballet-style pumps. Rachel imagined Hannah on her feet serving all day. There were a few leaflets, a couple from the bank offering loans and some vouchers for local shops that she'd seen on display on her way in. She checked the pockets of the cardigan and pulled out a folded leaflet that she'd seen many times before.

Interesting. The plot thickens.

In the other pocket she found a Post-it note with a website address and what looked like a password.

Adam bagged the Post-it note and leaflet as evidence, they walked back into the cafe and Rachel asked, 'Did Hannah ever use that?' pointing at the laptop.

'Oh yes, she did occasionally,' Jane replied, 'to be honest she was the only one that ever did. I'm thinking of getting rid of it, a waste of space.'

'Would it be OK if it's removed for examination? It may be helpful,' Rachel asked. She knew the likelihood of it being checked quickly was low at the moment. Emma had grumbled to her the night before about her department's budget being cut *again* and *too much work, not enough staff.* The usual mantra from them all. But she'd rather it was checked anyway, just in case; it would save them time later if they needed it.

'Yes of course, as I say, only Hannah used it. Oh, I do hope you find her, she's so lovely to have around.'

'Thank you,' Rachel replied as she turned to Adam, indicating to bag the laptop; *at least he could make himself useful.*

'OK,' he eagerly nodded, leaving the cafe to get a larger evidence bag.

'It would be helpful if I could talk to your other staff, would now be a good time?' Rachel asked, hoping she could speak to all of them and get it out of the way in one visit.

'Yes, yes, that's absolutely fine, we're quiet as you can see so that's OK, and we're all in today. Well, we will be when Amber arrives,' Jane said, looking at her watch.

Rachel spoke to two of the girls first and then Amber, who turned up half an hour late; Jane rolling her eyes as she came in, reprimanding her quietly, although loudly enough for Rachel to hear.

All three of them gave the same story as Jane. Lovely, kind, helpful, popular. Rachel didn't learn anything new, but the leaflet had intrigued her. She'd seen it many times before and she wondered if this was the first clue to Hannah leaving Liam, and all was not as it seemed in the relationship.

Rachel had of course seen the facade that people presented. At first there wasn't anything to indicate things were wrong apart from Hannah and Liam being *too* perfect. It rang alarm bells, and now she'd seen the leaflet those alarm bells were getting louder.

She'd worked in most areas of policing including Child Sexual Exploitation, Modern Slavery, and General Safeguarding. All areas that linked around coercive control. A seasoned officer, she had eighteen years' experience, and something with Hannah's disappearance didn't feel quite right. There was nothing to suggest any harm had come to Hannah though, other than her gut feeling. Liam was too attentive, he knew too much about Hannah's normal movements, in Rachel's opinion. He spoke to her far too much throughout the day; it wasn't normal and felt like possessive and controlling behaviour – but there was no evidence.

Because of the leaflet and her unease, she'd asked for the laptop at the cafe to be examined by Forensics, just in case. Hannah also didn't seem to have any digital footprint; no social media, very limited call history, it was unusual for her age. It seemed Liam was the only person she called or texted, and from what Rachel could derive she was pretty much estranged from her parents and family. She didn't have any close friends and was as good as isolated. She had no credit history either, having never bought anything on credit since meeting Liam. The house in Lichfield was in Liam's name only and she didn't own a car. She ordered the online shopping on Liam's credit card. She didn't appear to have a bank account; everything seemed to be joint, his accounts, his cards, his phone. Liam had said that's how Hannah wanted it; he'd try to get her to build up credit, but she said she wasn't bothered. She wasn't money savvy, he said. She was happy for Liam to do it all. She didn't want to drive either, she had learned when she was eighteen but she'd never owned a car; she cycled and walked, or Liam drove. She didn't use buses or trains normally, not since they'd moved out of Birmingham; she didn't really go outside of Lichfield, it seemed, unless it was with Liam.

Rachel knew it would take a few days for the laptop to be examined, maybe longer. She had nothing else to go on except a hunch. It was looking as though Hannah had left Liam and it would soon be a closed case, but, she still had a really uneasy feeling about him and she felt she was being manipulated. Why did Hannah have the leaflet? Rachel could see no other reason than her being a victim, and, if that was the case, surely Liam couldn't believe his marriage was perfect; his first thought would be that she'd left him, wouldn't it? Instead, he was adamant that she'd been taken, or something had happened to her. It was a big jump in his thinking; was he really that delusional about his marriage, or, did he have something to hide?

Just do it.

I know it's coming.

Why delay the inevitable?

Chapter 27

She wasn't sure how long she'd been there, was it five or six days? Longer? She didn't know. Liam had taken her clothes and left her naked, her only warmth a large bath towel that she wrapped around herself the best she could. It had been mostly dark apart from a camping torch and the light from a fridge when she opened it; Hannah had no idea where she was. She remembered Liam hitting her in the face in the car and a darkness closing in on her when she must have blacked out. She remembered coming round in the car, and briefly recognising she wasn't in Lichfield, before she felt a second blow to the side of her face. Her mouth had filled with blood leaving its metallic taste, the impact dislodging one of her molars. She thought she must have swallowed it when she passed out again.

When she came round, she was here; it wasn't home. She didn't recognise it; the smells, or the sound. It was cold and damp and had a vile musty smell that hit the back of her throat; it smelt empty, unloved. There were slate shelves set into large square holes in the wattle and daub wall; the holes disappeared into blackness. They reminded Hannah of something but she couldn't place it. The floor beneath her was stone slabs, dusty, cold, and uneven; they sucked any warmth her body created right out of her. The ceiling was the underside of old wide wooden floorboards; she could hear Liam walking across them above her each time just before he entered the room and descended the short flight of steps into what she assumed was a cellar. She could hear running water, ever so slightly, and the sound of cars passing. At times it sounded quite busy, the occasional horn and revved engines, but still quite distant. Just before Liam came down the steps, she'd hear what sounded like a car on gravel; she'd learnt this was Liam arriving before he came into her prison.

She didn't think he'd been there every day. The fridge was stocked with fresh food, the sell-by-dates within a week of the day she'd tried to leave. He'd left fruit, salads, ham and chicken slices, bread, and bottled water. She'd drunk the water and tried to eat some of the fruit, but her mouth throbbed from the gaping hole where her molar had once resided. Her face still stung from the blows she'd received from Liam in the car and she realised her head was cut, having dried, caked blood in her hair. There was blood in her fingernails too; she'd tried to clean them with some of the water, but decided she wanted to preserve it. She didn't know how long she had water for, how long she'd be here, or what Liam's plans for her were. He'd left a bucket for a toilet, but had emptied it only once; it had started to smell vile.

Each time he'd been down it had been in silence. He didn't speak, just checked the fridge, shone his torch at her, looked at her face, at her bruises maybe (his handiwork) and left. He never spent more than a few minutes; never said a word.

Each time he came into the room Hannah waited for more punishment, for Liam to punch her, kick her, pull her hair. So far it hadn't come, but she knew it would.

When he wasn't there, she'd tried the door. It was heavy and old, wooden and solid. It had huge iron hinges, with flaking black paint; rusted in place. There was no opening it. She'd checked the ceiling and the underside of the floorboards; they were solid too. She could see some light around the edges of the ceiling. There must be a rug or something, a piece of furniture maybe above her. She had nothing but her fingers to poke the gaps. She'd tried the plastic handle of the camping lamp, but it was too bendy and soft to get any real purchase.

It was pointless.

She was trapped.

Chapter 28

'Boss, I've been looking over these statements and I've got a really bad feeling about this,' Rachel explained to her Superintendent, John Weaver.

Rachel had read and re-read six statements from Hannah's parents and her work colleagues, and they all said the same thing. They talked about the perfect couple, how happy they were, about their holidays, their meals out, their day trips; all wonderful and rosy, all the same. Reading the same statement six times, Rachel felt as though she was hearing Hannah's voice, not theirs. It was the same story, almost rehearsed. It was what Hannah had told people; what Liam had told people. It was what Hannah was allowed to say. The 'story' of their perfect life was Hannah and Liam's, and these statements were just those words replayed to a new audience.

Rachel's growing suspicion was that none of them really knew Hannah. The leaflet from the abuse charity added to that.

Did they all really think that things were that good, all the time? There's always someone who points at the cracks, the gossip, the insightful little comments that open up a case. There was no mention of arguments, any discontentment, any signs that told a different story.

Rachel wondered if her own experiences through life and work tarnished her views, made her look for things that weren't there. Over her career she'd seen the best and worst of people. Their dirty little secrets, their impulses, and stained existences. She could never understand how evil and ruthless people could be, how manipulative and duplicitous. She'd arrested and charged rapists, murderers, traffickers, paedophiles, and violent partners. She'd picked up victims off the floor and held them, absorbed their pain and tears when they'd lost a loved one; a parent, a sister, a husband, a wife, a child. She'd held their hands and felt their grief. She'd lain awake at night knowing that giving everything of herself would never be enough; for every officer who did the same, it would never be enough. Society was broken, it was ugly, depraved, spoilt and rotten. Seedlings of joy and love were stamped on as soon as they started to appear by those who didn't want happiness and fulfilment for others. Did it mean she couldn't believe in happiness? That a couple could be so loving? That perfect did exist? She wished to her very core that she could believe it.

But she didn't.

Although there was no evidence, no real threads to pull at, no motive, Rachel felt as though something was wrong. Her instinct was that Hannah was abused and Liam had either done something to her, or she'd left because of him. Either way, she wasn't hearing the truth, and that meant she couldn't trust any of the statements; they were as good as useless. No one mentioned the extension, or them planning a family, but those were the sorts of things that people chat about, that Liam was so excited to tell her. Maybe they kept that sort of thing to themselves, maybe.

She had no evidence other than her instinct.

The laptop was now with Forensics and she wanted it bumped up the list. The caseload for the team was running at its highest, rising crime and less officers meant budgets were at the tightest she'd ever known, and caseloads at an all-time high. The one thing on her side was the veracity of the forensics team. It was headed up by her best friend Emma who had worked in Forensics for thirteen years. Her experience and integrity were exemplary, and she had an enviable reputation in her field. She'd made the unusual transition from traditional forensics to digital and if there was anything to find, Emma and her team would; Rachel just had to get the laptop bumped up the list. Easier said than done, when there were suspects in cells waiting to be charged, officers against the clock and evidence sitting in Forensics being the difference between them walking or being charged.

She needed to find something that would move it up as a priority; perhaps suggesting to John it would help her close the case quicker so she could move on.

She talked it through with John, but he wasn't budging. He agreed there was nothing evidential to move the laptop up the list and he couldn't bypass the process on a hunch, not when solid cases were waiting on Forensics, he'd told her.

'How's Adam getting on interviewing the neighbours?' he asked.

'Erm, I'm on it next.' Rachel said, a feeling of guilt stirred; she knew she could, should, have delegated it to him.

117

'Well why hasn't Adam done it? He's getting paid to work not shirk.' John shook his head. 'Bloody apprenticeship scheme.'

'I'm going to do it with him; he struggled with Mr James, so I thought he needed extra support,' she answered, feeling John was on her side.

'OK, well let me know how that goes, both the interviews and his performance.'

'Yes, boss,' Rachel answered and left the room.

Just because you choose not to see
doesn't mean you don't.

Sitting there, judging, but saying nothing.

I judge you.

I pity you.

To have the power to say something but not use it.

But,
I know you judge me too,
I know you pity me too.

'Why don't you leave?'
I know you say it.

But,
I can't…

I need your help.

Chapter 29

A large, balding man in his early fifties answered the door to Rachel. She noticed his ill-fitting pin-stripe navy suit did nothing for his physique, nor his profuse sweating which wafted past her nose along with a distinct smell of alcohol; whisky, perhaps.

'Hello. DCI Taylor, may I have a moment of your time?' Rachel showed her badge to the burly man.

'Uh, yes, what's wrong?' he said, startled.

'I'm investigating the disappearance of your neighbour, Mrs Hannah James,' Rachel said.

'Oh, OK, I thought there was something wrong with my son,' the man answered, then visibly relaxed.

'May I come in for a moment, and ask you some questions?' Rachel asked.

'Yep, but I don't know anything, I've got ten minutes,' he said looking at his watch and leading her into his lounge. It was neat and tidy – surprisingly immaculate, she thought.

'Does anyone else live with you Mr…?'

'Riley, Gary Riley.' The man stumbled his words out. 'No, just me here after my wife left. She took my son, and now I have to sell the bloody house to pay for the privilege,' he added bitterly; it explained the tidiness.

'I'm sorry to hear that, Mr Riley.' Rachel paused for a moment so as not to seem dismissive. 'I'd like to ask you a few questions about your neighbours, Mr and Mrs James.'

'OK,' he said tentatively, 'but I don't know anything. I don't know them.'

'Do you remember the last time you saw Mrs James?' Rachel asked.

'No, not really, a couple of weeks maybe, just around. You don't really notice.' He shrugged and continued, 'The way these houses are laid out you don't really see your neighbours. I prefer it that way, to be honest.'

'Can you remember how she seemed when you last saw her?' Rachel asked.

'How she seemed?' Mr Riley paused and thought for a moment with a look of confusion on his face. 'Well, I don't know; I've never spoken to her,' he answered, dismissively shrugging his shoulders again.

'What about Mr James, do you know him, ever talk to him?' Rachel asked, but got the distinct impression Mr Riley didn't really care.

'Nope, and never. Is that it? I've got a meeting to go to, a job interview,' he said abruptly.

It was time for her to leave and Rachel moved towards the front door. 'OK, thank you for your time, if you remember anything please ring me on this number.' She gave him her card as she left without any expectation that he'd call, or that he'd be getting a job that day.

Rachel had spoken to several of the neighbours, but the story was the same each time; no one knew the James's, they didn't socialise, they kept themselves to themselves, they were no trouble.

She knocked on the next door and a tall, thin, elderly gentleman with a mop of white hair answered, he stooped forward to listen. As Rachel started to ask him about the James's house, a short slim grey-haired woman, his wife she assumed, appeared from behind and said, 'There's a lot of shouting…'

Mr Lees shot her a look and said in deep, clipped English, 'Now, now, Jean, stop gossiping, you know what you're like.'

She stopped and smiled, bowing her head with embarrassment.

Rachel wanted to hear more and pull at the thread, but by now Mr Lees had stepped forward in front of his wife, blocking their conversation, his tall yet spindly frame dominating the space over his petite wife. Rachel felt just a little bubble of frustration as he tried to close the door. She put her hand out to stop it and he stepped back surprised, almost knocking his wife over as she moved out of the way; Rachel thought he was a man used to ruling the roost.

'Mr Lees, I know it may appear to be gossip but I would still like to hear it and rule it out if necessary. At this stage of an investigation all information is considered,' she said with authority.

Mr Lees nodded. 'Yes, I'm so sorry, do come in.'

As Rachel entered, the house smelled of lavender, it reminded her of her Auntie Maureen and Uncle Tony's house; warm and welcoming, cakes, biscuits and wine always on offer. She looked round and noticed the big bottle of sherry on the sideboard. She smiled to herself; they were definitely of the same generation.

Mrs Lees told her she'd heard shouting a number of times at the James's house and once, when she was walking her dog at night, it was dark, and she could see clearly into the lit room. She said, 'He was standing over her, shouting, waving his arms around and that poor girl was sat cowering on the settee, she looked terrified, the poor wee thing. I thought about knocking on the door, but, you know, I felt a bit embarrassed and a bit nosey. We all have our problems.' She looked at her husband and Rachel felt a little sadness for her.

Rachel asked if she'd ever spoken to Hannah, and she said although she'd tried to speak to both of them they kept themselves to themselves and usually just nodded.

At least she felt she was getting somewhere.

After she'd left their house, she saw Liam standing in his lounge watching her. What was he thinking? What did he know? Had Hannah just left? Had they argued and it had got out of control? Maybe he'd killed her and was covering it up. Rachel had dealt with every sort of evil and something about Liam made her uneasy.

Rachel looked back at him with curiosity as she walked to the next neighbour's front door.

Suddenly Liam came flying out of the house, swearing at her. There you are, she thought to herself.

'Why are you fucking talking to them? We don't know them. They're fucking nosey. If they say they know us, they don't!' he shouted as he flew towards her.

'Mr James, it's just part of our enquiries.' Rachel held her hands out in front of her; palms open to try and calm him and ready in case he got violent. Adam was now by Rachel's side; at least she had him for support, although limited, she was happy he was there for a change.

'Why the fuck are you talking to them, blackening my name? I don't know these people!' Liam shouted. His face was red, his hands in fists, his knuckles white.

'Mr James,' Rachel tried to speak and calm him down, but he continued, 'They're fucking nosey, that's what they are,' Liam spat. 'What the fuck do you think they know?' Suddenly he stopped, stepped back, and calmed himself. 'I'm sorry, I'm so sorry, I'm just so tired. This isn't me.'

Oh, but I think it is.

'That's OK, Mr James, I appreciate you're under a lot of pressure, it's OK. Let's go inside and talk.'

'It's OK, I'm sorry. I just need to go home and get some sleep. You don't need to come in,' he said.

'Rest assured, I'll keep in touch,' she replied as she and Adam walked to the next neighbour, leaving Liam to go into his house alone.

Rachel had now seen the side she'd thought was there. She expected to see an innocent person explode; we all have it in us. People can lose it when under pressure, and in extraordinary situations, but Rachel saw in Liam's eyes what she had only ever seen in the guilty. She knew at that moment her instincts were right; his marriage wasn't all it was cracked up to be, and he was an abuser. In that instant Rachel's mind focused on two lines of enquiry. Hannah had either suffered at Liam's hands, or she'd managed to get away from him. Rachel needed to urgently find out which one was true.

She got back to the station and found John sitting in the soulless canteen with its newly painted white floors and walls, with mismatched tables with varying plastic chairs sourced from the grotty old station; apparently the budget didn't stretch that far. John looked like he was just finishing up a meeting with his boss, Detective Chief Superintendent Owen, so Rachel got herself a coffee from the machine and loitered for a couple of minutes until John was free.

'I know he's done something to her, either now or in the past,' she said. 'Can you authorise the laptop to be pushed up the list?'

'Look,' John started, 'you know the law as well as I do, Rach, you can't bypass the process. We've got too much work on to make any exceptions, you know that. Now find some evidence we can actually work with. Then we can consider if it's enough to prioritise the laptop.'

Chapter 30

Liam stood in his bay window and watched the officer going to each house. The thick ones with the ugly, noisy kids weren't in, but the drunk bloke, Gary or Graham, whatever his name was, invited her in. *What was he saying, nosey bastard?*

Then she went to the dumb old bloke with his do-gooder wife. What were they saying? *Oh, we don't get Christmas cards from them,* or something equally stupid?

Liam tolerated his neighbours; he would pretend to be nice if they came to the door or waved at him, but he avoided eye contact if he could when he was out front. Where he grew up, he didn't have neighbours, just the staff and they knew their place, he wished his neighbours here did. The old bint Mrs Lees across the road was always waving like a lunatic. Liam would nod to her and get in the house or car as quickly as he could; once she started that would be it, and she talked absolute bollocks. The next house he bought would be private, isolated, more of what he was used to, what he longed for, what he deserved; where he could get on with his business without nosey prying eyes from the curtain-twitching brigade.

As he watched Rachel speak to each one, he could feel himself getting angrier and more wound up. *What were they saying? What had they seen?* They couldn't know anything. Anything they did say would just be gossip, uncorroborated gossip. Liam could see Rachel staring him down through the window, smirking as she went to the next house, looking at him, gloating. *You don't know fuck*, he thought to himself as his anger bubbled to the surface. Without thinking he stormed out of the house towards her, straight past the useless child officer.

'Why are you fucking talking to them? We don't know them, they're fucking nosey if they say they know us, they don't.'

Liam had had enough now. She came towards him saying something, but Liam was enraged. 'Why the fuck are you talking to them, blackening my name, I don't know these people. They're fucking nosey, that's what they are. What the fuck do you think they know?' Liam felt the rage overtaking his reasoning, and suddenly realised he'd gone too far; he'd been trying to keep calm, but his anger seeped out and he couldn't contain it any longer. He didn't know how he ended up on the pavement shouting and swearing at her. The red mist had come down and he couldn't help himself. He just needed to remain calm and once Judith had told them Hannah had left, he'd be OK, they'd drop the case. He was starting to wish he hadn't called the police, the only reason he had was because it was in the text. But Judith hadn't called them and keeping up the lies was taking its toll on him. There was too much going on now, and he was losing track of what he'd said and lost his cool.

'I'm sorry, I'm so sorry, I'm just so tired. This isn't me,' he said, trying to rescue the situation. The idiot officer said something about going inside to talk, but he made his excuses and went back in, shutting the door and Rachel out.

When is Judith going to talk to the police? he thought. He knew that was the plan as he'd seen the texts. *Who the fuck did they think they were? Stupid idiots.* He fetched the mobile he'd taken off Hannah and switched it on. The only number in there was Judith's with the texts Hannah had sent and the texts he'd sent pretending to be her.

He re-read the first text from Hannah to Judith.

I'm actually doing this, I'll text you tonight, so you know I'm safe, and I'll let you know to tell the police in a few days. Thank you so much for everything, you're a beautiful, amazing, selfless lady x

Shit, he thought to himself, Hannah is supposed to tell Judith when to tell the police. He'd been waiting for Judith to do it, but he needed to text her to tell her, and he hadn't realised it in his rage.

He re-read their exchanges as he paced around his kitchen. He needed to make sure he worded it correctly. He'd already sent a couple of texts to let Judith know Hannah was at the refuge. He re-read the three texts and sat down and wrote the next.

Hi, just to let you know you can tell the police now

He deleted it and thought about how Hannah had texted Judith before.

Hi, wonderful lady, hope you're OK, I am really happy here, you can tell the police now x

He re-read it and the previous texts to make sure they flowed, to make sure Judith didn't become suspicious.

He pressed Send.

He stood up and paced in his kitchen. He couldn't get out of his head that stupid officer with her smug little know-all face. He'd wanted to punch her when he'd gone outside, to show her, but he'd stopped himself. As he waited for Judith to respond, he could feel himself getting more agitated; his anger had nowhere to go, he felt it inside him, a blackness eating away, and he needed to let it out.

He grabbed his car keys and drove over to see Hannah.

I know you're coming to save me.

We had a plan.

I know you'll be here soon.

Chapter 31

It felt colder now, her towel pulled tightly round her helped a little but her feet weren't covered; they were so cold she could no longer feel them, apart from the occasional shooting pains that deep-set cold brings. She'd occasionally wrap the towel around them to try and warm them up as she sat shivering; it didn't help. Hannah kept trying to imagine herself somewhere else, somewhere warm – a beach in St Lucia, her garden in the summer, a country pub with a roaring fire in the autumn. Somewhere she could imagine herself – relaxed, happy, warm. Her stomach cramped from hunger. She knew she needed to eat properly and she longed for something hot, filling and comforting. She imagined eating a hot roast chicken dinner with crispy skin, Yorkshires, roast potatoes with piping hot chicken gravy, sage and onion stuffing burnt on the top, and slightly over cooked vegetables; the way she liked them. She inhaled thinking about it, almost tasting and smelling the perfect Sunday dinner; almost. Everything she had in her prison was out of the fridge – cold, uninspired, pointless. It hadn't gone any way to filling her up and she'd eaten nearly everything. All that was left was a cranberry and raspberry yoghurt, three wrinkled tomatoes, a cucumber that was watery and brown in the middle, and cooked chicken breast that had already gone off when she opened it her first day; it's pungent smell making her gag. She knew she couldn't eat that unless she wanted to poison herself; *maybe that's how I'll die, slow and painfully.* She picked up the tomatoes and examined them, squeezing them gently; they were squidgy but there was no mould, so she ate one and tried to imagine she was at a fancy buffet on a cruise ship, and she had just pinched a nice ripe juicy tomato. It didn't help; she still gagged as she forced herself to swallow it.

Over the last few days, she'd thought of everything that could happen next, fearing that Liam would kill her, or that she'd be stuck in the cellar or somewhere else, with him…for ever. Those were the only options she saw at the start. She'd thought about ending it all, but the only thing that was keeping her going was her plan with Judith, who knew how dangerous Liam was. As soon as she realised Hannah wasn't in Inverness, she'd know something was wrong and she'd tell the police. Once Judith had told the police about her leaving and

128

waiting for corroboration from Inverness Police, they'd realise she wasn't there, and they'd go after Liam, follow him, find her. It was her failsafe, her only hope, that someone would find her and rescue her, so she needed to eat and keep her strength up. She couldn't let herself starve and slip away.

She'd just reached to the back of the fridge to pick up the yoghurt when she heard the sound of a car on the gravel. Liam…it was only ever him.

Her stomach lurched; what now? She left the yoghurt, shut the fridge, and scuttled back to the corner she sat in, wrapping the towel around her shoulders, watching the darkness where the door would open. She heard Liam's footsteps boom above her, fast and angry footsteps flying across the room. She made herself as small as she could, wrapping herself into a tight ball. This was it, this was him coming for her; the inevitable beating.

The door opened, the light casting a dim shadow as he descended the steps. The room was small, and Hannah felt him closing in. The first blow came to her side, a crack below her ribs, the pain all-too-familiar as she choked and threw up the tomato. Over the years she'd learnt how to take a beating; always curled up into a ball, covering her head and face. Liam avoided her face most of the time and only bruised and cut anything other people wouldn't see. Only twice had he given her a black eye that they had had to make excuses up for. Today, though, she felt his hand at the back of her head, grasping her hair, pulling her head back, bringing his hand hard across her face. Her nose cracked, it knocked her sick, the taste of iron filled her mouth as her cut lip bled into it and her nose bled into to her throat.

'That fucking bitch thinks she's clever, thinks she know us. I'll fucking show her!' he raged.

Liam dragged Hannah upwards off the floor by her hair, put his hand around her throat and pushed her up against the wall. Hannah's legs flayed around, toes brushing the ground as Liam screamed into her face, 'You're all the fucking same; you think you're fucking clever, that fucking stupid little slag.' Liam's face was right in Hannah's, her feet off the floor and his body pressed so hard up against hers that it held her against the wall. 'I'll fucking show her.'

He released his grip, but, as Hannah's legs buckled, Liam turned her round and pushed her against the wall. He held her there with his forearm and she knew what was next as she felt him undo his trousers. 'I'll fucking show her, I'll fucking show that slag of a bitch.'

Chapter 32

Judith had called the station as soon as she'd received the text from Hannah; it was what she'd been waiting for.

Hi, wonderful lady, hope you're OK, I am really happy here, you can tell the police now x

She asked to speak to the officer in charge which turned out to be Rachel, who she'd known for a few years. After a couple of minutes on hold the call handler patched her through.

'Hi, Judith, how are you?'

'Hi, Rachel, I'm fine thanks. Thanks for taking my call – I know you're busy,' she answered.

'That's OK, I know if you're calling it's important. It's about Hannah James, isn't it?'

'Yes, it is, erm, just to start Hannah's OK,' she started.

'Oh thank god,' Rachel answered, 'I was starting to go down the murder route, if I'm honest.'

'No, no, and that's why I'm calling,'

Rachel interrupted, 'Look, is it OK if we meet in person? I can pop down to you in thirty minutes, I've got a briefing in ten.'

'Yes please, but I'll come to you,' Judith answered. relieved that she could see Rachel so quickly,

Judith felt a sense of relief as she walked to the car, being able to see Rachel so quickly; it was much easier than discussing it on the phone. As she drove up to the station she thought about Hannah, and how proud she was of her, and the courage she had to make her escape. She thought back to her own escape thirty years before and the similarities. Back then there was nowhere to go, but now there were refuges all over the country. As well as an accomplishment, it also brought her great sadness to know they were still needed, and demand for them was, sadly, at an all-time high.

Hannah was at the start of a difficult journey, but Judith knew she had an inner strength and support at the refuge in Inverness to do it. The team at the shelter would help her change her name by deed poll, find accommodation, sort her finances, and look for work. They'd give her practical advice, as well as the emotional support Judith had already started with her. It would be difficult, but she would be free to make her own choices and be in charge of her own destiny.

Judith understood the pressures and high demands on the police, and Hannah's ruse could be seen as wasting police time, but equally, Hannah had been left with no choice. She needed to leave him with no trace; Judith needed the police to respect Hannah's decision and to safeguard her against Liam. As she waited for DCI Taylor at the police station, Judith received another text from Hannah.

Hiya, lovely weather here, hope you're OK, have you told them yet? X

Judith replied just as Rachel entered the room.

Just at the station, I'll let you know when I've finished, stay safe xx

'Hi, Judith, how lovely to see you. We can use Interview Room 1.' Rachel guided Judith into the room.

Judith was all-too-familiar with the station; it was a new building and the team had recently moved from Frog Lane to Eastern Avenue, but she'd already spent enough time to know the rooms there. Two cups of tea were already waiting on the table as they sat down; Rachel knew her beverage of choice.

Chapter 33

Rachel often spoke to Judith when their paths crossed for different cases. She loved working with her and respected her immensely. She listened as Judith relayed the events of the past year, how she'd met Hannah, how brutal Liam was, that Hannah didn't want him prosecuted because it would make things worse. Rachel understood and had seen it many times before. The abused often couldn't be protected, were often cast out and not supported by their own families. It was a taboo, an ugly one, and when the abusers were released from prison, if indeed they'd even been in prison, the cycle would start again. Rachel understood Hannah's choices, and why the broken system meant to protect Hannah didn't do enough to support her, practically or emotionally.

Judith showed Rachel Hannah's messages. She didn't take any notes and kept the conversation off the record as requested. Rachel instincts had been right about Liam. Thankfully, Hannah was safe and starting a new life, free of the nasty, evil, bully. Rachel was disappointed that she couldn't prosecute him or protect any other women from him, but she'd be watching him. Although, with the ridiculous privacy laws she couldn't even tag him as someone to watch. His name wouldn't be registered anywhere, and his privacy protected, but at least Hannah had escaped him.

Rachel thanked Judith for her time and gave her a hug, as she often did, how many officers did. Judith was part of the police family and had helped and supported so many over the years; officers and staff as well as the public. After Judith had left, Rachel went straight to John's office and knocked as she stuck her head through the doorway.

'Boss, can I have a quick word?' she asked.

John Weaver looked up, nodded, waved her in and she sat down.

Rachel explained the conversation with Judith and immediately John agreed it sounded like a necessary course of action. Like Rachel, he trusted Judith implicitly. Rachel needed his advice now; she wasn't sure how to play it with Liam. She couldn't tell him Hannah had chosen to leave, but she needed to close the case without alerting him of the reason.

'We can close the case due to lack of evidence,' John said, 'or we can leave it open as a missing person, or we can close it due to the new information we have received.'

Rachel nodded as he stated each one of their options.

'But I agree, how we handle it needs to be managed carefully with Liam James,' he added.

They discussed the potential options in detail and how they could play out.

'He won't accept that she's left, and he'll do everything he can to find her,' Rachel said as it became clear that the only real option was the one she wanted to avoid.

'I agree, Rach, but I think our best course is to advise Mr James that she's no longer a missing person and he can't get any answers from us of where she is.'

Rachel tried to interject but John carried on.

'Rachel, you know we have cases like this every day, and we handle it as we would any other. I only wish we could charge the bastard, but we can't. That's against Mrs James's wishes, and, without any evidence from her, there's nothing we can do. Close the case and advise Mr James,' the superintendent ordered, 'and then get onto your case load.'

'Yes, sir,' Rachel huffed as she left the room and headed towards Liam's house.

Chapter 34

'Mr James, can I come in please?' Rachel stood at Liam's front door ten minutes after she'd left the station. She felt a little faint in the overwhelming heat, it felt as though they hadn't had a reprieve from the sun in weeks; she knew she shouldn't complain. She had Adam in tow for back-up, and a second pair of eyes and ears. She hoped Liam had calmed down after his explosive reaction to her talking to his neighbours earlier that day, but fully expecting much of the same; he undoubtedly had a side that he tried to hide.

'Have you found her?' he asked with concern in his voice. 'Oh god, you've found her, she's dead, isn't she? Oh god, no, this isn't happening.' The despair was visible on his face and in his voice.

'No, Mr James, Hannah is fine,' Rachel answered.

'Oh, thank god for that,' he said, taking a huge breath of relief, putting his hands to his chest. 'Thank you so much. Where is she? When can I see her?' he asked impatiently as he picked up his car keys and made for the front door. 'Or is she in your car? Is she here?' he asked in anticipation.

Rachel could see he was waiting for the news she was coming home, but she was about to him tell she wasn't.

'I've come to tell you that we're no longer treating her disappearance as a missing person. Hannah is safe and well,' Rachel said.

Liam nodded in anticipation, waiting for the news Hannah was nearly home.

She added slowly, 'Mr James, we're closing the case as that of a missing person. We have knowledge that Mrs James is safe and well. However,' she paused, seeing a look of confusion cross Liam's face. 'I'm afraid she doesn't want to come home, and this is no longer a police matter.' Rachel chose her words carefully.

Liam, stood motionless, mouth open, face blank, bewildered, perplexed. Rachel could see him trying to comprehend what she'd just said. Then he looked at her, silently for a moment, and sighed.

'Has she left me?' he asked quietly, with sadness in his voice.

From what she now knew of Liam James, he was clearly someone who was always in control of Hannah, and now she'd managed to get away from him, he'd lost that control. Rachel was quite taken aback by his response. She expected him to explode, that's why she'd taken Adam with her. Instead, he looked visibly broken, waiting for her to confirm his fears.

'It would appear that way, Mr James,' she answered softly.

'Can I have an address, or just a phone number please? I just need to talk to her. Whatever's wrong, I'm sure we can sort it out. All couples have problems, don't they?'

He looked so sad and broken, Rachel almost felt sorry for him, but she didn't; she'd met his sort many times before and wouldn't be sucked in by him.

Rachel kept her voice calm and low. 'I'm sorry, that won't be possible, Mr James. If Hannah wants to get in touch it will be up to her, but, as I said, it's no longer a police matter. I came to tell you as a matter of courtesy and to advise you we are closing the case.'

'But she's my wife,' Liam said in barely a whisper.

'As I said, Mr James, it's no longer a police matter.' Rachel stood and turned to leave.

'Stupid bitch,' she heard Liam say, just audible.

Adam was already out of the room and out of earshot.

'I'm sorry, what did you say?' Rachel turned back, shocked.

'Thanks for letting me know.' Liam offered out a hand to shake hers. Rachel took it tentatively, on her guard. She shook it and left the house.

She was aware of Liam watching her through the lounge window as she walked up the path to her car and Adam.

'I know he was out of order earlier, ma'am, but, I feel for him,' Adam said, 'he was heartbroken.'

'Don't believe everything you see or hear, Adam, it was all an act. Mr James isn't the victim here and Hannah is best off without him.' Rachel said, brusquely. 'I'll drop you back to the station and I'll go to see Hannah's parents, then we can get back to that stack of cases.'

As Rachel drove back to the station, she couldn't shift the uneasy feeling she had. Liam's reaction was not what she expected. The exchange they had should have been harder. And she was positive she heard him call her a bitch; she'd heard it enough times in her career and she'd met plenty of men like Liam to know they can flit between their presentable self and their real self. Something didn't feel right; did Liam know more than he was letting on? She trusted Judith implicitly and she'd seen the texts from Hannah. She hadn't spoken to Hannah herself, but Judith had, hadn't she? She tried to recall the conversation with Judith; she hadn't taken any notes and needed to check.

Rachel dropped Adam off at the station, instructing him to update the system notes; she'd check them for accuracy later. She called Judith, but it went straight to voicemail. 'Damn,' she muttered to herself and drove to her office. She felt sweaty and sticky and longed for a shower, just a quick blast to freshen her up. She could feel the pressure of a thunderstorm brewing, her head felt heavy with the start of a headache; she turned up the air con as high as it would go.

At the refuge she was greeted by Louise, a bubbly lady in her early forties she'd met briefly before. Rachel wondered if she was always so happy, she imagined she was nice to have around when you were having a tough day, although maybe a little annoying at times.

'Oh hi, Rachel, how lovely to see you. Business or pleasure?' she asked as she smiled.

'Business, I'm afraid. I'm trying to get hold of Judith. Is she around?'

'I'm so sorry, you've just missed her. She's off to a fundraiser. She's a guest speaker tonight over at Aston Wood, posh garden party affair, they've certainly got the weather for it.' Louise looked at her watch. 'I reckon you'll struggle to catch her now, the signal's awful there.'

'If you can get hold of her, can you ask her to give me a ring please? It's quite urgent,' Rachel said, thinking she wouldn't mind being at a garden party right now. She'd kill for a burger and beer; she hadn't eaten since breakfast again.

'Of course,' Louise answered brightly.

'I'll try and ring her as well,' Rachel said, 'but it is urgent; it's a safeguarding issue. As soon as you hear from her?' She nodded at Louise, who nodded back.

'Yes, as soon as I do. I'll try right away,' Louise assured her.

Rachel got back in her car and rang Judith again and left her a message.

'Hi Judith, it's DCI Rachel Taylor here. I need to check, have you actually spoken to Hannah James since she left, or did you receive texts from her? Call me or text as soon as you can.'

Rachel still needed to speak to Hannah's parents and let them know Hannah was safe and the case was closed, she headed to their house next. Although she wasn't sure whether she should hold back now; the sceptic in her thought, *this isn't over, there's more to this.* She rang John.

'Boss, look, I know I keep going on about this but, there's something not right here. I spoke to Liam James, told him what we agreed and he didn't react how I expected.'

'How so?' John answered.

'He was just, oh, I can't put my finger on it, you know what it's like?' she tried to explain.

'I do, but sorry, Rach, you know as well as I do, we go on the evidence.' She could hear the impatience in his voice.

'I know,' she interrupted, 'but I really do have a bad feeling, I want more time on this.'

'I'll refer back to my briefing, we need speed. I know that's not what you want to hear, but it is what it is. I'd love to spend more time on some cases but, as I said, we don't have that luxury. Have you informed Mrs James' parents yet?'

'No, not yet, I wanted to speak to you first.'

'Right, get over there and then back here,' he ordered.

'Yes, boss, will do,' she said, wishing she hadn't called him.

Chapter 35

As the idiot officer and her little pet sidekick walked out of his lounge, Liam laughed to himself at their incompetence.

'Stupid bitch,' he'd said under his breath. He didn't mean for it to come out.

The police had no idea where Hannah was, or that he'd been with her only an hour before. She was his again, and she wasn't going anywhere. *Stupid fucking police, she has no idea,* he thought.

He'd miss their little interactions; she reminded him of his sister, always poking her nose in, thinking she was better than him and he had to suck it up, be nice to her or face the *consequences*. At least with Rachel he'd won, he was home and dry; it was a relief. He could hide Hannah for a few more weeks at the house until his boss got back from his cruise. Then, once things had settled, he'd take her to another location and they could start their new life together. Her injuries needed to heal though, if anyone saw her now, they'd interfere, try and help her. He was angry at himself for damaging her face, he always managed to avoid hitting anything others could see. It was her own fault though, she'd made him like this with her lies, her scheming and conspiring with that bitch Judith. Now though, she was his, the way it should have always been. Things had changed though now and he just needed to be sure it's what he really wanted. What she'd done had spoilt them and he wasn't sure he could ever forgive her for it. He wanted things to go back to how they should have been, but Hannah, well, she did this, she broke them, ruined them. He could cut and run, go for the easier option. He thought for a moment, went upstairs, packed an overnight bag, got in his car and drove. First stop, Hannah.

Will you cry your crocodile tears when I'm gone?
Will you tell everyone…
I could see it,
I tried to help.

No,

you won't.

That's a lie.

You could see it,
but you didn't try.

It was too messy.

Too inconvenient.

It would ruin your day.

Better things to do.

Well, I hope you're happy now.

This is on you.

Chapter 36

Hannah was still shaking from Liam's visit earlier and she hadn't eaten anything for over twenty-four hours. She'd hardly moved from the spot she was in. The sharp pain of her bruises penetrated deep into her muscles; every tiny movement a reminder of what he'd done. Her thighs stung, as though she'd been scrubbed with sandpaper where Liam had forced her. She was damaged, inside and out; every inch of her soul was torn, and she was terrified.

When she heard his car on the gravel, she didn't move. She'd resigned herself to dying; there was nothing left, there was no fight. She knew Liam had planned everything better than her, he did everything better than her. He'd fool the police, he'd fool Judith. He was coming to kill her, and she accepted that; it was the best way out now, it was the only way out.

She heard his footsteps above, quieter than before, slower than before. The door opened and the dim light trickled down the steps.

Liam walked halfway down them, blocking out most of the light.

'They've closed your missing persons' case; they believed your stupid little plot, you idiot,' he scoffed. 'No one's coming for you.' He turned and left, locking the door behind him.

Hannah felt nothing, her body too weak to respond. There was no fight left, no hope, no reason to live. *OK*, Hannah thought to herself, *that's OK*. She pulled her legs in tighter and her towel round her shoulders as she heard Liam's car drive away from the house.

Chapter 37

Judith arrived home in a taxi just before midnight. She was woozy from too many proseccos and tired from the day. She opened the door, dropped her handbag in the hallway and headed straight to the kitchen. She flicked the kettle on for a cup of tea. She didn't normally drink at events – she saw them as work – but tonight she'd allowed herself to let her hair down; she was feeling particularly proud of Hannah, and thought she deserved a little celebration. She sat on her sofa with her peppermint tea and scrolled through her messages as she pushed off her shoes; her feet throbbed as they were released, welcoming their freedom. She realised she'd missed calls from Louise and Rachel. Rachel's message was short, but she sounded concerned.

'Hi, Judith, it's DCI Rachel Taylor here. I need to check, have you actually spoken to Hannah James since she left, or did you only receive texts from her? Call me or text as soon as you can.'

Judith realised she hadn't spoken to Hannah directly; she'd only received texts. She tried to call Rachel, but it went straight to voicemail, so she left a message. 'Hi, it's Judith, I tried to call you back, sorry, I've only just got in. I only had texts from Hannah, I'll try and speak to her and let you know.'

She then texted Hannah.

Hi Hannah, give me a ring when you can, hope you're OK and settling in x

The concern in Rachel's voice had really put her on edge. First thing in the morning she'd call the refuge as well to check Hannah was there.

Judith's phone was on all night, as it always was for emergencies. If Rachel or Hannah got in touch, she'd hear it. She had a restless night, worrying something was wrong, tossing and turning, seeing in every hour. As she drifted in and out of sleep, old thoughts entered her mind; sleeping in a public toilet of the local train station until the first train of the morning arrived. Her two toddlers – Amelia, six, and Melanie, three, – were crying because they'd seen their mum punched and thrown across the room once again. They were golden when she first woke them up just after 1am, putting her finger to her lips, Sshhh…they nodded; her husband passed out downstairs from his

143

usual drinking. She dressed them in silence, putting their warmest clothes on, black shiny wellies and matching red woolly hats, mittens and scarves, knitted by their grandma for Christmas. Their grandma, whose doorstep they'd be on the next morning, seeking safety and love. They stepped out into the frosty December morning, a child clutching each hand as they scurried through the empty, wet streets, dark as the lamps had gone out just after twelve as they did every day. The streets were lit in places though; houses adorned with Christmas lights, trees in the windows sparkling and flashing. They passed the tree in the main square, the one they'd all gone to see a month before being switched on by the local mayor. As they passed the tree they could hear a group of older men, shouting and swearing at each other. *Come on then, you wanker.* She felt the children tighten their grips and hug closer into her body as they passed. Glass was breaking as the men smashed bottles for weapons, swearing, egging each other on. They slid past them: quietly, quickly, silently. The train station waiting room was locked and Judith had held back her tears as she comforted her girls. She woke again, heart racing with fear; *you're all right, it's just a nightmare.* The more she thought about sleep, the harder it was to drift off, even though her body was trying to pull her in; her mind was too active. She must have dropped off again an hour before her 8am alarm woke her abruptly from a deep, dreamless sleep. She immediately checked her phone…nothing.

She tried to ring Hannah again. There was no answer, and she left a short message. 'Hi Hannah, it's Judith, just checking you've settled in OK, give me a ring when you've got five minutes.'

She rang the refuge, and it went to voicemail. She only had the main number and didn't have any of the staff's mobiles; she hadn't needed them before. Judith suspected that like her, they were running on a skeleton staff as they relied on charity funds and often unpaid volunteers, as well as a handful of paid staff. Sometimes it was all hands to the deck, and with too few hands, sometimes the phones would go unanswered. Judith left a voicemail and her landline number for the office, which forwarded her calls to her mobile. It would be easy for the refuge to corroborate her number to check Judith was who she said she was; it was on her website. They always had to be careful who they were talking to, just in case an ex-partner pretended they were someone else trying to get information about the very people they were there to protect. They'd had police and social services impersonators, people pretending to be friends, children, and parents, so their protocols were watertight. But Judith now started to worry. She was angry with herself for breaking her own number one rule and not corroborating who she was talking to. What if it wasn't Hannah texting her after all? Or was she just being paranoid? Either way, she needed to be cautious.

She made herself some toast, a cup of tea and checked her watch as she ate, listening to the morning news. It was 8:15am. She tried Rachel again – no answer.

'Hi, Rachel, it's Judith, just returning your call. I left a message last night as well. I hadn't spoken to Hannah, I've just called and left her a message. I've also left a message at the refuge in Inverness, call me when you can, my phone's on. I'm really worried.'

When she finished the call, she also texted Rachel, repeated her message and added that she was free all day and to ring back.

She needed to get some shopping in Lichfield, which wouldn't take too long. She had a quick shower and checked her phone as soon as she came out. Still nothing, it was now 8:30am. She dressed and drove over to her office. She always parked there when she needed to go shopping and always popped in, out of habit more than anything. She opened up the office and checked her phone, still nothing from Hannah or Rachel. She called the station and the call handler advised her that Rachel was due on shift at 10am. Judith thanked her and assumed Rachel must have been asleep when she called. She quickly checked her emails and walked into Lichfield; she'd try her again afterwards.

Chapter 38

Liam woke to the smell of the coffee being placed next to him on his bedside cabinet and started to come round from his deep sleep. She got back into bed and snuggled up to him, nuzzling her face into his chest. They'd stayed up for hours talking as he tried to get the measure of her. They'd met a few months before whilst he was weighing up his options. Hannah was becoming too high maintenance, and he felt they were going backwards. But Sarah seemed more pliable, more vulnerable. She hung on his every word and did as she was told; he only ever had to ask once. He toyed with the idea of keeping them both. Having Sarah meant he would still have his ornament on his arm at events, and she could cook and clean for him. Whereas Hannah always sparked something in him. Keeping her as well gave him the best of both worlds; how he'd keep her secret would be a struggle though.

'Are you staying all day today?' Sarah asked quietly as she straddled him playfully and kissed him on the forehead. She'd put his pale-blue work shirt on and had left it open, teasing him with her bare breasts. She pushed them forward, Liam opened her shirt and cupped them.

'I'm not sure yet,' he answered. This was the annoying thing; when they start asking questions, they get too demanding.

Sarah screwed her nose up and sat back, still straddling him and pouting playfully.

'I love having you here, all to myself. Now they've closed the case,' she started.

'OK, let's not talk about this now. What's for breakfast?' Liam asked, changing the subject. His hands moved down to her waist.

Liam could see she was disappointed, but he didn't need this hassle. Sarah seemed a little desperate, eager to please, lonely; easy pickings. She believed everything Liam said, a bit like Hannah in the early days; easy to control.

'I can do anything you want, I have everything in,' she said happily.

'Sausage, bacon and egg sandwich then,' he said.

She got off him and walked to the door, turning briefly to flash her naked body at him, giggling.

'Hmmm,' he said raising his eyebrows as she went downstairs.

He picked his phone up to check the time – just after 8am. He had a lot to do and organise and needed to get back home. He had a shower and shaved and thought about what he needed to do. If he stayed with Sarah as well, she could move into the Lichfield house and take over from Hannah. He had his routines, and it would be easy for her to pick them up. Where would he put Hannah, though? This house, in Hammerwich, was too small to hide someone so he'd need somewhere else, somewhere discreet. He could move somewhere new with Hannah. Somewhere no one knew them, but it would need to be far enough away from everyone, and he didn't want to change his job. He had the flexibility he needed there, and he knew he was overpaid for what he did, so getting something similar and cushy was unlikely. This was getting complicated.

He started putting his clothes back in his overnight bag and noticed Hannah's phone at the bottom. It had a text and voicemail from Judith. He read the text and listened to the message.

'Fuck,' he said to himself. Was it just Judith trying to talk to Hannah or was it that cop again, sticking her bloody nose in? He'd played it as cool as possible the previous day, but he was now in new territory, and he needed to be smart and think carefully about his next steps.

'Breakfast's ready, babe,' Sarah shouted up the stairs.

'OK, be down in a minute,' he shouted back.

After he'd considered his options, he went downstairs. 'Can you wrap that in foil for me, I need to go,' he said to Sarah, looking for his car keys.

'Oh,' she said, looking towards the dining table. She'd put his breakfast out with a glass of champagne and a single red rose in a vase.

Liam sighed. 'I'm sorry. I'll be back later tonight, but I need to go now.' He kissed her on the forehead.

Sarah quietly wrapped the sandwich and gave it to him, without saying a word.

'Babe, I'm sorry, come here,' Liam said, holding his arms out.

She walked over and loosely put her arms around his waist as he wrapped his tightly around her small frame, her head buried in his chest.

147

'I know this has been really tough on you too, her leaving like she has without saying anything, and her parents calling the police causing all this,' he said, perpetuating the lies he'd already told her.

'No, I'm sorry, I know you don't need the pressure, I know she's a psycho with all her mental health issues.' He felt her tighten her hold.

'Not long now hey, we're OK, aren't we?' he said, kissing the top of her head.

'Always…love you.' She looked up, eyes full of adoration for him.

'Love you too, I won't be long. Tell you what, I'll definitely be over later, let's have a nice meal, bottle of wine, how does that sound?' he said.

'Perfect, now off you go,' she smiled and patted his bum as he walked to the door.

Fucking woman, he thought, *want, want, want*.

He got in his car, drove to a layby and started writing.

Twenty minutes later, he drove over to see Hannah.

Chapter 39

Hannah heard the car on the gravel and curled up, pulling her towel tight around her; she didn't know what was coming next. He'd beaten her so badly, she felt every part of her body stinging and bruised; possibly broken bones. The pain was overwhelming, and she could no longer distinguish it in the different parts of her body.

She heard his footsteps on the floor above her, striding across the room, the sound of the key in the cellar door and Liam heaving it open as the old wood creaked. He walked down into the cellar, switching the light on as he entered. It was the first time he'd put the light on, and Hannah sat bolt upright; what was next?

'Have some water, I've got a little job for you.' He handed Hannah a plastic bottle, already opened and she took a sip. She kept her head down, not sure what was happening, and what the job was; she didn't understand what he meant by job. Was he letting her out of the cellar into the rest of the house? Did he want her to clean or cook? She took another sip in silence, avoiding eye contact with him.

He handed her a note. Her eyes hadn't fully focused having been in the dim light for so many days and it took a while to see what he'd written. As she read it to herself, she looked up at him and he smiled at her.

'A little message for your friend,' he laughed.

When Hannah had read the message out over and over, he left the room, switching the light off and Hannah sunk back into the darkness of her prison.

He'd won.

Chapter 40

It took five goes before he was happy, recording, listening, and directing her each time; he needed it to be perfect. After he'd left Hannah he'd driven home, left his car on the drive and walked through the warren of back streets in Lichfield to the alley opposite Judith's office in the hope that she'd be there. He didn't know where she lived and didn't think he needed to; he was hoping that the police dropping the case would leave him home and dry. Why was she still meddling? Was she suspicious?

He could see a light on in the office and a car parked on the pavement outside, but he couldn't see clearly who was in there. He'd only been there a couple of minutes when the front door opened and Judith stepped out. She walked towards the town centre. He followed at a distance and rang her mobile from Hannah's phone. She immediately went for it.

'Shit,' Liam uttered, and he rung off.

He watched her check the phone and, within a second, Hannah's phone was ringing. He ended the call and watched Judith talking; leaving a message.

He sent her a text.

Hi, really sorry, the signal's not great here, I'm out for most of the day. I will keep trying to call you, if not speak later when I'm back and I'll maybe try you on the landline at the refuge xx

Liam tried to call her twice more, but each time she'd tried to answer so he'd rung off and she rang back and left a message. Finally, when she was in Boots paying, he tried again. She wasn't able to take the call, so he played the message leaving Hannah's voice on her phone.

Chapter 41

Rachel had shared a bottle of wine with Emma the night before and had been about to open a second when Emma reminded her they both needed to be in work the next morning and sent her up to bed; she was exhausted. She'd slept heavily and didn't hear her phone ring. When she woke, she checked it, and realised Judith had texted and called her; she listened to the message immediately.

'Hi, it's Judith, I tried to call you back, sorry, I've only just got in. I only had texts from Hannah, I'll try and speak to her and let you know.'

She called her back straight away, but it was engaged. She started to leave a message just as Judith called her, but she rang off as she answered, and it was engaged again when she rang back.

'Damn,' she said to herself, frustrated.

Her phone pinged; Judith had left her a voicemail. She played it.

'Hannah's just texted me, she said she's fine and she'll ring me later today, she said the signal's awful in Inverness but promised to ring me later. I'll let you know as soon as I hear something, but I'll also ring the refuge again myself, I've tried a couple of times but no one's picking up.'

It sounded as though Hannah was OK, but Rachel really wanted to know that Judith had spoken to her properly, not just by text. She still had an uneasy feeling; Liam hadn't acted the way she expected the day before. Was she being overly cautious? Hannah didn't want to be found; she'd made every attempt to divert eyes away from her, particularly Liam's. The train trips she'd taken were just there to confuse him if he found out she'd left. No doubt he'd be trying to find her now. Best course of action was to wait until Hannah had spoken to Judith later that day.

She texted Judith back.

Hi, tried to return your call, it sounds as though I'm worrying unnecessarily but it would be good for you to talk to her, speak later, bye.

She checked her watch. *Just enough time.* 'You fancy a Maccies?' she shouted up to Emma, who groaned at her from her guest bedroom.

Chapter 42

When Judith had finished paying in Boots, she went for her phone and listened to the message.

'Hi, Judith, it's Hannah. I'm fine, everyone's lovely. I'm out for the rest of the day and all tomorrow, the signal's really bad here. I'll try you again at some point. Have you told the police yet?'

As soon as the message finished, Judith tried to ring Hannah back; no answer. She called Rachel; no answer and left a message.

'Hi, Rachel, it's Judith here. I've had a voicemail from Hannah saying she's OK. I have tried her again, but couldn't get through. You have worried me now, though, and there's something not right – it was her, but it wasn't. That probably doesn't make much sense, sorry. Can you ring me as soon as you can please?'

Judith knew Hannah well enough now to know when she was excited and when she was lying. Her voicemail sounded like she did in the earlier days; when she covered up how she felt, when she smiled through the pain, and through the terror. Something felt wrong, and experience told her that sadly, she was probably right.

She tried Rachel again, but it just went to voicemail. *I'll go up to the station,* she thought to herself.

Before the station moved it was five minutes' walk away, but now it was on the other side of town, a good thirty minutes' walk for someone strong and fit, but Judith was neither of those; she'd need to drive up. She walked back to her office to get her car, unaware that Liam still had her in his line of sight.

Angels crying golden tears,

Feathers falling from their wings,

With every tear drop, their souls wash away;

Angels dying every day.

Chapter 43

After he'd left Hannah's message for Judith, Liam watched her with curiosity. He followed her around Lichfield and watched her walking back to the office. How dare she think she knew Hannah; the lies she'd spun, interfering in other people's marriages. She'd started all this, it was her fault; the fucking evil bitch. Hannah had everything she wanted and this pathetic excuse for a woman was trying to split them up, putting stupid ideas in her head.

Liam needed to be patient though. He imagined himself walking over to her, startling her. He relished the thought of her finding out just before she died that Liam knew everything; that he had Hannah. He knew their dirty little stupid plan; he'd known for months.

At first, he felt rage as he stood outside the cafe watching Hannah and Judith plotting. He knew who she was, always in the local rags, raising money for her pathetic little charity; preying on innocent lives, ripping families apart. She was the worst kind of human, thinking she was better than everyone else, high up on her pedestal; her righteous views. She didn't know what love was, she'd never had it. She was jealous of people who did, and that's why she interfered; she wanted what Liam and Hannah had.

Watching Hannah talk to her in the cafe he wanted to know more, wanted to understand why she was talking to this woman. He'd been patient, watched and waited for months since he realised Hannah was spending more time with this woman. She hadn't mentioned her specifically, but it was clear she was talking to her more than the other customers.

The first time he'd noticed something different in Hannah's behaviour was when he'd seen the woman give her something; a piece of paper, bright-green. He saw Hannah take it whilst he watched her from his rental across the road. Carrying on his normal workday, answering emails and taking calls but with surveillance of Hannah now part of his norm. The best part of his job was being able to be mobile; not accountable to anyone. As long as his team performed, he was OK. He'd insisted on a satellite office that he'd chosen and work paid for. He was high enough in the company to get his own way; they were too worried about losing him to a competitor. So, his demands were met. He'd set up his office directly opposite the cafe and he could watch Hannah at his leisure, only occasionally needing to go into the Birmingham office.

Now, in the alley, he was watching Judith. He had his opportunity to end her pathetic existence and let her know who was in charge. *Who the fuck does she think she is?* he thought to himself. Liam grew more agitated as anger welled up, his fists clenching. He had to be patient though. *Just wait, now's not the right time.* It would need to be months before he exacted his revenge. It had to look natural, and he also had to wait for Judith to share the voicemail from Hannah with the police. He didn't know if she had already, he couldn't hear what she'd said on the call she made after she'd received Hannah's voicemail earlier that day; did the police already know about the call? He couldn't take the chance, he had to wait; he needed to control himself.

He remembered back to the day when he realised what was going on – the day he'd seen Judith give her the leaflet. He waited until the end of the day, watched Hannah leave and Jane lock up. Then, he walked round the back, let himself in and disabled the alarm; he'd suggested Hannah saved the code on her phone when Jane first let her have it, knowing he'd also have access to it. He looked through her locker and found the bright-green leaflet in her cardigan pocket. *Who the fuck does she think she is, nosey fucking bitch, she doesn't know anything about us. Hannah has everything, I give her everything*, he'd thought to himself as he read it.

Then he found her notepad.

He flicked through it quickly, not realising what it was he held in his hand.

Only the first couple of pages had something in there. He turned back to the first page. The first few lines were just rambling notes and doodles; a mind map of random thoughts. The words money, travel, food, refuge, stood out, radiating from the word ESCAPE circled in the middle. His stomach lurched, and his chest tightened as nausea passed over him; Hannah wanted to leave him.

I'll never let that happen.

He read in disbelief. *How has she got the nerve to do this, I give her everything.*

At this point it seemed these were just ideas. *Will she really carry this through?*

He photographed each page on his phone; he did this many times over the months that followed as more was added and her plans unfolded. Different routes, ideas, places to stop, a bank account. Until it was clear what Hannah's final plan was.

That first evening he'd seen the note pad and the leaflet, he'd got home and Hannah was all over the place; nervous and edgy. She'd dropped her dinner and had to go without. He'd enjoyed watching her squirm, trying not look him in the eye. He knew at that moment he was right not to trust her. It was as he'd always suspected; she was a filthy, lying little gold digger. He could read her like a book. It took every ounce of his strength not to knock her across the room. Dropping the plates gave him an excuse for a small bit of release. 'You idiot, what did you do that for!' he'd shouted. He'd smiled to himself as he sat down and watched her scrabbling on the floor. He was now intrigued how far she'd take it. *Does she really think she can take me for a fool? Does she really think she is better than me?*

He'd been back to the cafe week after week, checking her notepad, keeping abreast of anything new, anything significant. He also couldn't see properly to the back of the room, but he knew there was a laptop there. It didn't take long to check it one evening and he could view the history. He'd then set up a tiny camera hidden away so he could see the screen, and what she was searching for and checking. He knew exactly what she was doing, when she was doing it, and her plan to cover it up. As the day approached, Hannah finalised her plans, putting exact times and dates in. She had two specific pages that Liam had photographed and read over and over. Each page was headed: 'Real Plan' and 'Pretend Plan'. Liam had scoffed at the simplicity of it and why she'd gone to such lengths; if she'd have just got on a train and paid for it that day, he'd probably never have found her. But, Hannah's need for detail, for lists, for planning, that infuriated him when they were preparing for holidays was now her downfall. He visualised over and over in his mind what Hannah's reaction would be when he was there, at Blake Street station, when she thought she was leaving him and he was there, ready to punish her.

Not confronting Hannah and putting her in her place before that day was almost impossible, but he realised his end game; almost as immediately as he'd worked out what she was up to. All he needed to do was to play along whilst he made his own plans.

Those plans had brought him to where he was now, in the alley watching 'her'. Watching that self-righteous bitch. He'd been patient with Judith – he'd wanted to beat her to a pulp when he first found out. No one gets away with what she'd done, and not to him. He would be back in a few months and then she'd know who he was, and she'd pay. As he watched her the anger welled up inside him, rage brimming to the surface. He thought about their plotting, laughing at him, ridiculing him. *Fucking bitches*. He watched Judith struggling with her shopping, trying to get her car key out of her pocket. The more he watched, the angrier he got; rage was compelling him to go over, until he could hold back no more.

He walked straight up behind her, picking up a scaffolding clamp he'd seen on the floor in the alley. He brought the clamp up in the air above her head as Judith turned towards him, her hands coming up in front of her to shield herself. Liam's hand came down, smashing the clamp into her skull; he smiled as he did it. Judith's look of fear and surprise disappeared as she dropped to the floor in a crumpled heap. A pool of dark crimson spread across the pavement beneath her head.

He turned and ran across the road, up the alley and he was gone, throwing the scaffolding clamp over a fence into the undergrowth at the side of the railway. It sank into the bushes and looked like any other piece of rubbish discarded over the years. Liam was disappointed in himself for not holding back, but he also felt a sense of overwhelming relief and calm. The anger had gone and all that stood in its place was pride; he'd dealt with that bitch.

As he reached home, he could hear sirens. Assuming they were attending to Judith, he checked his watch; a bit early for a drink, he thought, but he'd excelled himself today and needed to relax. He poured himself a beer, switched his TV on, and kicked back to watch the sport.

Chapter 44

'Emergency, which service do you require?'

'There's a woman, I think she'd dead.' The caller could just about get their words out, their voice breathy and cracking. 'He hit her, he hit her, oh god.'

The caller taker took the details as other contact staff received multiple calls and it was clear a major incident had occurred, and…there were witnesses.

Within minutes, Police and Ambulance were on the scene and Lichfield came to a standstill as roads closed and the area was cordoned off. Judith was pronounced dead. Her lifeless body lay on the pavement; no indication of the woman she was, the work she'd done, the lives she saved. The pool of blood trickled over into the gutter, congealing as it cooked in the sun. Crowds gathered, some looking on in horror, others with their mobiles held high trying to grab the gory scene to share without any thought. A forensic tent was quickly erected to shield her; to spare her indignity in death from the selfish eyes. Police pushed the crowds back and spoke to some, hoping to appeal to their conscience to delete any images they'd captured that served no purpose other than to promote their own selfish involvement in the heinous act.

SOCO got to work, collecting forensic evidence and the police started their investigation. The witnesses who rang in were interviewed as more came forward at the scene. There were five in all, each with the same story. A man walked up to Judith and hit her on the head, stood there for a few seconds and then ran across the road towards the industrial units. They all said the same: blue jeans, blue hoody with the hood up. None had seen his face, but all were sure it was a tall white man.

Whatever Judith had been hit with wasn't at the scene, so the police started the laborious task of searching the area for the murder weapon, and for a suspect; a lone individual.

With Judith's history, and because of the charity she'd started thirty years before, she was always a target for disgruntled ex-partners. She'd been threatened on numerous occasions, particularly by men, turning up looking for their wife, girlfriend, children. The staff at the refuge were distraught and helped police check records to try and find potential suspects; it was going to be a long investigation.

Detective Chief Superintendent Carl Owen headed down from Stafford to the team on the ground, to take charge. Judith was one of their own; she was part of the police family. Carl Owen had the sad task, along with John Weaver, of breaking the tragic news to her daughters, who'd thirty years before escaped the clutches of an evil man, and now they'd still lost their mum to an equally evil man.

Within hours a press statement was being prepared, describing the work Judith had done, the woman she was. It asked for any more witnesses to come forward and the suspect's description was circulated. As the day turned into evening and the light faded across Lichfield, officers continued to search the area, off-duty officers also turned up to help as the sad news spread across the force. There was a vast area to search and a warren of side roads, alleys, gardens, and hedgerows. CCTV was being pulled wherever possible, door-to-door enquiries had started and social media campaigns shared the story as it spread through the region.

I'm ready to go now.
Just make it quick.

Chapter 45

Hannah wasn't sure how much time had passed, but it didn't feel long since his last visit; it felt they were getting more frequent. Sitting on the floor in the corner, naked, bloody, and bruised, Hannah pulled her legs in tighter. She didn't think the human body was designed to survive the beatings Liam had put her through, but here she was, still alive, still hanging on. She thought she must have either slept or lost consciousness at some point, but she still felt it was the same day as she heard his footsteps above her.

There was nothing more he could do now; he'd stripped her of everything, she was ready to die – she wanted to die. She just wanted him to finish her off, and she accepted that. She shivered from the cold and looked up as the light from the doorway entered the room and Liam's mass filled the space. She was ready now, she felt it would be over soon, and she welcomed it. The pain would stop, the torment would stop. He'd won, but she didn't care now. Nothing mattered, just that it needed to happen soon.

He came over to her, grabbing the hair on top of her head as he pulled her up to her feet, his other hand coming up below her jaw and pushing her up higher against the wall. He stared straight into her eyes, but nothing stared back. She could see him, but her spirit had already gone. *Just do it.*

'Ding-dong, the witch is dead,' he scoffed at her, his spittle hitting her face. 'That stupid witch is dead, and no one's coming for you.' He spat the words she couldn't bear to hear.

The realisation of what he'd done, who he meant, took hold of Hannah as her body kicked into life. Shocked by a rush of adrenalin as she screamed, 'Nooooo...nooo...noo...' The sadness and pain overwhelmed her as she fought him, kicking and screaming. Judith was dead because of her. She tried to kick at Liam, but her legs gave way as he let go and she dropped to the floor, sobbing inaudible sounds.

'You thought you could trick me, didn't you? You thought you were special and better than me, but you're pathetic. You stink, you're a fucking disgrace,' Liam snarled as he spat at her slumped on the floor.

He left Hannah realising that she wasn't going anywhere. That he could do worse to her than kill her – to kill those she loved, her family, the few friends she had, then to keep her locked up and tortured; treated worse than an animal. Hannah had never felt sadness so profound; Judith was dead because of her, a sweet, caring, amazing and selfless woman who at the worst point in her life decided to help others.

She was dead and it was her fault.

Chapter 46

The news of Judith's murder ricocheted through the police like a bullet. Rachel had heard almost immediately as the calls came in. She'd received a text from John, and it stopped her in her tracks. She'd tried to ring Judith back less than an hour after she'd received her call and said she'd try her again, but within half an hour she was dead; the brutal finality hit her hard.

At the devastating news she'd got up from her desk and gone into the toilets. She replayed the conversation with Judith; it had closed Hannah's missing person's case. She felt her stomach knot and a sickness start to well in her throat as colour drained from her face; she stumbled as her legs gave way. She leant on the sink for support and threw up. The awareness that Liam could have done this was at the forefront of her mind. She splashed her face with cold water as tears welled and she threw up again.

Her mind was racing as it made connections between Hannah's case and Judith's, but it was asking more questions than she had answers, and the connections were becoming foggy and confused. She calmed herself and wiped away her tears, took a few deep breaths, and walked back to her office.

She cleared a whiteboard, her head spinning with a constant commentary. She needed to get it out of her head and onto something visual so she could make the connections meaningful. She needed to talk to John; she wanted a second, experienced mind on this, but he was offsite dealing with Judith's investigation. She'd seen him walk out earlier and he looked grey. She'd already sent a text asking him to contact her urgently about the call from Judith relaying Hannah's message, but he'd not got back to her. She imagined his phone was stacking up with calls, texts, and voicemails as they found evidence and witnesses; her message just one amongst many.

Rachel needed to bring clarity to her own thoughts, to make her suspicions about Liam credible, so they'd be taken seriously and considered for Judith's investigation. Hannah was the link, so she needed to start there. She started drawing a timeline of when Hannah was reported missing. When she was last seen; CCTV at home and the train station.

She researched all the train and bus routes times on the day Hannah left for Inverness and she called Inverness Police Station. Judith said the plan was for Hannah to go to the local station to corroborate Judith's story; Inverness police said they'd not had any reports from Hannah. Rachel asked about refuges in the area. She asked if they could enquire on her behalf; had Hannah arrived? There was no point her ringing them directly, they wouldn't divulge any information; a local station with its connections, however, they may have cooperated.

Rachel rang Emma. 'Do you have Judith's phone yet?' she asked.

'Yeah, it's here, it's just being booked in. I can't believe Judith's gone, my team are…'

'Can you send me the texts and voicemails Hannah sent her including dates and times,' Rachel interrupted.

'OK, are you onto something?' Emma enquired as Rachel ended the call.

Rachel continued drawing the timeline. She remembered what Judith said; Hannah was going one way, but she was getting off early. Rachel checked stops between Lichfield and Birmingham. Hannah caught the 7:44am in Lichfield, that was the time of the first text and fitted with the CCTV footage. Shenstone 7:49am, Blake Street 7:52am, Butlers Lane 7:53am, Four Oaks 7:56am, Sutton Coldfield 7:59am. Her mobile rang.

'Hi DCI Taylor, this is Inspector Wilson of Inverness police.' The officer spoke in a slow Scottish accent.

'Oh, hi, did you get anywhere?' Rachel said impatiently, realising she probably sounded a bit rude.

'Yes, I spoke to my contact at the centre, and she's confirmed, although I had to pull a few strings,' he continued slowly.

For god's sake hurry up.

'It's not easy getting information out of these places you know.' The officer was dragging it out.

'Confirmed she's there?' Rachel interrupted.

'Oh no, she's not, they were expecting her but she never arrived, they said they'd called a Judith Millar down there to confirm it. It happens a lot you know, these women.'

'Thank you,' Rachel said and ended the call. She didn't want to hear where the conversation was going. *These women?* She sensed a draconian view was about to come out of Inspector Wilson's mouth and she didn't have time for crap like that.

Rachel thought for a moment and went back to her board. Instead of Hannah's departure times, she looked at the arrival times of trains in Inverness. The first arrived at 6:26pm, that was the earliest possible arrival in Inverness. She wrote down later trains and buses, just in case she'd changed her route.

Her phone pinged. It was a text from Emma.

Sent you an email

She opened the email and found the first text she was after.

I'm actually doing this, I'll text you tonight, so you know I'm safe, and I'll let you know to tell the police in a few days. Thank you so much for everything, you're a beautiful, amazing, selfless lady x

She found the next text she was after.

Hi lovely, I'm here, so excited. Just getting off in Inverness, I'll let you know when I'm at the refuge

Received at 5:05pm. It was an hour and a half before Hannah could have arrived in Inverness.

Two hours later, 7:08pm and the second text.

Arrived safe and sound, they're lovely here. Going to bed x

It was to confirm she was there, but it was impossible. Unless Hannah had also lied to Judith about where she was going. It was highly likely she hadn't even sent the text. *She's not safe at all.*

The next message was the voicemail from Hannah, she clicked the audio link and she heard Hannah's voice for the first time. A soft, lonely voice, Judith was right, it didn't match the happiness of the message; was it coerced? Rachels chest tightened, *Where are you, Hannah?*

But…it meant Hannah was still alive, well at least when the message was sent. Rachel felt relief tinged with fear, they needed to find her soon.

The final transcript of Judith's phone was from the refuge in Inverness confirming that Hannah never arrived, received too late, after Judith's murder; a message she never heard.

Her next thoughts went to Liam. Did he know about Hannah's plan and Judith's involvement? If nothing had happened to Judith, she'd

166

have no reason to suspect anything, so why would he risk that? Surely, he'd have realised she'd make the link. *If he killed Judith, he's unravelling*, she thought to herself, *this means you're unpredictable.*

Rachel looked at her timeline again and listened to Hannah's voicemail. *Did you change your route, Hannah, and lie to Judith about where you were?* The facts were: Hannah had tried to leave, she was terrified of Liam, and she didn't go to Inverness. This was a plan that had taken months in tiny slots of time. She didn't have an opportunity to plan anything else. Rachel genuinely believed Hannah wouldn't have lied to Judith and gone somewhere else; Hannah trusted her implicitly. Judith had given her the confidence to leave, to make her own choices. If Liam had found out the plan, he'd definitely have tried to stop it, he'd definitely have a motive to confront Judith, or worse; this was a man who could see no wrong in his own actions. He was narcissistic, selfish, and highly manipulative. Was he capable of murder? And where was Hannah? If she was even still alive. Liam could have killed her after the message. *Are you tying up loose ends?*

Rachel had to go with the working assumption that Hannah was alive. She needed to speak to her boss, decide what to do next, re-open her case and talk to him about the link with Judith. The only real evidence they had was that Hannah wasn't where she said she was going to be. There wasn't any evidence that Liam was involved other than a hunch. No evidence that he'd sent the texts, coerced the voicemail, or been anywhere near Judith. The description of the suspect could have been pretty much anyone.

She picked her phone up to ring John again just as he walked past her office. 'Boss, have you got a minute?'

He turned round and sighed, clenched his jaw; she could see the didn't want to talk, he must have been exhausted. He stood in her doorway. 'Can this wait? I'm up to my neck,' he said.

'It's to do with Judith,' she answered, and John looked confused.

'What, how?' he answered.

'I think there's a link to Hannah and Liam James. Take a look at the timeline.'

Rachel quickly walked John through the board, the train times, Hannah not being in Inverness and sending texts that didn't corroborate with the timelines. The voicemails and texts with Judith and Liam's odd behaviour the previous day.

'OK, I can see where you're going with this but it's circumstantial at best. We've got a list of people with potentially similar grudges and there's nothing here to make Liam James standout,' he started.

Rachel protested, 'But I'm positive he did it, and there is something that makes him stand out – the timing. It's so close to Judith receiving the voicemail from Hannah.' Her frustration came through.

John sighed, exhaustion etched on his face. 'I agree he needs to be a suspect, Rach, but more so for Hannah's disappearance, not Judith's murder. Re-open Hannah's case and talk to Bob about what you have here.' He was referring to DCI Bob Moore; the officer in charge of Judith's case.

'OK, boss, I'll get onto it now.' Rachel sighed as he left the office. She hated working with Bob the Knob as he was known behind his back, but needs must, she thought, and she picked up the phone to call him.

Chapter 47

Bob Moore ran his briefings with military precision, and Sunday morning's about Judith was no different. Although he'd seen Rachel's timeline and listened to her suspicions the previous evening, he smugly said he was with John Weaver and didn't see Liam standing out as a main suspect over anyone else. He seemed to take great glee in telling her to work harder to find something useful as though she was his junior officer. Rachel didn't rise to his taunts and remained professional.

She'd had many run-ins with Bob over the years and she knew he enjoyed taking any opportunity to discredit or belittle her. They'd started their careers at the same time and whilst Rachel knew she did her job for the right reasons, she felt Bob always had his eye on his career path. His decisions were influenced by who was watching, and whether he'd get a promotion or commendation from it. He wasn't well liked, but he still had his own inner circle of likeminded cops who scratched each other's backs through the promotion routes. However, even though he'd gone for every promotion at the earliest possible opportunity, he'd still made DCI a year after Rachel following a number of failed attempts, and she knew he felt the sting of that. She'd also been told the chief wasn't best pleased he'd been made DCI and knew Bob had fallen lucky with the interview panel that year; it wouldn't happen again, she'd heard.

Bob gave Rachel one minute in the morning briefing to share her thoughts with the rest of the team, but Rachel felt she was still on her own. Four other officers talked through different suspects, and Liam was added to the pile of persons of interest. Through Sunday she shared the background check information she'd already gathered with her colleagues, but felt they were getting nowhere. When her shift ended at 6pm she called Emma.

'Hey, are you free?' she asked.

'Yeah sure, just about to eat in thirty, do you want to join us? I'm actually cooking a proper chicken dinner,' Emma laughed; her lack of cooking skills was well known.

'Is it safe?' Rachel laughed.

'I don't know, we'll find out tomorrow, I guess.'

'I don't think I've eaten today since brekky, to be honest, just realised I'm starving, so I'd even eat your cooking today,' Rachel said. 'I'll head over. I need to talk to you about Judith and Hannah James. I'll explain when I'm there.'

Rachel took photos of her timeline board, grabbed the files and her laptop, and drove over to Emma's house in Fradley; fifteen minutes away.

As she drove, she grew more concerned about Hannah's whereabouts. Was she still alive? She was sure Judith had been murdered by Liam, had he done the same to Hannah? If not, where was she? They'd seen some of Liam's house but not all and there was a small shed in the garden and a double garage. She needed enough evidence to get a warrant for a complete search.

She pulled onto Emma's drive and took a deep breath; it also meant an evening with Laura, Emma's girlfriend, who Rachel had never really taken to, and she knew the feeling was mutual.

Emma opened the door. 'For god's sake, rescue me will you,' she whispered, rolling her eyes, meaning Laura was in a mood again, no doubt due to Rachel's impending arrival.

Rachel pulled a jokey grimacing face. 'Eyes and teeth darling, eyes and teeth.'

'Hey, Laura, how's it going?' Rachel chirped brightly as she walked into the kitchen.

Laura forced a smile. 'Fine, thank you for asking.'

Rachel knew she wasn't fine, she never was, and Laura was well known for her childish outbursts and unreasonable demands of Emma.

'Right, dinner's ready,' Emma declared, 'we have something that once resembled a chicken and everything else I could stick in the oven straight from a bag or tray.' Meaning Aunt Bessie had come to the rescue as usual with pre-prepared roast potatoes, Yorkshire's and the veg was no doubt microwaved.

Emma and Rachel made small talk whilst Laura did her best to say as little as possible whilst pushing her food around the plate.

'It's not that bad,' Emma joked.

'Oh piss off,' Laura replied. She stood up and left the room stomping loudly up the stairs, slamming the bedroom door behind her.

'Sorry about that,' Emma said, sighing and rolling her eyes again.

'Did I interrupt something?' Rachel asked.

'She was fine earlier, but you know what she's like, doesn't want to share me with anyone, she's bloody exhausting,' Emma replied.

'You really need to end it with her, Em, the longer you leave it the harder it gets.'

'I know, I know and I will. Look, forget her for tonight, let's eat,' Emma pointed at Rachel's plate.

'It really is shite, you know,' Rachel laughed, 'how can you burn a chicken in a bag? You've only got two instructions, the heat and the length of time!'

'I know, I was distracted. I've been looking at the evidence for Judith. I just feel sickened by it,' Emma answered.

'Me too, I just can't get my head round it, I'm sure it was Liam James but Knobby's got the case and he's treating me like something he stood on as usual; he's not listening properly. He needs sacking, the fuckwit. God only knows why they gave Judith to him.'

Rachel knew it was luck of the draw; Bob was on duty and picked Judith's case up, just because he was there.

'You should have seen him in this morning's briefing thinking he was running a boot camp or something, shouting, not listening as usual. Twat.' Rachel could feel herself getting more wound up.

'If you're not going eat that I'll order a takeaway and we can look at the case together,' Emma interrupted.

'I'm OK, I'm past eating to be honest,' she smiled, pushing her plate away.

'No worries, I'll chuck it.'

They tidied up and Rachel started to explain her hunch to Emma.

She showed her the photos of the timeline, the texts and voicemails, the train times and talked about Liam's behaviour. Emma listened, taking it all in.

'Can you see anything else?' she asked Emma in desperation. 'John said it's circumstantial. But they need to take it seriously. I'm positive it's Liam, and Hannah may be alive somewhere, and who knows what he's going to do next.'

'Honestly, Rach, I agree with them. I can see exactly where you're coming from but we have no hard evidence, nothing forensically that joins them. So far, we haven't got a murder weapon for Judith and there's no DNA, fingerprints, or anything to link Liam. The description of the assailant is too generic – tall white man in Lichfield, it could be anyone.' Emma sat quietly with Rachel for a moment, then continued, 'Tell you what, I'll take a look at the cafe laptop first thing tomorrow, see if I can find anything.'

'Thanks, hun, that would be great,' Rachel said, exhausted.

'Look, you get off home, get some sleep and I'll talk to you tomorrow.' Emma often mothered Rachel, knowing she didn't look after herself.

'Ok, thank you,' Rachel answered, feeling defeated, gave her a hug and made her way home.

Chapter 48

Rachel's mobile rang the next morning; a mobile number she didn't recognise.

'Hello, is that Rachel Taylor?' The woman's voice was shaky and breathy; speaking before Rachel had a chance to talk.

'Yes, this is Rachel Taylor, how can I help you?' she answered.

'I, I, erm, er, oh this is really difficult, I may be overreacting, but…' Rachel could hear her take a deep breath. She often found people who weren't used to dealing with the police struggled on the phone and it was harder to settle someone when you weren't face to face. 'I found your card in his office,' she blurted out; her voice got faster.

Rachel intervened. 'OK, just take your time. What's your name?'

'It's Lucy, Lucy Hassall.' She took a deep breath.

'Are you ringing about a particular case, Lucy?' Rachel's voice was calm and steady, slowing down the conversation to help Lucy speak more clearly.

She heard her take another long breath. 'Yes, it's about Hannah James, do you know about her?' She was calmer, but her voice was still shaky.

'Yes, I'm the officer in charge of the case. You said you found my card?'

'Yes, I found it in Liam's office, and I could see the number on his call history,' she blurted out again.

'How do you know Mr James?' Rachel asked.

'I'm his, er, secretary, well I'm actually an Executive Marketing Manager, that's my job title, but he calls me his secretary.' Her voice speeded up, more animated; evidently she was annoyed at the injustice of his belittlement of her. 'I graduated with a First in English Language and speak French, Italian, and Mandarin, and he's got the nerve to call me his secretary,' Lucy added, on a roll. She took a breath; Rachel took the opportunity to interrupt.

'OK, Lucy,' she said calmly, 'let's just take it slowly. What is it you want to tell me?'

Her response was much slower and quieter, almost as if she didn't want to say it out loud and make it true. Lucy was tearful and could just about get her words out. 'I think he's done something to her,' she said, her voice cracking.

Sensing how upset she was, Rachel wanted to see her face to face. 'Lucy, would it be easier if we met up? I could come to you?'

An hour later, Rachel was sitting in Lucy's apartment just off Brindley Place. It was 12:15pm and Lucy had agreed to meet on her lunch break. She was slim, in her early thirties, looking flushed, with short blond, bobbed hair and a smart navy business suit with a white open shirt underneath.

'He's not nice, you know, he treats everyone like shit. He's horrible, it's a real boys' club at work. He's slept with most of the women, not me though, I wouldn't let him, although he's tried, slimy git.' Lucy had undoubtedly been bottling it up for a while.

'There's no point going to HR as he's the golden boy in the company's eyes, he gets away with anything. Gift of the gab; he's manipulative and clever. There's been loads of complaints against him, I know there has, but nothing ever happens and so many women have left because of him, or been sacked, he's vile.' She got it off her chest almost in one breath.

Rachel paused for a moment and looked at her directly. 'OK, just take it slowly,' she smiled, still trying to calm the pace of the conversation. 'You mentioned you thought he'd done something to Mrs James,' Rachel questioned, 'can you tell me more about that?'

'I just have a feeling,' Lucy answered.

Rachel smiled but was hoping for hard evidence, not a feeling.

'Hannah was lovely, she was so quiet, hardly spoke. He'd bring her to parties and events, but she always looked so distant. He was rude to her in front of other people, and she'd just smile and take it.' Lucy sighed, 'I had a boyfriend like him once,' she shook her head slowly, 'I maybe reading into things, maybe seeing things that aren't there because of my own experience, but, well, sometime you know, don't you?'

Rachel nodded, she could see Lucy drifting off thinking about a previous time; an unhappy time.

'Anyway,' she continued, 'The first time I met her was about five years ago. I think they'd only just started going out and she was full of life, but now, well, the last time I saw her, she was grey and withdrawn, and so quiet. She hardly looked up. I mean she'd smile and laugh and try and make conversation, but,' she shook her head and sighed again, 'it's like she wasn't there.' Lucy's eyes welled up. 'I should have said something, reached out. But,' she sighed again, 'you don't get involved, do you? I feel so guilty.' Lucy reached into her handbag and pulled out a tissue to dab her eyes.

Rachel thought for a moment how to proceed. She believed Lucy, but she couldn't show bias; she needed to question her without leading her. 'Is there anything specific that would suggest Mr James was involved in Hannah's disappearance?'

'Well, he's hardly been in, he's been at his office in Lichfield the last few months; it's been really difficult trying to get things signed off by him,' Lucy explained.

'You mean his home office?' Rachel asked.

'No, his office in Lichfield. He made a right fuss about, had to have it, and it was like, what he wants he gets,' she huffed. She was getting more annoyed and bitter again.

'He's got an office in Lichfield?' Rachel asked, trying to hide her surprise and anticipation that it may lead somewhere. 'Do you know the address?'

After a couple of minutes Lucy had found the address, checking the records using her work tablet. Rachel put the postcode into Google Maps and her heart raced. It was on the opposite side of the road to the cafe, directly opposite; this was the breakthrough she needed. What if Hannah was there? Had he been spying on her? Was there any evidence there? Was he there now? Questions streamed through her mind.

'Thank you, Lucy,' she said calmly. 'Do you know where Mr James is today?'

'No, and I'm really annoyed about that too. He told me I had to work today. I don't normally work Mondays but he was adamant I had to be in, and he's not even turned up. That's what made me ring – I'm so angry and he can't keep getting away with things. In the week, when he does come in, he goes straight back out, and it drives me mad. I mean, what's the point?'

Rachel let Lucy carry on, she didn't want to break her stride; her getting things off her chest was helping her glean useful information.

'And that's another thing,' she continued, 'he can go to appointments in his own car, he doesn't need a pool car, that's just supposed to be for spare when other people need it, but no, he ties up two cars and then other people can't use it.'

'He uses a pool car? Do you know where he, er, Mr James goes?' Rachel asked.

'Just work, I guess, clients maybe, he's started using it more over the last year,' Lucy huffed and added casually, 'I can check on the vehicle tracking if you want?'

'You have tracking?' Rachel tried not to show her excitement. 'Can you show me?'

'Yeah, sure, we had them put on all the pool cars last year, he probably doesn't even know. I mentioned it was happening ages ago and he ignored me as usual. He gets regular reports which include the data, but I know he doesn't even read them; the read receipt on his emails never shows it. He does that a lot, just ignores everything and gets away with it.' Lucy talked faster as she logged onto the app on her tablet. She clicked the car registration and it showed up in Hammerwich, just outside Lichfield.

'There he is,' Lucy said, smugly pointing at the screen.

Rachel could see the car was moving. 'Can you see where it's been?' she enquired.

'Yes, but I need to go back to the office, I'm going to get into trouble if I'm late back from lunch. I can't let him, or anyone know I've spoken to you,' Lucy said nervously. 'He checks my clocking-in time on my pass; it's not even supposed to be for that, I'm supposed to have flexi time but, no, not according to him, just another reason for him to pick holes,' Lucy continued. 'I'm not even supposed to work today, why am I even worrying? I need to leave that place, I hate working for him,' she scowled.

'OK, thank you, Lucy, you've been a real help.' Lucy sat up and Rachel could see she was pleased with herself. 'You have my number. Can you have a look at the tracking, and I'll speak to you later today? When it's OK for you to ring, maybe when you're back home?' Rachel suggested, and Lucy agreed.

Rachel hoped this was the breakthrough she needed, but she also knew getting a warrant to search the office or the tracking software would be difficult. There was still no evidence to suggest Liam had done anything wrong, with Hannah or Judith. And particularly with Judith the list of other suspects was growing, and Liam wasn't near the top. Those who'd threatened staff at the refuge were way ahead of him on the pecking order for interviews, and it was a slow process. None of the conversations she'd had with Judith were recorded; everything was off the record, other than the voicemail she left for Rachel just before she was killed. Rachel thought it through on her drive back to Lichfield, and she called Emma.

'Hey, how's it going? Have you checked the laptop yet?' she asked.

'I'm so sorry, I got pulled into Knobby's briefing at 8am and he's prioritised a stack of evidence. I just can't get to it,' Emma answered.

'You're kidding, this is ridiculous. He wouldn't see proper evidence if it slapped him in the face. I'm going to talk to John.'

'Be careful, Rach,' Emma warned her.

'I know, I know, I've just had a fucking 'nuff now. Thanks anyway.'

Next stop: her boss's office.

Chapter 49

'Boss, can I have a word please?'

John looked up as Rachel walked into his office.

'About the Hannah James and Judith Millar cases,' she continued, 'I really do think there's a connection and I don't think Bob's taking me seriously.'

John wasn't always the most approachable when critiquing another colleague's work, but on this occasion the sting of Judith's death was palpable in the station; anything that could help catch the bastard would be worth a listen.

Superintendent John Weaver had almost done his thirty years in the police, and had met Judith almost as soon as he started. Back then she was in her early twenties and her charity was in its formative days. She wasn't really taken seriously; domestic violence wasn't even a crime back then, and certainly not coercive control which had only recently gained any support for prosecuting perpetrators. Now domestic violence and abuse was one of the highest demands on the force.

As a young gay man, John joined the police knowing his life choices were a crime in many people's eyes. He'd married Philippa, had two lovely children, but always knew he was carrying on a facade. His friendship with Judith had developed over the years; both outcasts. Him with his secret he wanted hidden and her on a crusade to change the world, constantly coming up against prejudice and blockages.

Judith had found out his secret when he'd been with the force for two years. He'd been posted as a decoy at the top of Barr Beacon, Great Barr, the highest point in the West Midlands. It was a park for walkers and families during the day and a known dogging site at night. He was there to trap and catch, 'the puffs and queers at it', his sergeant had said. John had been left on a bench to try and attract some random bloke. They'd made two arrests; one had been roughed up without cause and suffered a broken jaw. 'Resisting arrest', he'd been ordered to put in his report. John felt sick at what he'd been involved in. These were two innocent men just trying to meet up. Yes, it wasn't the best place, and it was sordid but with the hype in the media and regular gay bashing, it was a choice out of necessity.

Judith had seen him the next day, when he'd been called to the refuge to deal with an angry husband looking for his wife and causing a disorder. Judith could see John was upset, distant, and asked him to come round later that day, when he was off shift. He told her what had happened; he knew she knew about him being gay and felt comfortable talking to her. She had that insight into people, she could sense it, and she soon became a friend, a confidante. She'd been the one years later who encouraged him to come out, to tell his wife, his kids. She'd said to him, and he'd repeated the same phase over the years, 'Choice, the most important tool you have, use it wisely.'

Judith was at his wedding when he married Mike three years ago. They'd often meet up for a drink, family parties, charity events. She was more than just a police partner, she was his friend, probably one of the closest friends he'd ever had, and now within seconds some mindless yob had ended her life. What she'd done over thirty years was far and above greater than anything he'd done or could ever do in his career, he thought. She'd changed hearts and minds; she'd been involved in case law to change legislation. She protected thousands through her actions, not just the ones that had been through her refuge, but men, women, and children across the country; she'd created a legacy, and now she was gone.

Rachel stood before him explaining the link between the cases. He already knew that Judith had come forward and told Rachel about Hannah going to Inverness. He knew about the messages Hannah had sent and understood the need for absolutely confidentiality. The case had been closed under his guidance; he trusted Judith without question. As Rachel explained her thoughts about the link, she told him about her meeting with Lucy and her suspicions. John agreed with her, but without solid evidence there was no way round getting the warrant to search his office or the tracking software. There was nothing to stop him having an office in Lichfield, nothing to stop him using a pool car.

'Boss, I know we closed the case, but what if we were wrong? We still have the laptop from the cafe and Emma's was trying to look at it this morning, but she can't get to it because of other work Bob's prioritised. We have Judith's phone, we can make the link, I know we can, this is all too much of a coincidence.' Rachel was pleading and

John looked at her, understanding her need to make the connections. 'I also want the tracking software looked at – if we can see where's he's been we may be able to get a lead,' Rachel added.

'We definitely can't get a warrant for that. What about this Lucy? Do you trust her?' he asked.

'Yes and no, she's a bit flighty so there's a risk she'll blurt it out at the office. I know she hates Liam and I think something may have gone on sexually between them, so there may be an ulterior motive. She may be lying, but I don't think she is.'

'What's your gut really telling you? Do you think Hannah's alive?' John asked.

'I'm in two minds. I definitely think he killed Judith because of Hannah leaving, but is she alive? Honestly, my gut says yes but I fear I may be wrong, and I think he thinks he's going to get away with it if we don't focus efforts there. He's been taunting me, he's being clever, manipulative and I want to nail this bastard.' Rachel's voice cracked.

John trusted Rachel, she was one of his best officers, but without evidence for a warrant his hands were tied. Never one to break any rules, he considered the options for a moment. 'Right, talk to this Lucy again and see how much she can volunteer to tell you. Find out where that pool car's been, if he's used any others. See if she can share any of his diary information. We need to know if he was using it on the day Hannah disappeared, where he's been over the past few weeks, but remember, this is on the down low for the moment. We just need one lead, and we can go after him.'

'Got it, boss. Thanks.' Rachel turned and left his office.

John sat for a few moments running the information through his head. The right thing to do was ring his boss, DCS Owen. John wanted Bob off the case and Rachel in charge – someone he trusted – but equally he felt she was too invested now and could be making connections where there weren't any. They needed at least one piece of hard evidence to link the cases; failing that, they may have to be creative. He reached for the phone and dialled.

'Emma, are you free for a catch-up in ten minutes?'

180

Chapter 50

Lucy was relieved she'd had the courage to call the police; she felt quite proud of herself. Time to get him back. Finally. Rachel seemed really nice, she'd definitely listened to her.

Lucy had got the measure of Liam early on when she first started working with him. He'd just got a promotion to director, and she'd started at the company taking over his old job; she could do it standing on her head and started performing really well. She'd made great strides as soon as she started, landing three major accounts, and had started to get noticed, but Liam soon put a stop to that. He called her into his office one morning.

'I'm restructuring the team. It doesn't affect your job title or basic salary, so there'll be no griping about it,' he'd said matter-of-factly.

She nodded slowly and sat in silence, waiting to hear what *restructuring* meant.

'I'm splitting your top three accounts, Barnard, Gresley and Shentons. So arrange handovers with Rob, Mark and Leyton ASAP.'

His drinking buddies, funnily enough. Who were now getting her three new accounts that she'd worked her butt off for and managed to land in record time. One every three months is good, but three in one month was unheard of. She could feel her heart racing; she was livid. He'd just disregarded what she'd achieved; she should be getting promoted, not downgraded. She'd sat in stunned silence for a moment, thinking how best to challenge his decision, then said. 'But that takes my bonus down by fifty percent.' Also meaning he'd given his buddies a pay rise each.

To which he'd said, 'Well you need to get some more accounts in then, don't you? If you don't like it, you know where the door is. I have no hesitation helping you through it, you're still on probation, remember.' He'd flicked his hand at her to leave his office.

She could feel the tears welling and her bottom lip tremble. She bit it to try and keep her composure. *Don't cry at work.* She stood and left the room, went to the toilets and let her tears flow. That evening she phoned her best friend Meg.

'You'll never guess what happened,' she'd sobbed on the phone, and Meg came round immediately to console her. Meg had been her best friend since the age of four; they'd got into various scrapes along the way as they grew up and always had each other's back. Lucy had been her bridesmaid three years before and godmother to her daughter, Lily, aged two. Meg had her hands full nowadays, but would still be there for Lucy at the drop of a hat.

'Babes, I know you, you're capable of anything you put your mind to. This is just temporary, you'll get something else,' Meg had said as she followed an exploring Lily round Lucy's flat.

'It's going to look really bad on my CV though, leaving somewhere so quick, and he's not going to give me a good reference, is he? He's shafted me, good and proper.' Lucy envisaged herself sitting in interviews trying to explain.

'Have you spoken to HR, though?' Meg had asked.

'What's the point? And, besides, I don't want to work there,' she'd responded.

That was five years ago, and Liam had gradually reduced her responsibilities, along with her confidence and self-esteem. She'd been to numerous interviews; she looked great on paper, but, when in the hot seat, she just couldn't perform. She was too honest and would start moaning about Liam. It looked really unprofessional, but she couldn't help herself.

Then she'd met Matt, who she'd dated for eighteen months. At first, he seemed lovely, and charming, but turned out to be possessive and controlling. Her self-worth plummeted even further, and it was only when Meg's husband Joe had intervened that the relationship ended. They'd been out for a meal, the four of them, and Matt had been obnoxious throughout the evening. Matt and Joe never really hit it off; one supporting Blues, the other Villa, so there was always tension and the banter was uncomfortably strained. Meg was seven months' pregnant at the time, and as they left the restaurant Matt had made a jibe, *Who ate all the pies*? Within a split second, Joe had him up against the wall.

'You never talk to my wife like that, you spineless piece of shit,' he'd said.

'Just a joke, mate, chill out,' Matt had retorted, pushing him off.

182

'It's not a fucking joke and it's not a joke when you treat Lucy like you do, she's too good for you,' He turned to Lucy, 'I'm sorry, bab, it's got to be said.'

'She's too good for me? Are you having a fucking laugh, I could do better than that skinny ass, no tits ugly bitch.'

Joe then punched him square in the face. Matt fell backwards holding his nose, threatening to call the police. That was the last Lucy saw of him; his sister picked up his belongings from her apartment, apologising for his behaviour as she did.

She could see Liam was the same as Matt. Lucy watched him at work with disdain, always working the room, charming, manipulating. Always for his own benefit. When she'd met Hannah the first time on a works' night out, she remembered thinking, *You could do so much better than him*. She was beautiful, funny and intelligent, but, over the years, her personality had melted away. After Lucy had split up with Matt, she remembered thinking Liam must be just like him at home; a bully. Now though, she felt she had the upper hand; he was going to get what was coming to him.

After meeting Rachel, she'd got back to the office and spent the afternoon researching the tracker on the various pool cars that Liam used and his own company car. She'd created a spreadsheet, colour coded it for similar places and made various notes against it. She'd ring Rachel when she got home, get her email address and send it over. *Justice will be served*.

She left bang on five and walked quickly home stopping only to pick up a salad from Marks and Sparks. It was another scorching day and she didn't feel like eating much, besides, her stomach was churning with the day's events.

She got home, opened the door, kicked her heels off and quickly changed into a pale-blue summer dress; floaty and loose. It felt so refreshing to get her tight work suit off. She found the card in her bag with Rachel's number on it and started to dial, her hands shaking a little. *Relax*, she said to herself, just as there was a knock at the door.

Chapter 51

By 9pm that evening, Lucy still hadn't called her back. Rachel sat legs sprawled on the sofa trying to cool down; the humidity was stifling, and her Hendricks and slimline tonic wasn't helping to cool her down. She'd found the loosest strappy T-shirt and shorts she could find in her drawer; pale pink with pandas on. A Christmas present from her mum; the panda's a reference to police cars, her mum had giggled.

She rang Lucy; she didn't answer.

This was so frustrating – not only couldn't she get a warrant without the evidence she needed, now she couldn't see what evidence there was. She tried twice more and left a voicemail, just a short one, without giving away who she was. 'Hi, just waiting for you to ring about our meeting today.'

She'd had a long day, head throbbing, still trying to make connections, trying to make sense of Hannah's timeline. She took another sip of her drink, *I'm sure you're not helping my headache*, she thought, then took another. She sat on the sofa for another hour; she could feel her eyes getting heavy as she fought against the sleep.

She woke just after 3am with a stiff neck and weighed up the effort of moving to get to bed, versus her knowing how bad she'd feel the next day if she stayed on the sofa. Her bed won.

Back at the station the next day, she thought of ringing Lucy; it was mid-morning. She'd driven past Liam's house first thing and could see the car missing. He could be at the Birmingham office, she thought, so now wasn't a good time to ring her; Liam could catch her on the call. Rachel was thinking what to do next at her desk, tapping her pen in frustration when her phone rang – it was Lucy. *Thank god*. Now we can get to the bottom of this and start to get some background on Liam's movements, she thought.

'Hi, Lucy, how are you today?' she asked.

'Sorry, Lucy won't be available to talk today.' The voice, by now, was all-too-familiar. The call cut off.

'Oh shit.' She shot up and ran to her boss's office.

John looked up, startled. 'What?'

'I think he's done something to Lucy, the secretary I was telling you about. I've not been able to get hold of her, then she just called me, but it was him, I recognised his voice. He said something about her not able to talk.' Rachel felt panic like no other; she'd never in her career put anyone at risk, witnesses, or victims. 'Oh my god, what has he done?'

'OK, calm down. I'll get in touch with City Police to get round to her flat, and we need to find out where the hell Liam is as well,' John said.

He reached for his phone. Rachel checked hers and scribbled the address for him then ran out the office, shouting, 'I'm going over there, call me if you hear anything.'

Rachel got into her car and raced into Birmingham along the A38, her sirens blaring on her unmarked vehicle. Twenty-three minutes later and she was pulling up outside Lucy's apartment block. She could see a police response vehicle parked outside. She raced into the building and up the three flights of stairs to Lucy's apartment. The door was open and a young PC was standing in the doorway. He turned and saw her. 'Sorry, miss, you can't come in,' he said, putting his arms out to block her entrance.

'DCI Rachel Taylor of Lichfield City Police, my boss called this in,' Rachel just about said, hardly able to breathe after the three flights, showing the officer her credentials.

'Oh, sorry, ma'am, they said you were coming. We need to preserve the scene, we've been here ten minutes; my sarge is in there with the body.'

'Oh god, what's happened?' Rachel asked, desperate not to hear the answer she was expecting.

'Looks like suicide,' the young officer replied.

Rachel put her hand to her mouth, and she felt nauseous as a heaviness descended on her.

'OK, thank you. Who's the officer in charge?' she asked.

'That'll be my sarge, ma'am.' He turned back into the room, 'Boss, DCI Taylor's here from Lichfield, can I let her in?' He turned back to Rachel. 'Sorry, I don't know the rules about other force's access and the like, this is my first proper week – my first dead body, too,' he added brightly.

Rachel looked at him with disgust as a male voice from inside the apartment shouted, 'Let her through.'

Rachel walked into the lounge and saw Lucy slumped on the sofa, her head dropped to one side. A bottle of vodka was empty next to her, a tumbler broken on the floor and an empty pill bottle near her on a cushion. Her mascara had run, and Rachel could see she'd been crying. Streaks of black and grey down her cheeks, her mobile was in her hand and a note in her lap.

'This is for you.' The officer indicated to the note with his pen.

Rachel could see her name at the top, the note upside-down from where she stood. She carefully walked round to the side of the sofa so she could take a closer look without disturbing the scene. She imagined that only half an hour before Liam had been there. No doubt forced Lucy to drink, to write the note, to take the pills and end her life. He'd then had the audacity to ring Rachel and goad her.

Before she read the note, she turned to the sergeant, and looked at his badge. 'Right, Gavin, we need to check anyone coming and going to this building, any CCTV and we need Forensics down here. This wasn't suicide. I spoke to her killer, Liam James, thirty minutes ago. His office is ten minutes that way.' She pointed towards Brindley Place and gave him the address. The sergeant tried to protest, saying it wasn't Rachel's patch, but quickly backed off when she used her seniority; she wasn't taking no for an answer.

'Yes, ma'am, I just need to talk to my boss, but yes, we'll get onto it,' Gavin answered.

Rachel leant in to look at the note.

Dear Rachel

I'm so sorry for wasting you're time I shouldn't of said anything, Im so ashamed of myself. I thought when she was gone he'd want me but he didnt he never has. I guess I was just jealous but that doesn't make it right does it Im so sorry I just made it up to get back at him He'll never want me though I know that now I'm sorry

Lucy

The note was badly written, both grammatically and scribbled almost; the paper was crumpled and dirty with what she assumed was tears and mascara smudges. Had Liam written it or Lucy? If Lucy had, she'd certainly written it badly on purpose to let Rachel know she

186

hadn't killed herself. She'd made a point of telling her she was an English graduate and undoubtedly knew how to write properly, even under stress, it would be a natural habit for her.

Within the next thirty minutes SOCO were in the room, taking photographs, swabs and fingerprints; they took Rachel's for elimination purposes. They were on the Staffordshire database, but it would be quicker to take them whilst she was there, they said.

SOCO agreed it looked like suicide at first, but there were some things troubling them over and above the phone call Rachel claimed to have received.

'Where's the pen?' one of the SOCO said, a young woman called Claire. 'I'd expect to see a pen near the body but there aren't any pens in this room. Has anyone bagged a pen?' she shouted with replies of 'no' coming back to her.

'There's some in the drawer in the hall,' one of the team shouted.

'But why would she put it away?' Claire asked and screwed her nose up. 'Why would she tidy up? Everything else is untidy where she's sitting. Why would she put it away? There's no need.'

Rachel knew she had a point. Plus, it was likely a generic ball point pen, so to find one on Liam with forensics was unlikely.

The sergeant walked back into the room. 'Ma'am, can I have a quick word?' he asked Rachel.

Rachel walked out of the room onto the communal landing, face-to-face with the sarge.

'My officer has just spoken to Mr James at his office and there are plenty of witnesses who can give him an alibi – he's been in his office for the last three hours. It couldn't have been him you spoke to on Miss Hassall's phone. It was either her, or someone else, but not him.'

Rachel was stunned, lost for words. It didn't make any sense; she knew it was him she'd spoken to. *It must have been him.*

The sarge asked her to stay and took down the exact details of what had happened, but made it clear they'd be handling this case. He'd obviously had some direction from above and was more confident dealing with her seniority; if they needed any assistance, they'd let her know.

Driving back to Lichfield, she rang Emma. She updated her on the conversation with Lucy and the events that had followed. 'Can we catch up when I'm back? I just need to talk this through, if anything,' she asked.

'Of course, I'll be staying late tonight and I'm really sorry I still haven't had a chance to check the laptop; every time I go to look at it, Bob's either on the phone asking about other evidence or popping up in my office. He's like a meerkat on heat.'

Rachel sighed. She was weary with the treacle they were wading through. 'OK, I'll be about thirty minutes, maybe more, the traffic's shite.' She felt deflated, but she knew she was so close; she needed to push on.

Forty minutes later and Rachel was in slow-moving traffic just coming into Lichfield along London Road. She thought about the events of the past two weeks, still angry at herself for closing Hannah's case without corroboration from Inverness; but that was hindsight, and it wouldn't help her now. At the time there was no reason to think anything else. It was Hannah's plan; they'd respected her wishes.

She eventually pulled into the station and texted Emma.

Here

Emma texted back immediately.

OK, we're in Room 1

What more can you take?

There's nothing left.

Chapter 52

It seemed as though he hadn't been for days. There was no food left, apart from the now-mouldy remnants of the fridge and there were two litre bottles of water. She didn't feel the cold anymore, she didn't feel anything; she was numb with sorrow and regret. If only she'd been a good wife and done as she was told, Judith would still be alive. She was an idiot for thinking she needed more, selfish that what she had wasn't good enough. Liam had provided a perfect life for her, but she was greedy and spoilt. She could hear his words resonating in her head.

She knew that when the water had gone, she'd drift into starvation or die of thirst. She remembered watching a documentary but couldn't remember which way round it was, water or food. Should she just stop drinking now and allow the inevitable to happen? As she thought it through, the cellar door opened and Liam stood there. He switched the light on. 'Get up.'

She hadn't even heard the car or his footsteps. She squinted and held her hand over her eyes, shielding them from the brightness as she tried to stand. She managed to get up on her feet but dropped again. She put her arms in front of her to push herself up and saw she was covered in blood and dirt; scratches and bruises at different stages. She leant on her right wrist and it buckled, she yelped with pain realising it must be broken.

'You're pathetic. Get the fuck up, you lazy whore,' Liam yelled at her. 'Fucking pathetic.' He strode across the room and pulled her up by her broken wrist as she screamed and sobbed. He let her wrist go, hooked his arm around her waist and dragged her up the steps, bashing her legs against each one. At the top they were in a small hallway. He let go for her to stand on her own, but she dropped to the floor in a heap. She tried to push herself up and winced as he came towards her to lift her again.

The room was familiar, but she was dazed and everything was so blurry that she couldn't work out where she was. Liam lifted her again and she felt carpet bashing her feet as he took her up another flight of stairs.

'Fuck!' Liam snapped. 'Shit.'

Hannah looked down and could see the beige carpet had dirt and blood scraped on it.

'Look what you've fucking done,' he snarled.

He lifted her fully off the floor and carried her up the stairs, every movement painful. His arm was crushing her ribs whilst he was being careful not to touch any more of the pristine decor.

Hannah knew she'd been there before, but only once. The cheese cellar, she thought, and she knew where she was.

Liam pushed the door in front of him open with his foot and dropped Hannah into the wet room. The polished Italian porcelain tiles were £100 a square metre and had taken over twelve weeks to deliver. *But it was worth it, we work hard for our money and we deserve it.* She replayed the conversation in her head with Liam's boss, Stuart.

Liam turned on the shower and threw a bottle of shower gel at Hannah; it hit her shoulder and dropped to the floor. He walked out, leaving her on her own.

Although the water hitting her body stung, it was welcome, and gave Hannah the first warmth she'd had in what must have been over two weeks. She didn't know how long it had been, but it was long. At first, she just sat curled in the ball on her side how Liam left her, but as the water thawed her, she loosened. She was still too weak to stand, so she sat up slightly, wrapping her arms round her knees and pulling them in close as she let the water run over her. She slowly uncurled and tried to gently clean her body. The shower gel stung her cuts but gradually the blood and dirt washed away, and Hannah could see what was left of her. Bruised, scratched, swollen, cut and scabbed. Her body didn't look like anything she'd seen before. Her stomach under her ribs was dark purple, almost black, different shades and sizes of bruises all over her. Green, blue, purple, yellow; mapping the beatings she'd endured.

She eventually stood, pulling herself up with her good arm using the, no doubt expensive, chrome bar installed in the luxury bathroom. She looked down and watched her diluted blood swirl and disappear down the drain She tried to remember when Stuart and his wife Lilia had left for their three-month holiday and, more importantly, when they'd be back.

Hannah picked up the extra-thick white towel and wrapped it around herself. It felt like the softest and warmest thing she'd ever touched. She closed her eyes and visualised being in a luxury spa, sipping champagne, waiting for someone to massage her weary body and bring her back to life.

Liam walked in and she abruptly came back into the room; the reality of where she was hit her. He pulled the towel off her and looked her up and down with disgust.

'Get dressed and come downstairs,' he ordered.

He left the room and Hannah looked at the clothes he'd put out for her on the bed. The ones she'd run away in. She dressed in difficulty because of her presumably broken wrist and even though her clothes were too loose, they still irritated her bruised and broken skin. Then she heard it and it stilled her to her core; Louis' inimitable voice echoing through the house. Barefoot, she tentatively walked down the stairs holding onto the rail for support as the music got louder. She protectively pulled her broken wrist into her chest. She could smell food – fish and chips; something she hadn't eaten for five years. She walked into the kitchen and could see two plates with the paper wrappings opened and a glass of red wine next to each one. Liam sat on one side of the enormous solid oak table that stood in the vast designer kitchen. She waited...should she sit, was it a trap? He nodded, indicating for her to sit and watched in silence as she took her place; silent, apart from the velvety tones of Louis' voice.

It was a beautiful house for sure. She'd been shown around by Lilia; stealth bragging about everything that was there. It was old, she didn't know how old, but she remembered going into the cellar. *It was a cheese store, that's what the slates are for – to keep the cheese cold,* Lilia had told her. In the kitchen Hannah remembered standing on top of the reinforced glass. *Go on, it's safe, just stand on it, it won't break.* Hannah had peered in and looked down the well. It was lit at the sides by spotlights with ferns and moss growing up the sides of the green and grey stone and the dark, murky iridescent water below.

Hannah remembered joking, *I'm expecting to see a dead body float past.*

It was beautiful but scary to think there was a well with its hidden depths.

The road's named after the well, and we've got the well in our kitchen, how cool's that? Lilia had said. It was cool, but now Hannah was being held there captive, beaten, and raped. Was this where she would die? Would she be put into the well and disappear? Her final resting place; no one would ever find her.

'You need to eat and build your strength up,' Liam said brightly as if she'd been out on a long run and they were getting home to a treat of fish and chips to celebrate her achievement.

Hannah didn't know what was happening; what would come next. Was he taunting her? Was he going to feed her, then kill her? Her last meal. She sat down opposite him with the fish and chips inches from her face; hot food. Was this a test? Would he let her eat and then reprimand her for eating fattening food? Everything was a trap. She felt a finality in the moment, but at least it would end; she just wanted it to be quick.

He pushed the glass of wine towards her. 'We need to celebrate.' He nodded towards the glass, smiling. Hannah picked it up cautiously. Her hand shook so much the red wine sloshed around, and she lowered the glass back to the table to steady it.

Liam held his glass high. 'To Lucy,' he exclaimed in a cheery voice as if he were celebrating her birthday. 'Long may you rest in peace, you stupid bitch,' Liam added as a broad smile crossed his face. 'I wonder who's next on the list?' He looked directly at her, the smile gone as his face screwed into a grimacing smirk. 'Not you though, I've got special plans for you.'

Hannah felt herself go as the familiar feel of fainting swept over her, nausea rising and disorientation as she fell.

Chapter 53

'OK, there's a number of explanations for the phone call,' Emma said, clearly and confidently. She was used to giving evidence in court; only ever the facts, never speculation, but calculated probability was often a factor.

Rachel listened intently. John had already heard Emma's suggestions and stood patiently whilst she ran through it with Rachel.

'It could have been Lucy who rang you herself,' Emma started.

'But...' Rachel tried to interrupt.

'Just bear with me,' Emma said. Rachel nodded. 'If she was crying her voice could have sounded differently, maybe deeper. If it was suicide, she probably wouldn't make any sense. It is a possibility.'

Rachel nodded reluctantly. 'I honestly do believe it was a man though, not Lucy,' she said.

'Another possibility is, you could have misheard what they said,' Emma started.

Rachel bit her lip, stopping herself from interrupting.

'It could have been someone else, who'd seen her commit suicide, or found her. Maybe called the last number in her phone, panicking and said she wasn't available, or something like that, and you misheard. They maybe, decided they didn't want to get involved and changed their mind whilst they were ringing. That's a high probability.'

Rachel thought about it; possible, but unlikely. 'He said, "Sorry, Lucy won't be available to talk today," That's not someone who was asking for help, and they knew her name,' she said.

'OK, but we don't know who it was for definite, so we don't know how they'd have handled it. It could have been genuine. Finding a body is traumatic for most people, or they could have disturbed someone else. As I said, they may not want to get involved for any number of reasons. People don't always say what you expect them to in these situations,' Emma suggested.

Rachel nodded. 'Why didn't he call an ambulance or the police?'

'We can only guess at that, Rach, as Emma's already said; they may have panicked,' John answered.

'It was definitely Liam James, I know his voice,' Rachel said quietly.

'You know his Birmingham accent, Rachel,' John intervened. 'Can you genuinely recognise different Birmingham accents? They pretty much all sound the same to me.'

'It was him.' She was firmer; she was sure.

'So, next explanation, it could have been someone else who killed her, whether they made the call or not, or whether it was Liam James or not. It's a genuine possibility and the absence of the pen suggests this is a highly likely explanation.' Emma looked sympathetically at Rachel; they were all frustrated, but Rachel felt personally responsible for Judith and Lucy's deaths. She wasn't, and there was no way she could have predicted the events of the last few days, but both deaths weighed heavily on her conscience.

'So, let's assume for a moment it was Liam. We know he has an alibi for three hours from 8:30am to 11:30am. The call to you was at?'

'10:04am,' Rachel responded.

'Yes, 10:04am. Now, the tablets would have taken a while to take effect, and until we know her stomach contents, what she took and when, and her time of death, we won't be able to work out if Liam had a window.'

'We're assuming the time of death was the call, but she could have died earlier,' John added.

'Of course, I just assumed.' Rachel put her hand to her mouth. She'd made too many assumptions; she was tired and making mistakes.

'That's why we trust the forensics, Rach. City Police are letting me know time of death and likely time of taking the tablets as soon as they know,' Emma added.

'How did he make the call from her phone, though?' Rachel asked.

'Ok, I've been thinking that one through. It could have been a cloned phone so we're looking into that as a possibility. I'm liaising with City about that too,' Emma said, adding, 'We need to accept it's their case unless we can make a clear link to our cases. At the moment though, that's not happening.'

'But why take the pen?' Rachel asked.

'It could have just been a mistake, Rach. How many cases have we solved because of mistakes these idiots make?' John stated. 'If it's him, and he's done this to Judith, I'll string him up by the bollocks myself.' John's voice cracked.

'I'm so sorry, boss,' Rachel said as Emma rubbed his shoulder. 'We know you were close.'

'She…' John tried to speak but couldn't. 'She...'

'It's OK, boss, we understand.' Emma put her arm around him and gave him a hug.

In all her years Rachel had never seen her boss cry. He could deal with anything, but now his eyes were full as a single tear broke rank and trickled down his cheek.

'We'll get him, John,' Emma said softly. 'We will.'

He took a deep breath and wiped his cheek. 'I'm sorry.' He pulled a seat out and sat down. Rachel wondered how much sleep he was getting and when he'd last had a break.

'OK, what about this tracking software?' John asked, composed and back on his game. 'How much did we learn?'

'Very little. All I could see was he was driving through Hammerwich at the time I was with Lucy,' Rachel answered.

'Could you see the logo of the app?' Emma asked.

'Er, oh god, er yes, it was like a blue circle with a car in the middle, erm, I think it was yellow.' Rachel closed her eyes and visualised Lucy's tablet trying to remember what she'd seen. 'Yes, blue circle, yellow car.'

Emma tapped her phone. 'Like this?' Emma showed her a logo on her phone's app store.

'Yes, that's it. Does that help?' she asked.

'It may do,' Emma answered.

'I don't think we'll get a warrant on the evidence we have to search the tracking app; everything is speculation. It may have the evidence we need, but we don't have just cause,' John said, stating the annoying fact they already knew. He was clearly frustrated with a system that at times was more in favour of criminals and their human rights than their victims. 'Leave that one with me, I'll see what I can do,' he added.

John stood up, his big frame filling the room. At well over six feet, with his high emotional IQ when dealing with victims and witnesses, he was known as the gentle giant; although neither Rachel nor Emma would like to see him lose his rag. On the times he'd come close at arrests, Rachel had on a few occasions winced, but he'd always managed to control himself; his record was exemplary. He left the room.

Rachel turned to Emma. 'What time are you finishing tonight?' she asked.

'About 8pm-ish.'

'My place after, I'll get a Chinese?' Rachel asked.

'Yeah, sure.'

'Usual?' Rachel smiled.

'Usual.'

Chapter 54

Emma arrived at Rachel's at 8:30pm. Her house in Tamworth wasn't much; two up, two down. She'd bought it off plan with Jay about fifteen ago. It was three years since they'd split up and Emma had been there for Rachel through the breakup. Different paths, and no time for relationships; Rachel put her career first too many times Jay had said. Rachel didn't see it like that – she put other people first every day, not her career. Jay, as much as she loved him, never needed her as much as others did, and they gradually drifted apart, leading virtually separate lives until he eventually moved out. She still missed him though and suspected it was more the lack of children in their lives that that caused the split; a toll on their lives they both had to pay.

Rachel's house was decorated exactly as it was when she'd first moved in. White walls, pale-oak-effect laminate floors, gloss-white kitchen units, black-gloss laminate worktop, and a standard housebuilder bathroom with floor-to-ceiling white tiles and a turquoise mosaic border. It was looking tired now, but Rachel didn't really notice; she didn't spend much time there.

'Glass of wine?' Rachel asked. 'I'm on my second.'

'Not tonight, early start tomorrow, and I'm driving,' Emma answered with defiance that she 'would' be going home.

'You can crash here if you want, you'd just need to make up the bed.' Rachel smiled, knowing what was coming.

'Oh, go on then,' Emma laughed.

This was standard practice whenever she went over. Emma could count on one hand how many times she'd actually gone to Rachel's and gone home the same evening. She knew Laura would be pissed at her again, but that relationship was on its last legs, so it didn't bother her. She was hoping she'd get home one day and Laura would be gone; she didn't have the time, effort or emotional capacity to deal with splitting up with her at the moment. It would be horrendous with Laura's mood swings and constant outbursts and accusations. Emma knew she was delaying the inevitable, but she just didn't have time for the drama at the moment.

She took a full glass from Rachel, they clinked and she took a sip, savouring the taste of the wine and the relaxation she felt.

'Chinese should be any minute now,' Rachel said just as the bell rang on cue.

As they ate and drank, Rachel and Emma discussed all three cases, Hannah, Judith and now Lucy.

'If he has killed Judith and Lucy, what are the chances of Hannah still being alive?' Emma asked.

'It's not high and I really fear she's dead. But, this is a man who controlled everything about her life. When he lost that control, I don't think he'd have let her go; if anything, I think he'd have tightened control and punished anyone who got in his way,' Rachel suggested. 'Or maybe he has killed her and is tying up loose ends, I don't know,' she sighed.

'You're making the facts fit the narrative, Rach, be careful. And,' she paused, 'if what you say is true, that also puts you in the firing line; I think you need to extra vigilant at the moment.'

'You don't need to worry about me,' she answered, 'I can look after myself.'

They both knew Emma was right. Someone like Liam was unravelling and he was unpredictable; Rachel needed to be careful.

'We need to search the Lichfield office and the tracking software. We need to know where he's been,' Rachel added, frustrated that the evidence they needed was protected because they didn't have enough cause to search. It was a system that constantly obstructed itself.

By now they were on their second bottle of wine and Rachel was tired and emotional with the alcohol taking effect.

'Could you hack into it?' Rachel said tentatively.

'No, I could not,' Emma shot back sternly. She knew it was the alcohol talking; in Rachel's right mind she would not even suggest it.

'But we need a lead,' Rachel slurred, and gave her friend doe eyes.

'Apart from it being illegal, it would be inadmissible, you know that.' Emma stood her ground.

'But we need to do something,' Rachel pleaded.

'Rachel, I'll say this only once: firstly, it's highly illegal, secondly, if you get caught it's a slap on the wrist, but if I get caught every case I've ever worked on could be reviewed, meaning guilty people could be released, as well as losing my job and probably prison time. The answer is no, and I think it's time we called it a night, don't you?'

Rachel had never been reprimanded by her friend before. She nodded and stood up to clear the dirty plates and Chinese boxes away.

'I'll tidy up,' Emma said, giving her friend a hug. 'Off you go,' she added, with more compassion.

Rachel went to bed.

Emma was annoyed at her friend. Rules were there to protect, and as much as they hindered at times, they were there for a reason. It was a slippery slope to consider other options. She knew her friend would be remorseful the next morning, so she wouldn't make it difficult for her; she knew she was in the wrong and she needed support not judgement at the moment. She thought back to her conversation with John about the very same thing after Judith was killed.

Chapter 55

Rachel lay in bed thinking about the case; she regretted saying anything to Emma. Neither of them had ever bent the rules, even a little bit, but she was out of options. People were dying, they didn't know where Hannah was, and she didn't want to feel responsible for another death if she could have done something. She felt lonely and lost; it was unfamiliar. Her head span with the wine. She'd had about three-quarters of a bottle, normally that wouldn't affect her as much, but she was tired and emotional. As she drifted off to sleep, she thought about how she could get Liam James; there must be a way.

Chapter 56

'If we re-open the missing person case, do we need to tell Liam James?' Rachel asked her boss the next day.

'Honestly, I don't know. As far as the evidence shows she wanted to leave, she did leave, and she doesn't want him to know where she is. If we take this case in isolation, by reopening it we could be putting her at more risk if she is somewhere in the country of her own volition. We could find her and risk him finding her too.' John thought for a moment as Rachel leant on the table with her head in her hands; they were at a crossroads. 'If we take the three cases together there's a high possibility that he's either got her or he's killed her; we need to proceed with caution. We can't let him know we're investigating him,' John added.

'Although, boss, being questioned over Lucy by City has already risked that. We don't know how they handled it with him.' Just as she said it Rachel's phone rang, a withheld number which usually indicated it was the police. 'Rachel Taylor speaking.'

'Ma'am this is Detective Sargent Johnstone of Birmingham City Police, you asked me to ring you with any updates.' The officer sounded nervous.

'Yes, go on.'

'This is to inform you the death of Lucy Hassall is continuing to be treated as a suicide and is likely to be ruled as such and closed.' It was as though he'd rehearsed the sentence.

'What do you mean, closed? What about the call and the pen?' Rachel demanded.

'I'm sorry, you know what it's like, it's resources. I can send the forensic report so far, but we're not doing any further investigation. It will be passed to the coroner.' The officer was no doubt in a chain of command, it was probably not his decision and out of his hands.

Rachel was furious, but answered calmly. 'Thank you, that would be helpful. Your forensics team are already in touch with our team so please send it over and cc me in,' she said and ended the call.

'I don't believe it, those incompetent up-their-own-arse idiots have done a shoddy job and are ruling Lucy Hassall a suicide, without doing a proper investigation.' Rachel lost it more than she ever had in front of her boss.

'What?' John shot up, 'You've gotta be kidding me.'

'We've all got resource problems, we still do our jobs.' Rachel was incensed. 'That bastard's getting away with it, he's fucking getting away with it.'

'OK, Rach, calm down.' He gestured with both hands to calm her down. 'We need to look at options here. I know you're angry, so am I, but we need to deal with the facts and evidence we have and what we can use,' John said with authority. 'We have no evidential link to Lucy Hassall or Judith,' he added.

Rachel's phone rang, again another withheld number. 'Taylor,' she snapped.

'Whoa, calm down, it's me,' Emma said.

'They've closed the Lucy Hassall case,' Rachel said in dismay, 'you're on speaker, John's here.'

Emma answered, 'I know, it's not technically closed but it's heading that way. City sent me the forensics just now. Lucy most likely took the tablets around 8pm the evening before. The call you received definitely wasn't from Lucy but equally the call wasn't registered as coming from her phone, it wasn't in the call history. They've not got anything in the report about you receiving a call, and suggested she used a pen and put it back in the drawer; my guess is they needed to do more work, they didn't have anyone, and they'll close the case. I'll be putting in a complaint and a referral.'

'Me too, the lazy bastards,' John said angrily.

'Can we prove in any way that Liam made the call?' Rachel asked.

'Unlikely. If he did have a cloned phone, there's no way we can find it now and it could have been anyone who made the call. I need to go, I'm late for a meeting with the ACC,' Emma said.

As the phone went dead it rang again, and it was Liam James. Rachel froze and showed the screen to John.

'OK, be calm,' he said.

'DCI Taylor speaking, how can I help you?' she answered as calmly as she could.

'Hello, this is Liam James,' the familiar voice said quietly. She knew for sure he was definitely the person she'd spoken to the day before on Lucy's phone.

'Yes, Mr James, what can I do for you?' Rachel voice was steady.

'I don't know what to do, with Hannah going missing. I know I was angry the other day and I'm sorry about that. I'm just so worried about her, but now my secretary, oh god, I don't know what to say…the police said she's killed herself. They haven't told us much else. It's awful, it's just so sad,' Liam finished and sighed deeply. Rachel felt the amateur dramatics in it.

'She was so sweet.' His voice cracked. 'Why would she do that? It doesn't make sense. It's just so sad,' he whimpered and tailed off. Rachel kept her calm.

'Would you like to meet up, Mr James?' Rachel knew he was playing her but two could play at that game.

'Yes, please, that would be so helpful of you, thank you. I'm at home. I went back to work too early, I thought I could manage, but this has pushed me over the edge.'

Rachel could feel her anger bubbling under the surface, and she used all her will to keep herself calm. 'I can come over now, Mr James, if that helps?' she suggested.

John looked at her intently; he could only hear half the conversation, and he waited quietly for Rachel to finish the call.

'Yes, thank you, I think that would help, thank you so much, I really appreciate your support.'

Rachel started to understand him more now; he wanted to control her, for her to march to the beat of his drum, to react when he clicked his fingers. He was enjoying this. What had started as him trying to hide his crime, was something he now wanted to show off about.

'OK, I'll be about fifteen or twenty minutes. Just sit tight, Mr James, we can talk it through when I'm there.'

204

Chapter 57

Before she got out the car, John gave her a pep talk. 'Now, remember, you're trying to get evidence, anything that gives us a clue. You need to keep calm, stay alert. He may try to push your buttons – don't react. If it was him who called you...'

'He did, it was him,' Rachel interrupted.

'If he called you,' John took back control of the conversation, 'he was doing it to taunt you. Why is that? What does he get from it? So, you need to be vigilant and don't read into things that aren't there, it's easily done when you have a strong suspicion.'

'I know, boss, I'm ready,' Rachel said confidently.

'Remember, I'm just round the corner – leave your phone on and I'll hear everything. I'll be recording it too. If you need me, I'm there. Remember the call for support?'

'Do you have a dog?' Rachel answered.

'Yes, if you say it, I'll be there,' he reassured her.

Without time to set up a wire properly Rachel and John needed to improvise, and this was the best option. Rachel arrived and she could feel Liam watching her through the lounge window. She took a deep breath. *Stay calm, don't let him get in your head.*

Liam welcomed her into the house. 'Thank you so much for coming, I didn't know who else to ring. I'm not sure if you'll be able to find out anything,' Liam rambled as she entered, his eyes red. Rachel was now used to seeing Liam like this. *Crocodile tears.*

'I'm so sorry, I'm forgetting myself, cup of tea, coffee?' he asked.

'No, I'm fine thank you, honestly.' She forced a smile. 'You sounded very distraught on the phone, Mr James,' she continued. 'Do you want to talk it through?'

'Yes please, that would be helpful,' he answered and led her into the lounge. 'Please, take a seat.' He indicated to the sofa.

They both sat. He perched on a brown leather armchair and leant forward, his elbows on his thighs, wiping the tears from his eyes with both hands.

Rachel's phone was on in her top pocket so John could hear.

'I think all this is too much. I don't know if you'll be able to find anything out, what's happened to Lucy, I mean.' He put his hand to his mouth and shook his head slowly, and more tears followed.

Rachel used every ounce of her very being to stay calm and professional. She wanted to tell him she knew he'd done it. She wanted to tell him she knew it was him taunting her the day before. She imagined herself getting up, walking over, and punching him repeatedly. Releasing all her anger, for Hannah, for Lucy but mostly for Judith. For the kind, pioneering woman who had done nothing but help others.

'I'm not sure what you're asking me, Mr James,' she said.

'I think there's a link to Hannah, someone's out to get me, I know it,' he blurted and stared at her intently.

'Why do you believe that?' she said calmly.

'Because it's all too, too. Oh, I don't know, it's too coincidental. Why would Lucy kill herself? I don't believe it. There's absolutely no reason. She was happy at work and probably one of my best members of staff, nothing was too much trouble, she was content, I know she was, I refuse to believe she killed herself.' His voice was pleading. 'And it's so close to Hannah going missing. There has to be a link, there must be, someone's trying to get me, I'm sure of it. I'm scared,' he added, staring at her intently, with arrogant confidence.

He was taunting her, and she knew it, but did he know she knew it? Did he know she thought he was involved with all of them, Hannah, Judith, and Lucy? Rachel tried to clear her mind to gather her thoughts – she needed to remain focused.

'Mr James,' she paused, 'Liam,' she said softening her voice, 'I know this is a very difficult time but there's nothing to suggest a link. Birmingham City Police are investigating Lucy's death and it is highly likely that they will rule it suicide. There's no evidence to suggest otherwise.'

She knew there was evidence but the idiots in her neighbouring force were too busy to even look. 'Is there anything you can think of that would suggest otherwise,' Rachel asked, knowing he was playing a game. He wanted her to tell him about the pen and the call and the letter, but she wasn't falling for it. She was going to draw it out of him;

she felt he wouldn't be able to resist. That was his game now, *her* – he wanted to control her like a puppet.

'You mentioned someone was out to get you,' she paused, 'why do you think that?'

'There's no specific reason, I just know they're linked.' He stared directly at her, into her eyes, into her soul as though he was trying to see her thoughts, to see if she knew it was him.

'And is there anyone you can think of who may bear a grudge?' She knew there was probably a long list which included her.

'No, no one, I always get on with everyone. My colleagues and friends say I'm very amiable,' he said and smiled as though he imagined a halo hovering over his head.

'I'm sorry, but without any evidence, there's nothing to go on,' Rachel explained.

'What about the pen and the call, surely that's enough evidence,' he blurted out.

'Er, what do you mean?' she asked.

Liam couldn't help it, and she had him, knowing about evidence she hadn't told him about.

'An officer said there was something suspicious about a pen and a phone call,' he said, clearly trying to taunt her; she didn't rise to it, she didn't even flinch.

'I don't know about that, Mr James, I'll have a look into it,' she said as calmly as she could. She thought she had him, but he was clever. She couldn't prove that City hadn't told him, and he couldn't prove they had – catch twenty-two. Rachel was positive City wouldn't have shared that information, but who knows; they were incompetent and may very well have leaked confidential case information.

'I'm sorry to have wasted your time,' Liam said, standing, 'thank you for coming round.' He opened the lounge door.

Rachel stood, surprised. Was that it? He just wanted to waste her time and let her know he knew more than he should?

'OK, if there's anything else, you have my number,' she answered as she left the house.

She walked round the corner to where John was waiting in his car and shook her head as she approached. She got in.

'No idea what that was about,' she said to John.

'He's showing off, but I'm more than sure now, it's him,' he answered. 'We need evidence.'

I don't want to die

I just want it to stop hurting so much

Chapter 58

Hannah woke and the familiarity of the coldness and smells of the cellar engulfed her. She came round, disorientated and still hungry, having not touched the food upstairs. The realisation hit her that Liam's anger was no longer just about her. He had killed twice that she knew of, and he'd said, 'Who's next?'

She couldn't just give up and wait to die. Was Liam now going after her family, her parents? She didn't know who he meant, but she couldn't just sit there feeling sorry for herself and do nothing. She needed to get out, she needed her strength, she needed to do something positive.

She looked in the fridge and could see it was now restocked; Liam wanted her to eat so he could prolong her agony as he tortured and tormented her. She needed to eat to get her strength back to escape, to end this. She opened a pack of cooked chicken breast and ate it, struggling to swallow it, so washed it down with some water. It made her gag as her stomach reluctantly accepted the unfamiliar presence of food. She ate some tomatoes, ham and cheese. She decided to eat as much as she could rather than ration it; if he wanted her alive, he'd restock the fridge, surely. She ate with the fridge door open, allowing the dim light to trickle into the blackness of the cellar. Hannah sat thinking; she had to escape.

She understood now that the water she could hear was the well, just a few feet away, through the wall; could she dig through to that? What with, though? Her hands? And would she then drown if the water came in? It was a stupid and impossible idea. The only way out was through the door, which meant either getting it open when he wasn't there or getting past him when he was; the options were dismal.

Hannah left the fridge open to light the room, but it wasn't much use. She walked to the steps, with her left hand in front of her to feel her way in the half-light, her right arm protectively held against her body; her eyes started to adjust. The stone steps were smooth and worn in places from years of use. This had probably been a well-used room when the house was built, full of cheese and no doubt other food; the perfect larder. She wondered if the house had servants years before.

She thought about previous owners and what had gone on in this place, nothing like she'd endured she thought – she hoped.

She reached the top of the steps and ran her left hand over the door as she had done previously. She'd decided before it was impossible to get through, but maybe that was because she'd already accepted her fate; her will extinguished. With her renewed ambition to escape she touched every part of the door, scraping, pulling, and trying to twist the bolts and find weaknesses in the wood.

I can do this.

She kicked it with the bottom of her bare foot which pushed her backward as she stumbled down a couple of steps. She grabbed the banister to stop her tumbling to the bottom, mistakenly with both hands, and a searing pain shot through her broken wrist. She let go and slipped two more steps, twisting and landing on her backside as it sharply hit the step and the side of her head bumped the wall. She got up and went back to the door; it wouldn't defeat her, her mind was clear. Her determination to stop Liam's killing spree would get her out that room.

I can do this.

Chapter 59

It was just after 2am, dark and a bit damp from the day's heavy downpour when the weather finally broke. Rachel stood at the back door of Liam's Lichfield office; her black hoody covered her face, and her tied-back hair was also covered under a plastic forensic hat, beneath a woolly black hat. She'd only worn clothes that couldn't be recognised, no distinguishable marks, all black, gloved hands, black plimsolls, and a black face mask; everything she could throw away, only her eyes were visible. She knew her stuff catching criminals, so she knew how not to get caught herself. She just wanted to look round; she was sure Hannah wouldn't be there as there only seemed to be one room for Liam's first floor office with a window facing the pedestrian area below.

Earlier that day she'd discussed with John getting a warrant but there were no grounds. John knew what she was doing; he was putting his whole career on the line, they both were, but they were out of options and they'd agreed they had no choice. If they could find something to give a lead elsewhere, even though the search of the office would be inadmissible and as John said, 'downright illegal' they would at least have some direction of what to do next.

The back door was old and wooden and easy to get into as she quietly slid inside. There was no alarm; she'd been able to check with the agent pretending to be interested in one of their other properties in the block. They only gave the basics, but there was nothing to suggest an alarm. She also guessed Liam didn't want anyone else alerted in the event of a break in; especially the police.

The back door led directly into a small hallway the length and width only of the stairs ahead of her and the door to the right for the estate agent's office below Liam's. She walked up the stairs quickly with her torch lighting the way and she entered the room, again quickly opening the locked door; it had an old lock not designed to keep anyone out. There was a single chair at a cheap desk at right angles to the wall under the window facing the cafe. The slatted blinds were angled so Liam could see out, but it would have been harder for someone to see in. There was nothing on the desk other than a docking station for a laptop, but no laptop. A small printer sat in the corner on top of a metal filing cabinet. Against the back wall were three kitchen cabinets and three base cabinets with a basin, kettle and microwave, and a door to the right to a single toilet; the office was stark and grotty. Rachel opened the filing cabinet; empty, as though it had never been used. The kitchen cabinets had a bottle of washing up liquid, a couple of mugs, coffee and tea. There was a space for a fridge, but there wasn't one. The base cabinets were empty except for a pile of clean tea towels.

Rachel was disappointed; she expected to find something, but there was nothing. She left as quickly as she arrived and was in and out in less than five minutes.

Chapter 60

Liam was intrigued as he watched Rachel on his phone; the tiny camera in the light fitting had activated when she entered the room and streamed straight to his phone, alerting him of the intruder. He watched her hurry round the room, opening drawers and leaving quickly. He wouldn't report it straight away; he needed to remove the cameras facing the cafe first, that would be a job for the next morning.

He waited until 8:30am the next day to report the break-in; the camera facing the cafe had been removed and he left the ceiling one in place. He needed to leave it there otherwise it would look suspicious as he had the footage and intended to use it. The call-taker at the police station listened with sympathy as he explained about the break-in, his wife being missing, his secretary. *Just one more piece of bad luck,* he said and, *why is this happening to me?* They gave him an incident number for the break-in and said they'd inform the officer in charge of his wife's disappearance as he'd suggested.

Liam smiled as he put the phone down; he couldn't wait to see the bitch squirming when he showed her the footage of her breaking in. He knew it was her, who else could it have been?

Fifteen minutes passed and his phone rang – it was Rachel. Liam smiled to himself.

'Thank god you rang, someone broke into my office. It's all connected, it has to be,' he pleaded with her, 'it's all connected, can't you see?'

'Yes, Mr James, it does seem very suspicious. Are you at home today?' Rachel asked.

Liam imagined her having to control herself and feign ignorance, and he loved this new game; he had her where he wanted her.

'No, I'm at my office in Lichfield.' He grinned as he said it.

'OK, I'll bring a scene of crime officer with me. Can I have the address, please?' she asked. She already knew where it was; he smiled as he gave her the details.

Thirty minutes later Rachel was standing in the office Liam knew she'd broken into the evening before.

'Was there anything taken, Mr James?' she asked.

'No, no, nothing, it was really strange. I got an alert on my phone, but I was asleep and only noticed it this morning and came straight over. Here, have a look.' He pushed the phone under her nose.

He watched Rachel watching herself moving round the office, without showing any emotion; Liam intently staring at her as she watched, waiting for any flicker of reaction. He wanted her to suffer. As she watched, Liam walked behind her and looked at the phone over her shoulder. He leant in to watch with her and he smelt her hair; newly washed, fresh shampoo smell, apples maybe, he inhaled, breathing her in. He looked back to the phone.

'Look at him, who the fuck does he think he is, just walking around like that? Sorry, I didn't mean to swear, I'm just so angry. I've had enough,' he said, smirking behind her back.

Rachel turned to him. 'It's OK, Mr James, it's understandable and you don't need to apologise.'

Liam could see Rachel acting and talking to him as though he was a victim whose feelings she cared about, but behind her words he knew she was pretending. He loved having the upper hand. She reminded him again of his sister, always easy to manipulate, usually getting her own way; but not today.

'Do you have any idea who it could be?' she asked, and he wanted to say, *Yes, it was you, you stupid bitch.*

'No idea, he looks quite short and a bit fat if you ask me,' he said, peering at the phone again, hoping to get a rise out of her, but she didn't react.

'This is Paul from our forensics team, he's going to have a look round and see if he can find anything of note,' Rachel said authoritatively.

'OK, knock yourself out,' Liam nodded and indicated to the room. He watched Paul checking different places, the doors, windows, the desk, dusting for prints and picking up fibres. He watched Rachel touching places herself, no doubt to make sure any fingerprints of hers were discounted; *clever.*

As she did, she turned to him. 'Mr James, obviously for purposes of elimination can we get your fingerprints please?'

Fuck. He hadn't thought this through. *You idiot,* he chided himself at his overconfidence, his complacency. He didn't want them to take his prints just in case; they had no reason to. 'Why? This is my office, it's going to have my prints in.'

'Yes, we know, that's what I mean. We need them for elimination purposes,' Rachel repeated.

Liam wasn't sure what to do; it would only be an issue if they found evidence on Judith which he was sure there wouldn't be, or in Lucy's flat, and they'd closed that case already. What if they hadn't? What if this was a trick? 'I'm not sure I'm happy with that,' he said.

'It's purely routine,' Rachel started.

'No, no, I'm not happy. I want you to leave,' he demanded, 'I want you to go now.'

Liam was fuming as he watched Rachel and Paul leave.

'I'll get you, you fucking bitch,' Liam said to himself once she was out of earshot. 'You'll get what's coming to you.'

Chapter 61

When Rachel got the call about Liam's office she told John.

'OK, you know there's no evidence of you being there and if you go there now, anything they do pick up, hairs, fingerprints etc, will mean nothing cos you're in there investigating. He's doing this just to mess with you, you know he is.'

'I know, I just feel stupid,' Rachel answered.

'Don't be, and under no circumstance is anyone to be on their own with him, OK?' John ordered.

'Yes, boss.' Rachel left the room and headed down to Forensics to get someone from SOCO to go with her. She avoided Emma; she didn't want her to get suspicious that she'd done something she shouldn't, she'd already had her wrists slapped by her.

She found Paul Chadwell, Chad, hidden away in the back office and he agreed to go down with her. They drove down together in a SOCO van and Rachel told him to be vigilant with Liam; that he was a person of interest, but they had nothing on him. When they arrived, Liam was up to his usual games; she felt him breathing down her neck as she watched the footage of her moving round his office, and his breath stank of bitter coffee. She knew he knew it was her and his smarmy comments were there to try and get her to react; she remembered John's words and remained professional. When she'd asked for his prints his reaction was priceless. She and Chad had left as requested and she could see Liam's rage brewing, about to boil over; she got into the van feeling quite pleased with herself.

'Did you get any?' she asked Chad.

'Yep, loads,' he nodded and smiled, 'I dusted a few places he touched whilst we were there, so we've definitely got his prints on file now. Boom!' he added with exuberance.

Rachel laughed.

'Too much?' Chad asked.

'Just a bit.'

Chapter 62

Rachel stood outside Hannah's parents' house thinking about her approach. She needed to talk to them again with the new information she had, but she had to be careful; she wasn't sure how they would react, how they'd take the news that she thought Hannah's life was in danger.

'So, you tell us less than a week ago that she left him and was safe, but now you don't know where she is and that she may be in danger? I don't understand. Terry, what's happening?' Pat pleaded as her husband put his arm round her.

'We've been worried sick. We've called everyone we could to try and find her,' Terry added. 'Why do you think she's not safe, what's that bastard done to her? We've been ringing him all week and we've been to the house, but he's not answered, he's never in.'

Rachel was disappointed to hear that they'd tried to contact Liam. When she'd visited them before to tell them about the case being closed, she'd specifically told them, for Hannah's own safety, they should not contact him. They were parents though, and she couldn't imagine how she'd act in the same situation. She was beginning to think she should keep them in the dark, but she needed more information to try and locate Hannah; it was a risk she needed to take.

'Initially we closed the case as a missing person based on the information we received at the time. Hannah had been planning this for some time and as you know a friend of hers had come forward to tell us this.' Rachel paused and took a breath. If she told them about Judith's death that had not officially been linked to Hannah and was an open investigation, she'd be stepping way over the line. 'Due to recent events that I can't go into, we-we…' she stuttered, 'I believe that Hannah may not be safe,' she finished.

'What do you mean, you can't go into? This is our daughter.' Pat angrily shot the words at Rachel; the quiet woman she'd met before finally showing some passion and real concern for her daughter.

'This is ridiculous,' Terry added, 'bloody useless.'

They were both worried and their reaction was exactly as Rachel expected, but she needed to press on. 'I'm sorry, but if I'm being absolutely honest this is a hunch and this is my gut feeling. I'm on my own here. I'm putting my job on the line. I'm sorry, I have no evidence, but I am really worried about Hannah. I've got her best interests at heart and I need your help,' she paused, 'but I also need you to keep this from Liam James, it is in Hannah's best interests. I can't stress that enough.'

'I'll rip his head off!' Terry shouted as Pat quietly wept.

She tried to calm them down. 'I need your help. Did Hannah ever try to reach out to you or did you see any signs that things weren't right between them? I know I asked the other day, but is there anything else you can think of? Anything at all?'

Rachel stayed with them for over an hour, but it was clear they knew nothing about Hannah and Liam, and hardly saw them. They were as good as estranged from their daughter and had no part in her life; if only they'd shown the same sort of passion and concern towards Hannah, and made an effort to look out for their daughter's welfare before she disappeared, then perhaps Hannah wouldn't be in this position.

As Rachel left them, she reiterated, 'Please do not talk to Mr James about this, it's imperative for Hannah's safety.'

You're spineless.
You say it's not right.
You talked among your little groups and pitied me.
But did you do anything?
Did you make a stand and help me?

No!!

It was too much trouble.
It would take up too much of your precious time.

I saw you looking, talking, pitying me.
I didn't need that.

I needed help.

I needed action.
I needed you to do something.

Just one little thing.

It could have made all the difference.
I pity you for believing your own lies.
For not caring, for not getting involved.
I pity you for being the person you are.

And this is the result.

221

Chapter 63

It felt as though hours and hours had passed. Hannah couldn't find anything to help her get through the door. Her fingers were raw, cut and splintered with rust and wood. At the top of the steps, she'd knocked along the wall all over and the underside of the floor above; the other side being the hallway. *Tap tap tap* to see if there were any weaknesses. In a newer house it would have likely been cheap materials and a hope of getting through them and out into freedom, but this house was old, and each tap returned the same dullness and solidness of an aged building. It would take days to get through even with the right tools; Hannah had one useful hand and nothing else.

She'd stood lower on the steps reaching up to the underside of the wooden floorboards, pushing along the edge to find any looseness, any weakness, any opportunity. She tried to remember what was above her – furniture, or rugs? Was it the solidity of the floorboards she was pushing against or was there a mass above them as well, pushing down? Either way her efforts were futile; nothing moved, not even a creak to indicate weakness in her prison walls.

Hannah started to fall inside herself.

I can't do this.

She was angry that she was here, angry that people were being killed because of her, would be killed; she was useless, Liam was right, she was useless, a useless piece of shit, stupid and ugly.

Stop this, she thought to herself. She could feel herself getting pulled into the familiar insular comfort of depression where she only thought of herself, her situation; a place where she didn't need ambition, so it didn't matter if she failed, it was only herself she was letting down. Now was different though – other people needed her, they didn't know it, but it was down to Hannah to save them; she didn't know who they were, but it was up to her.

If only someone had fought for me, she thought; her family, her friends, they'd all abandoned her, left her with him and no one helped. No one was interested in her plight, no one cared, she wasn't important to anyone. The darkness pulled her further into a place where she didn't need to try, where she was used to hiding, where a complacency of 'this is my life' was acceptable and her identity could melt away; unmissable.

'Stop this,' she said again, out loud this time. She'd built the wall that hid her life, she'd protected Liam's real identity, she'd lied to stop people seeing what was really there. If they had seen, why would they help though? No one wanted her, cared for her, missed her. Why hadn't she been found, had she been forgotten already?

'Stop this,' she said louder. Judith cared and she was dead, she'd fought for her, she'd inspired her, she had shown understanding and compassion that Hannah had not felt for a long time.

Why was Lucy dead? Had she seen something? Maybe she'd recognised Hannah's plight and stood up and said something. Maybe now that Hannah was missing, people were coming forward and saying what they'd seen, and that's why people were dying. Hannah was exhausted and her exhaustion was fuelling her spiralling fall into the dark. She needed to look after herself, she needed her strength to get out, she needed to sleep to beat her own demons if she were to beat Liam.

Think of something positive, she thought to herself; she'd heard about research into people who were in hopeless situations such as the horrific and tragic stories she'd read about Auschwitz. She'd heard that people in that same situation who focused on getting out, imagining their life afterwards, when they would be free, coped better than those who thought about the hopelessness and tragedy of their situation. *Focus on something positive*, she thought again. As she did, her garden came to mind, her lily opening and flowering. She imagined the bees, butterflies and birds filling her garden, enjoying the flowers as much as she did. For them it was survival, for her, back then, it was for pleasure – but now it was for her survival, too. *Think happy thoughts*. She focused on the sounds, the bird song and buzz of the bees, filling the air above her as they flew from blossom to blossom on the cherry tree; the sounds of the pond bubbling and splashing. She imagined the aromas of the flowers - lavender, honeysuckle and jasmine. The smell of fresh, newly-cut grass and the earthiness of the soil as she planted up new bulbs and seedlings.

She was a seedling, trying to break through the earth to find new life. To open up and welcome the sun, and the rain splashing her to help her grow, to survive. A calmness enveloped her as she allowed herself to imagine the pleasure of being free; she lay on the floor, and let herself sleep.

Chapter 64

'What have you done with her?' Terry shouted through the lounge window. Liam had been woken by him bashing the front door and ringing the bell over and over. As he descended the stairs, he realised it was Terry and looked at him through the front bay window. Terry saw him and scrambled through the bushes shouting through the window, 'Where is she, you wanker, what have you done with her?'

Liam stood and watched him and picked up his phone; he'd managed to avoid them all week. He couldn't deal with their petty lives and stupid, inane existence.

'Terry, please stop, you're making it worse, please,' Pat pleaded with her husband.

He bashed the window with his hand again.

'Terry, please, she said not to do this.' Pat was in the bushes trying to pull her husband back.

'The police are onto you, you fucking wanker, where is she?' he said with his face against the window.

Liam showed him the phone and with a small smile he gestured to the CCTV camera pointing at Terry.

'Emergency, what service do you require?'

'Police, someone is trying to get into my house. I'm being attacked.'

Chapter 65

'I want to make a complaint. Your officer has a clear vendetta against me, she's turned Hannah's parents against me at a time I need them most. She's harassing me, she's unprofessional and she's making unfounded claims against me. My wife's case has been closed and I'm beside myself with worry and your officer's behaviour is a disgrace.' Liam sat with his arms crossed opposite John Weaver.

'Mr James, obviously we take complaints very seriously, and we will of course investigate your allegations. Is there anything we can do now, today, that would help?' John asked. It was the first time he'd met Liam James face-to-face, and he needed to put the knowledge he had out of his head and make his own judgement of the man before him. He knew Rachel had concerns about Hannah's father in particular having it out with Liam but he didn't expect to be sitting opposite him having to listen to his diatribe against Rachel.

He's got brass balls, that's for sure, he thought to himself. There was no evidence to suggest Liam was guilty of anything other than being an arrogant cocky bastard, but seeing him eye to eye he realised that Rachel's gut feeling was well-founded; this bloke gave even John the creeps and he feared he really had had a hand in Judith's death.

'Firstly, I want an apology, and secondly I want that woman nowhere near me. I want someone else on my wife's case,' Liam demanded.

'Yes, Mr James, I agree an apology is in order.' John skirted round reallocation of the case. In reality it was closed as a missing person case and was now reopened under the radar, without Mr James's knowledge. 'If you can give me a moment I'll be right back,' John said as he stood and left the room.

'Rachel, he wants an apology,' John said, back in his office where he'd told Rachel to wait.

Rachel nodded slowly rolling her eyes; they'd already been through the scenarios once Liam had called 999. Terry was nearly cautioned but Liam had said he would drop the allegations and instead wanted to lodge a complaint against DCI Rachel Taylor for her 'reckless and inept investigation' John and Rachel both knew it was part of his game; that he wanted to humiliate her.

Rachel took a deep breath and exhaled slowly. 'Let's do this and get it out the way,' she said. John nodded and they both walked back to the room where Liam had been left.

John and Rachel sat, Liam's gaze fixed on Rachel, his arms firmly crossed.

'Mr James, I want to apologise for any distress caused at what I know is a difficult time for you, and I apologise if talking to Mr and Mrs Chattaway created this situation through a misunderstanding. As you know, the missing person case has been closed as we had, have,' she corrected herself, 'reason to believe Hannah is safe, and I was trying to establish where she may be, for my own satisfaction.'

'So you're still trying to find her, that's good,' Liam said brightly. John noticed how quickly Liam switched his mood, it made him uneasy.

'We are, Mr James, but as you know we have been advised that Hannah does not want to divulge her location and I'm afraid I've been unable to find her.' Rachel played along with the game.

'Well,' Liam exclaimed, 'I accept your apology and I am grateful to you for thinking of my wife's welfare.' Liam stood and put his hand out to John. 'And thank you for listening and arranging this to clear up the confusion. It has restored my faith a little.'

John shook Liam's hand firmly. Liam turned to Rachel and extended his hand, she took it and Liam put his other hand on top of hers. 'Thank you, Rachel, thank you,' he said gently and winked at her.

'I'll take you out, Mr James. DCI Taylor, please wait here,' John said sternly as he directed Liam out of the room through to the exit.

When he returned, Rachel was sitting, her hands clasped in front of her on the table. 'He winked at me when he shook my hand, when you couldn't see,' she said calmly. 'What do you think?'

'Guilty as hell, the arrogant cock.'

Rachel nodded.

I don't know how I ever loved you.
Why I ever loved you.

How I didn't see your demons.

You let them out to ravage me,
To strip me of who I once was.

I can't remember who that was.
It was a different lifetime.
But I know I want her back.

She deserves more.

I deserve more.

Chapter 66

Hannah had completely lost any association with day and night, or how long she'd been there, but it had been at least a week since she'd been allowed out of the cellar and upstairs. Liam had been twice since the day he'd told her he'd killed Lucy; he brought food both times, in silence as he did before. It was a relief. He'd been more erratic than he'd ever been in their marriage, his violence was worse, and his silence was deafening; she didn't know what would happen each time he opened the cellar door.

Hannah had started to notice when the traffic sound was heavier and associated that with day and when it was quieter with night, but it made no difference to her day to day. She was eating better and regularly, and was starting to gain her strength back. She'd also made a makeshift splint for her wrist out of plastic bags wrapped tightly round and tied with her good hand and teeth.

She spent her time still trying to work out how to get out and was now planning a way to get past Liam; she hoped he would take her upstairs again, and if he did, she'd go with the right head on her shoulders and take note of what was around her.

A car rolled onto the gravel, and she heard the door shut, footsteps above her, the cellar door opened, and Liam entered the room. He didn't have any shopping bags with him, and Hannah braced herself. If he wasn't there to bring food, what was he there to do?

'Come up,' he said, as though they were in their old life and things were normal; well, as normal as could be.

Hannah complied and slowly walked up the steps and into the brightly lit hallway which hurt her eyes once more. She followed Liam into the kitchen and sat as instructed at the kitchen table; Liam stayed standing. There was no food or drink, and she didn't know why she was there. She took in as much as she could, purposely walking slowly, looking for potential ways out but now sat with her head down, not daring to look at Liam.

'Look at me,' he said quietly, and she complied, slowly lifting her head. 'We will be going on a little trip soon, once you look respectable.' He looked her up and down. She was still wearing the clothes she'd attempted to escape in and, although originally naked in the cellar, Liam had let her keep them on after he'd allowed her to shower. She'd only showered once in the weeks she been there, her clothes stank, her hair was matted and greasy. Her bruises and cuts were healing apart from the fingers on her good hand which were red raw, and her broken wrist was bent and misshapen, wrapped in its makeshift plastic bandage.

'Let me see.' Liam indicated to her wrist, and she pulled it closer to her. He pulled up a chair next to her and put his hand out. Hannah, terrified of what was to come, started to cry as she offered her broken wrist supported by her other hand. Liam gently laid her right hand in his lap and turned to her left hand to examine the cuts and splinters. 'You need to stop trying to get out, it's impossible. I watch you every day.' He tapped his shirt breast pocket with his phone in it. Hannah looked with sadness into his eyes, and she felt like the pathetic useless idiot he said she was.

Liam unwrapped the plastic bag around Hannah's wrist. As it loosened, Hannah yelped as the pain was released. Her wrist was various shades of purple and blue through to green and pale yellow; it was healing, but it wasn't set right. Liam looked closer to examine it, then he offered it back to her and Hannah cradled it on her chest. Liam stood and she flinched, waiting for him to hit her, but he left the room briefly, returning with an unopened wrist support normally used for sport.

'It will have to do for now,' he said matter-of-factly. He gently put it on Hannah's wrist as though the monster inside him was locked away, and the loving Liam Hannah knew when she'd first met him was back.

'You need to shower, so we'll wrap it in cling film and there's clean clothes on the bed for you too.' Liam stood and Hannah knew she was to follow. 'Don't bother trying anything, I can see you everywhere in this house,' he said as he pulled out his phone. Hannah didn't know if he was telling the truth – it wasn't his house – but she wasn't taking any chances. She was too weak and vulnerable, and he did say they were going somewhere soon; maybe that would offer a way out and an opportunity to escape.

She followed him to the en suite again, a clean towel awaited, and various clothes were laid on the bed for more than a few days. She showered and this time enjoyed it, relishing the hot water as it soothed and warmed her broken body. She closed her eyes as she lathered herself, washing away the pain, the grit from her grazes, the dirt and smell of the cellar that seemed to have seeped deep into her pores. The luxurious Molton Brown shower gel felt silky smooth on her skin. She breathed in the aroma; sandalwood. It reminded her of a spa; somewhere safe. She'd just washed the last of the soap off her as Liam stuck his head through the door with a remote. Within a second the shower stopped abruptly, and Hannah stood naked, vulnerable once more. Liam helped her dress in silence, putting on soft tracksuit bottoms, a t-shirt, hoody, clean underwear, and socks; she'd never felt so happy to wear them. Her feet were sore, chapped and blistered but they felt warm as the socks cocooned them. She couldn't brush and dry her hair with her broken wrist, so Liam tried to brush it for her, but it pulled on the matted strands. So, she took the brush and gently brushed it herself whilst Liam blew it with the hairdryer. Then he helped her walk down the stairs as though he cared about her, and was helping her recuperate; a loving husband, there for his wife. Her trainers were also at the bottom of the stairs and she felt relief that at least she'd be warmer, and more protected in clean clothes and trainers. He took her back into the kitchen to where she'd sat an hour before.

Liam sat opposite her. 'We will be leaving in a few days for our new life together and you will do as you are told. And just so we're clear, no one is coming for you, the only stupid bitch looking for you has been told to stop and she won't be bothering us anymore; she won't be able to,' he smiled. 'You need to start showing me some respect. I am your husband.' Liam stared at her.

Hannah assumed they had to leave because Liam's boss would be back soon, but she didn't know where they'd go. They couldn't stay in Lichfield or anywhere nearby; she realised that Liam planned to pick up as he'd left off but in a new place. She was his wife, she'd do as she was told but she expected she wouldn't be allowed out anywhere except with him. The boundaries had changed. Liam had gotten away with murder and all he had to do was set up home somewhere else, and she would be the loyal dutiful wife once more.

She looked at him and nodded, but thinking to herself that he was deranged. *How could he think things would be the same?*

'Now let's get some food,' Liam said as though it was a normal day, and he was planning a nice night in with a takeaway.

Chapter 67

The next day was Rachel's day off. Emma had texted her first thing.

Right madam, I promise I'll try and get to Hannah's laptop today so you have a proper day off, no work and make sure you eat properly !! xx

She'd texted her back.

yes mom!

Rachel decided to take the rare opportunity to go shopping to get some fresh veg, pasta, chicken and chorizo to make her favourite meal, but mostly to stock up on wine. She knew she'd been erratic of late and she needed to take more care of herself, but her wine was one thing she wasn't giving up – it kept her sane.

In the grocers she picked up a red pepper, checked it for marks and was suddenly aware of someone pushing past her and reaching for a pepper. Rude, she thought. She moved to the side and as she turned, she stood back, upright, and stunned.

'I think Hannah always shopped here,' Liam said, his face blank and stern, still looking straight ahead. 'I wonder where she's shopping now?' He put the pepper back and moved along to the broccoli. Rachel stepped back out of his way.

'Mr James...' she started to say.

'Oh, you don't know where she is do you, you stupid bitch? Poor PC Plod doesn't know anything.' He carried on looking forward as he picked up some broccoli and put it in his basket.

'What the—' Rachel tried to speak.

'Can't do a fucking thing, can you? Can't find her, can't ask questions, no one believes you. Fucking useless waste of space.' He turned and smiled and indicated to walk past her. To anyone else looking it would have seemed like a normal, pleasant exchange; no one else could hear what he was saying.

Rachel stood silently, not sure what to say or how to react. Her immediate thought was to press him for more information to antagonise him, but she needed to pretend he was right, that no one had her back, when, in fact, John Weaver was baying for his blood.

Liam paid for his shopping and turned to Rachel as he left. 'Lovely to see you,' he called across the shop, louder so others could hear. 'See you soon!' He waved and smiled.

Rachel watched him as he left the store. *Bastard, two could play at that game.*

Chapter 68

Rachel was used to dealing with people who threatened her, but she felt he had the upper hand and he unnerved her being in the grocer's. He'd already killed twice, she was sure of it, but he'd evaded even being questioned let alone arrested and charged. There was no proof and the evidence she needed was locked behind bureaucratic red tape.

She'd called Emma as soon as she left the grocers and told her briefly over the phone. Emma had then eaten with her and stopped over that night, she felt safer with her there, and they discussed it in detail. The next day she sat in John's office, relaying the conversation with Liam.

'Cheeky bastard,' John said, shaking his head. 'He's got some fucking nerve, that's for sure.'

Rachel nodded.

'I mean, what does he think he's playing at? I don't get it, is he really that stupid?' he added.

'Honestly, I don't think he can help himself,' Rachel answered. 'He's a player, we know that from Lucy.'

'Well, the good news is, it means he will likely trip himself up if he's that cocky.'

Rachel nodded again, waiting for John's words of advice. She didn't want to show it, but Liam had really rattled her.

'OK, this is what we're going to do, firstly, everything by the book from now on, the office search backfired, and Owens would have me hung up by my short and curlies if he ever found out.'

Rachel nodded, 'Sorry, boss.'

'I don't want him getting off on some stupid technicality, having some flash solicitor playing the system.'

He reached for his phone and dialled, 'We're talking Liam James.'

Rachel could only hear half the conversation.

'...are you free ?'

'Yep, my office...sure, not a problem...as soon as you can.'

'Emma's on her way,' John relayed to Rachel. 'Cup of tea?' he asked.

'Good idea,' Rachel replied, knowing it meant she was making it. She went to the kitchen and made three teas and thought about options for Liam. She swore to herself when, once again, she couldn't find a teaspoon, they were like gold dust in this building. She carried the drinks precariously spilling some as she navigated her way back to John's office. Emma was there as she walked in.

'What about tailing him?' Rachel asked as she put the cups down, spilling a bit more. 'Sorry,' she said as she mopped it with the side of her hand.

'We could but, we just haven't got enough bodies, they're all on Judith's case and we all know that Knobby's driving blind on that.' John answered.

It was the first time Rachel had heard John call him Knobby, she looked at Emma with a small smile, Emma winked at her, smiling too.

'What about this tracking thing?' John asked.

'Still need a warrant,' Emma stated, 'I think old fashioned tailing is the only thing you can do at the moment and I'm still trying to get to the laptop, but yesterday, well, that was a wipe out.' She shook her head.

'I'm OK to do it, I can watch him,' Rachel said.

'Nope, we need more bodies, it's too risky on you own,' John answered.

'Even if I just do a bit, from a distance, we might just get a lead,' Rachel tried to change John's mind.

Her and Emma waited as John thought.

'OK, you carry on looking at anything to connect the three cases forensically when you're not looking at Bob's other stuff' he said to Emma rolling his eyes, frustrated at Bob's direction of travel in his investigation of Judith's murder. 'And you watch, but from a distance for now.' He nodded towards Rachel. 'Set up surveillance at his house and see if we can get any leads of where he goes. I'm sorry it's only you for now, but I'll try and get some more resource on this. Until we've got something more solid the boss won't support us.' DCS Owen, was well known for the 'by the book and nothing but the book approach' but was also influenced by the findings in Bob Moore's inept investigation which was now following the lead of a different prime suspect, who Bob was convinced was their man. He'd been lording it up the previous day about his 'breakthrough' and had pulled his suspect in for questioning, even though Emma had pointed out there were no forensics, and a stronger lead was emerging with Liam James. Bob had dismissed Emma's and Rachel's protests and arrested the other suspect on even weaker evidence.

Rachel and Emma left the room.

'Be careful,' Emma said, 'I don't like where this is going. The last thing I want is you losing your job over this. We need to do this by the book, or he'll walk.'

Rachel nodded to her friend and took off towards the car park.

She booked out a different pool car to her usual just in case Liam had clocked it on previous visits to his house. She drove to the park opposite his house, picking up some food and drink on her way there; she didn't know how long she'd be watching, and experience told her to always stock up. Although Liam had a good viewpoint of the park from his house, Rachel had spotted plenty of places where she could watch from a distance, long enough away so that Liam wouldn't notice or recognise her. She parked in a car park off the same main road that Liam's estate was on; if he drove away, she could quickly follow.

Rachel walked slowly around the park keeping an eye on Liam's house, but his car wasn't on the drive; she assumed he wasn't in but couldn't be sure. She moved further into the park away from his house, maintaining a good view and sat under a tree for shade from the afternoon sun, blending in with other park users. She knew Liam wouldn't recognise her that far away, but she had clear sight of his house.

An hour passed and Liam arrived home, driving slowly onto his driveway. Rachel watched him get out. He had a laptop bag on his shoulder, some files under his arm, and he went into his house. She watched and waited for another four hours. She'd finished her water and eaten her sandwich, but the sun was blazing on the hottest day of the year so far. She was desperate for another drink, desperate to solve this case and be somewhere else; today would be a perfect day to sit in a pub garden drinking pink gin, if only. She was parched, her throat was dry, her lips tacky, thinking of pubs gardens wasn't helping. She had another bottle of water in the car; it would probably be hot having cooked in the sun all day, but she needed to drink something. Could she get there without losing sight of the house? She walked over towards it, still with Liam's house in her eye line. She was a few feet away from the car – bugger, she thought. She should have parked it in the first space near the park entrance. Instead, she was four spaces in and too far from the edge of the grass to see the house. She quickly ran over to the car, losing sight of the house. She pulled open the car door and was hit in the face by the heat as it vented. She leant over the passenger seat to the water in the centre of the car, grabbed it, got out, shut the door, and ran back to the edge of the park, all done within thirty seconds; Liam's car was still on the driveway. She watched from the edge of the park for a couple of minutes then walked back to her spot under the tree to continue her surveillance.

She texted Emma.

Any progress?

Ten minutes later and Emma responded.

Nothing yet, you?

Rachel texted her back.

Nope, been watching ages. If you fancy dropping off a frappe latte I wouldn't say no ;)

Emma responded

Sure, I'll pop out at 5, will ring you when I'm there xx

Rachel looked at her watch – not long. She looked at Liam's house. Still no movement.

Chapter 69

Liam stood behind Rachel's car watching her in the park; he'd been watching her for days.

He'd followed her home the day he complained about her, watched her squirm in front of her boss; *stupid bitch*, he'd thought. Whilst he was sitting opposite her at the station giving her half-assed apology, he imagined himself fucking her and making her realise what it was like to have a real man; she was probably a lezza by the looks of the woman who'd stopped over the night before. She didn't know what it was like to have a real bloke – he'd show her.

He'd followed her to the grocers and enjoyed their little exchange; she was fit and attractive with her long brown hair and brown eyes, but she needed to dress like a woman. All the female officers look like dykes, he thought, and she needed putting in her place; he could make her a real woman.

He'd watch her get into a car at the station earlier that day, not her usual car, he thought, and he'd followed her as she pulled into the car park near his house. He carried on past the entrance and continued round the other side of the park to watch her for a bit before he went home. As soon as he got into his house, he'd found a couple of timers for his lights and set them at different times for later that evening. From his study he watched his CCTV and could almost see her sitting in the park, zooming in and magnifying the area, examining her, but she was just a blur. He thought it comical that he was watching her, watching him. *Stupid bitch.*

He watched her from his study, angling the shutters slightly so he could see out, but no one would see in. He'd seen her walk over to her car and as soon as she was out of sight, he'd quickly left the house, and crossed the road into an alley way that ran alongside the park; it wasn't used much and was overgrown in places giving Liam plenty of spaces to hide as he snuck along it. From a distance he could see her appear from inside the car with a bottle of water then ran out of his view. He moved along to the end of the alley and could see her standing at the edge of the grass. He looked to see who else was there; it was still light and there were families getting in and out of cars, children getting shouted at for running by the road.

240

Too many people. He needed to be patient this time.

He planned to drag her into the alley out of sight, show her what it was like to be a real woman and kill her, knowing his face would be the last she'd see. It was too light, and too busy, but he didn't want to lose the opportunity before she drove off.

Liam stayed out of sight and watched her go back to where she'd been sitting. An hour passed and he watched her typing into her phone and looking at her watch. Twenty minutes later a car pulled into the car park and he stepped deeper into the bushes in the alley; the same woman from the night before got out and rang someone.

'I'm here,' a pause, 'yep, I can see you,' and the woman made her way across the park to Rachel. The woman had two takeaway cups with her; she gave one to Rachel and they chatted for a few minutes.

Liam watched with curiosity. I could do both of you, he fantasised. He'd enjoy that, fuck them, and kill them; the thought of killing them was intoxicating to him. Now he'd killed he realised this is what he'd been missing all his life, the thrill of the chase and the release it gave him; it gave him purpose. He had no regret, no emotion about Judith or Lucy, just pure pleasure. He thought of his sister again, back to his childhood; now he understood.

He watched the other woman get up and walk back to the car park – he could take her now, right under the nose of that stupid copper. He stopped himself, though; he had his eye on a bigger prize.

The other woman drove off and Liam continued to watch Rachel.

Chapter 70

It was just before 9pm and the light was beginning to fade. Rachel had texted John twice earlier in the day, giving brief updates that there was no movement, whilst he was at the station trying get extra officers released from other jobs. She texted him again.

Still nothing going on here, boss, any luck with the extra support?

He answered.

Unfortunately, not, Bob's got Owen's ear on this. I'm leaving in a bit so can be over in thirty and give you a break for a few hours

She texted him back, relieved he was able to help.

Thanks, boss, that'd be brilliant

Rachel looked over to Liam's house; it was harder to see as the light faded. She saw the lights go on, one on the driveway and the other in the lounge. She couldn't see in from where she was, but at least she'd see him leave, if he did. She got up and walked closer. There were shutters on the windows so she could see some light, but the angle of the shutters meant she couldn't get a clear view inside.

As she walked past Liam's she saw John turn up and pull over at the other side of the park. He got out and she started walking towards her own car without talking to him; they didn't want it known that they knew each other.

It was now dark and as Rachel got to her car she turned back, and she could just about see John slowly walking round the park as she had just done. He'd brought his black German Shepherd, Luna, with him, a retired police dog who was old and on her last legs. Luna made it easier for John to loiter and Rachel watched him stroll towards Liam's house, Luna waddling behind him as he stopped and waited for her as they gradually made their way past.

Rachel walked to the driver's side of the car and just as she was out of John's view, she was aware of a presence. She half-turned to see Liam's fist coming towards her; she tried to duck but it was too late – he struck her on the side of her temple and she blacked out.

Chapter 71

Rachel came round face down in the gravel and dirt and she could feel a weight on her, and pain at the side of her face where Liam had hit her. The weight shifted and she was flipped onto her back. Liam was straddling her, his knees keeping her arms pinned down and his hand over her mouth. As she came round she started struggling, her eyes wide with fear as she tried to fight him off, but she couldn't shift his weight.

'Got you,' he laughed, 'you weren't expecting that were you, you stupid bitch.'

She couldn't move, his full weight was on top of her. He leant down his face right next to her ear as she struggled. 'I'll be the last thing you'll ever feel inside you,' he whispered.

Realising he was going to rape and kill her she tried to bite his hand, but it was forced down so hard, she couldn't even open her mouth. She tried to scream with every cell of her being but only inaudible muffled sounds disappeared into the night air; no one would hear her. She kicked her legs and tried to twist her body from under him, trying everything to make it difficult for him. As well as her police training, she'd also been on self-defence courses for rape and assault and knew to make it as hard for her assailant as possible, to give her more time. She wasn't going to submit; she had no choice, she had to fight. She felt him rise up, his knees still pinning her arms down as he scrambled to undo her jeans with his free hand. She struggled more, freeing her right arm, swinging it upwards, her nails scraping his neck. He kept his hand over her mouth and tried to grab her arm with his free hand as she struck out, trying to hit him. As she struggled the hand over her mouth slipped

'Joooohhhhhn!' she screamed as loudly as she could. Liam's hand came smashing down into her face, covering her mouth again.

She felt him pause.

'Fucking whore,' he said, and she saw a rock coming towards her face.

Chapter 72

John heard Rachel scream his name and he ran as fast as he could towards her car, calling her as he went. Luna was some way behind, but she leapt into action when she saw her owner run and went from a docile old lady to ready to attack.

John reached Rachel's car and he could see her lying on the floor in the alley. He looked around for her assailant, but there was no one there. He went for his radio and pressed the red button to send out an alert for emergency assistance, automatically giving his location.

He leant down to her and checked her pulse; she was alive, but in a bad way and he could see the cut above her eye, blood pouring from it.

He went back on his radio. 'Officer down, I need an ambulance now, Beacon Street car park.' He could already hear the police sirens as local response vehicles headed his way.

He looked down the alley, but it was too dark to see anything. Luna was now by his side attentively awaiting instructions.

'Stay with me, Rach, help's coming.' John looked at Rachel and to Luna. He pulled Luna over to sniff Rachel; her assailant's scent may be on her. 'Luna, go,' John commanded. Luna sniffed the floor for a moment then shot off down the alleyway.

'Stay with me, Rachel.' He checked her pulse and her breathing again. He didn't want to move her; he didn't know how bad her injuries were and the paramedics were already on their way.

He could hear the sirens getting louder, and the first police car arrived. John instructed them, pointing across the park to Liam's house. A paramedic arrived next on a motorbike. He checked Rachel and straightaway called for the air ambulance; it didn't look good.

Chapter 73

When he realised she wasn't alone, Liam knocked her out and ran down the alley towards his house about 300 feet away. He neared the end looked back and was aware of a dog speeding towards him.

'Fuck!' he shouted, trying to find his car keys in his pocket as he ran. The dog exited the alleyway as Liam was on his drive, clicking his alarm to open the car. He got to his car, the dog closed in twenty feet, ten feet. He scrambled to open the door and slammed it as he got in. The dog jumped up the side of the car, growling and snarling at him through the window, its claws bashing the glass.

Liam reversed off the drive and heard a thud as he made off towards Shenstone three miles away. He passed two police cars and a paramedic as he left Lichfield and drove down the back lanes through Wall to avoid cameras and police cars.

When he neared the end of the lane, he abandoned his car and ran the last quarter of a mile to Shenstone train station. He kept to the edges and out of sight of the CCTV as he'd done many times before, making his way to the work's pool car where he left it each day. He got in, kept his head down and left the car park driving through the lanes, staying off the main roads as much as he could on his way to Hannah, not sure what to do next. He'd planned to kill Rachel and hide her body, but now, now he knew he'd fucked up. He needed to think and think fast.

Being strong isn't about strength.
It's about courage.
It's about doing the thing you're most scared to do.
It's about seeing the end game.
It's about fighting when the odds are against you.

It's about taking that step without knowing what's next.

Just watch me.

Chapter 74

Hannah was woken by the car on the gravel, and she heard Liam open the door and run into the house. Normally she'd hear him walk above her straight to the cellar door; he was rarely in the house long, but she could just hear him walking around, his shoes loud on the wooden floorboards.

She braced herself – were they leaving, would this be her moment to escape? She was ready, she'd planned what she was going to do if they left. She would take the first opportunity when there were people around and scream and run and make as much noise as possible. Liam thought she was compliant again and too terrified to leave, but she needed to get out, she needed to stop him from hurting or killing whoever was next.

She froze, rooted to the spot as she intently listened, trying to imagine where he was in the house above her; the hallway, the kitchen. Then he stopped moving. She stood listening harder – nothing. Ten minutes passed in silence, she dared not move. Then she heard him again, walking faster across the room, the key in the lock and the door opened.

Liam came flying down the steps.

Oh shit.

She was standing as his hand came up to her throat. He was angry and pushed her up against the wall, her feet losing the floor and flaying around. He let go and she dropped to the floor, and he kicked her in the ribs and then her lower back. She lay crumpled, then his hand was on the back of her head, pulling her up by her hair, up and over as he forced her down onto her front, pulling her loose jeans down so he could rape her once more.

Chapter 75

Emma had heard about Rachel from John; he'd called her just after 10pm the night before. 'The fucking bastard,' he said, 'she's in a right state. The Air Ambulance and paramedics are with her now, getting her ready to go. It was him,' John said, 'he fucking tried to kill her. She might not make it. Oh shit, I should have got more officers. And he hit Luna – she was lying on his drive. He fucking hurt my dog the bastard and he fucking killed Judith, I know it!'

John had cried on the call, she'd never heard him so distraught, even over Judith; she could hear another officer trying to console him who then took the phone from John and spoke to Emma. They told her they were searching for Liam James as the prime suspect and that Hannah James was now being treated as missing, possibly kidnapped, or worse, dead.

Hearing the news about Rachel hadn't impacted her the same way it had John and her other colleagues. She was as angry and furious as they were, and she wanted more than anything to kill Liam James herself but instead of crying and talking it through with her colleagues she became more focused and determined and her thoughts were clearer than ever. Hannah was still missing, and evidence was needed to help find her and finding Liam James was the route to that. She thought through the evidence they had and pulled the cafe laptop from the evidence store. Fuck Bob, she thought, this was a new case and he couldn't stop her looking at the laptop.

It didn't take her long to get into it and she set to work systematically, checking the history and logging the sites visited. There were a lot of searches for holidays, trains, buses, the refuge in Inverness, a bank. She logged each one in a spreadsheet and wrote her own notes alongside them. A post it note recovered at the cafe had a clothing website and password on; she logged into it and the password let her in. Emma searched through the account; there were no orders, payment history, credit, debit, or bank details set up. Hannah had set up an email address. Emma opened the account, and it went straight in without needing a password. Finally, she was getting somewhere.

She opened the inbox, but it was empty. The deleted folder contained one email from the clothing website for the account set up, and nothing else, then she checked the recycle bin, nothing there; it led nowhere. Frustrated, she carried on looking at the other sites, but apart from the clothing site there was nothing else but generic searches. She couldn't be sure which sites had been searched by Hannah or a customer, although they did know the laptop wasn't well used by others so she could predict a high proportion of the usage was Hannah.

By 3am she had a long list of sites and made notes of other enquiries to make. As she worked, she kept track of the investigation and by 3:30am Liam's car was found near Shenstone and police were searching the area and checking CCTV. Emma had already advised them of the pool car registration, and they were also searching for it but so far nothing had come to light. Liam James had disappeared.

By 9am Emma's team were given permission to access the tracking records for the pool car. They could see it going to Hammerwich, as Rachel had mentioned before, and they could see it had been parked in Shenstone train station several times; it had also visited an address in Four Oaks a number of times. Emma called the team on the case and fed back to them the Hammerwich and Four Oaks locations and two teams were dispatched. Within minutes ANPR records showed the pool car had been clocked just outside Four Oaks at 9:50pm the night before. The focus was now on the Four Oaks address on Hartwell Lane and information started to come in about who it belonged to and who lived there; Stuart and Lilia Farrington, aged forty-four and forty-six.

It didn't take long to establish that Stuart worked at the same place as Liam and, according to Lilia's Facebook page, they were on holiday in the Caribbean; photos suggested they'd been there a couple of months. The team carried on digging to find out more about the couple, the house and the links to Liam and Hannah, to feedback to the officers on the ground.

Emma carried on her own quest, trawling through the evidence she had for Judith, Lucy, Hannah and now Rachel. She allocated the leads on the laptop to two of her staff, Ravi and Derek, and they started trying to find anything else to help find Liam or Hannah.

At 9:30am Emma was drinking another strong black coffee, desperately trying to stay awake. She'd had an hour's sleep when she'd drifted off at her desk around 5am, only to be woken by a police siren outside the station. Chad knocked on her door.

'Hi, are you free?' he said.

'Sure, what's up?' Emma said, wearily.

Chad looked uncomfortable as he explained his trip with Rachel to Liam's office. He'd logged the evidence but hadn't allocated Liam's name against anything. He'd guessed it was Rachel who'd broken in by the way she acted but wasn't 100% sure and now that Liam James was a prime suspect, he thought it best to let Emma know.

'Look, Chad, that's fine.' Emma was too tired to go into his suspicions. 'What have we got from the office?'

'A stack of fibres, hair and fingerprints that I'm 99% sure are from Liam,' he answered.

'OK, get the records updated and tag him to the evidence and then get down to Liam James's' house. There's a team already there but I want something that links his evidence in the office and the house so we can get a closer probability that we have his prints and DNA on record,' she asked.

'Will do,' Chad answered, and he left.

Although Liam was in the frame for Rachel's attack and Hannah being missing there still wasn't a link between Liam, Judith, and Lucy. Emma turned her attention to the link between Judith and Hannah, specifically the texts and calls between them after Hannah had gone missing.

Chapter 76

The team dispatched to Stuart Farrington's house liaised with Four Oaks police to organise a joint operation, and armed response were mobilised; officers from Lichfield and Four Oaks gathered for a briefing two roads away from the property. The driveway was long, and the gravel would have made it difficult to approach quietly so a drone was mobilised and was flying over the property.

The drone hovered lower, and an image of the pool car came into view streaming back to the officers waiting to go in. There was a chance Liam James was there, possibly with Hannah, but they couldn't risk alerting him; there was no guessing his next move. Would he flee, kill Hannah, kill himself or, most unlikely, would he surrender? The team discussed their options and watched the drone footage intently as it hovered outside each window upstairs and down; there were no lights on and no movement. The drone switched to heat sensor and after ten minutes of inactivity and no heat signatures being found, the decision was made to go in.

The only entrance was along the drive and armed officers quickly approached, crunching the gravel, and circling the building to cover the exits. They waited and listened for any signs of occupants, as two of them carefully checked the windows to get a closer look; still no sign.

'Go, go, go!'

Officers rammed the front and back doors. They entered and dispersed into the house filing one after the other, through the ground floor, upstairs and into each room shouting, 'armed police', as they went.

It was obvious someone had been there recently; there was food left on plates, fish and chip wrappers in the bins, a half-drunk cold tea. There was blood and dirt on the stair carpet and a bloody handprint on the wall.

'There's a cellar,' shouted one of the armed officers and two colleagues joined her. She pulled the door open and one of the other officers stepped in, followed by another; their torches on and their firearms held high and ready. As they stepped in the smell of shit and piss rose out of the room, but they ignored it and made their way down the steps, their torches scanning the room trying to find signs of life.

The light came on as an officer found the switch at the entrance to the cellar and the room lit up. Empty wrappers and mouldy food lay in one corner along with a bucket that must have been used as a toilet, in the other a fridge, and around the room what was clearly a lot of blood spatter on the floor and up one wall.

'Clear,' one shouted to indicate it was empty. 'We'll need SOCO down here ASAP.'

'Clear,' echoed through the house as each room was searched. Liam James had gone, and it was obvious someone had been held in the cellar, with Hannah James being the most likely person.

Breathe.

Breathe slow and steady.

Just breathe.

Take your time.

Take your chance.

Then run.

Chapter 77

When she woke, Hannah couldn't move her legs and arms. They were bound, and her mouth taped shut; she was tied up, lying on her side with her arms behind her back. She quickly realised she was in the boot of a moving car and although she'd started to get used to the darkness and loneliness of the cellar, this was different, and she became claustrophobic, panicking and struggling, trying to move in the tiny, enclosed space.

She screamed through her taped mouth as hard as she could and tried to kick and wriggle out of position. Her broken arm was bent and in an awkward position causing pain to flood over her as she passed in and out of consciousness as the car moved onwards in its journey.

Eventually the car came to stop, and she heard the car door open and shut, then the boot opened and she braced herself.

What now?

It was the first time she'd seen proper daylight for weeks and the glare of the sun hurt her eyes. She couldn't make out the blurry shape in front of her, but she knew it was Liam. She screamed as hard as she could and wriggled and kicked as his fist came down and hit her temple. He slammed the boot shut, got back in and the car started moving again.

Hannah tried to control her breathing and her mental state to calm herself. She needed to stay alert and take any opportunity to escape and panicking wouldn't help; she was fighting for her life and needed to be clear-headed. She focused on the steady hum of the engine and breathed in and out slowly to bring her heart rate down.

The car seemed to drive for hours. Liam stopped and checked on her twice more and she just lay there when he did. *Don't antagonise him.* She needed to make her escape when she was in a better position, outside of the car and not tied up in it; she needed to submit and be compliant, for now.

Chapter 78

SOCO had been at the house on Hartwell Lane for three hours bagging, boxing, and marking evidence. Word was coming into John and Emma that there was a lot of blood, DNA evidence, fibre, and fingerprints in a number of rooms, including the cellar; particularly the cellar.

SOCO were also at Liam and Hannah James's house collecting evidence to compare, and at Liam's office in Lichfield. They already had Liam's fingerprint evidence from there thanks to Chad but now they could corroborate his evidence as being that of Liam James, and if it was at each location.

The working theory was that Hannah was alive, that Liam had held her captive at the house in Four Oaks since she disappeared and was now on the run with her. The conditions she'd been held in were squalid with basic provisions and it had been reported back that it was bitterly cold down in the cellar, considering it was now the height of summer. Emma looked at the pictures taken as they were logged. She must have been freezing down there, she thought to herself. Dates on food wrappers went as far back as being within days of when Hannah had first disappeared at the start of June. Bloody fingerprints were found on the inside of the door and the ceiling where she had been trying to get out, the fridge was filthy with more bloody fingerprints and mouldy food; there were two clear set of prints in the blood, one of them definitely belonged to Liam James.

Two discreet cameras were also found tucked into the corners of the ceiling, and an iPad and been found with an app that the cameras streamed to. Emma shook her head as she viewed the evidence; he'd been watching her the whole time so any attempts to escape had been feeble.

That poor girl, she thought, *he'd thought of everything.*

John called Emma to let her know an officer was trying to contact Stuart and Lilia Farrington, and it was assumed that Liam had taken Hannah in Stuart's car, a BMW X5. It wasn't on the drive, but they needed to establish if they'd parked it at the airport or whether it should have been at the house; assuming Liam took the car ANPR and CCTV were being checked to try and find it but as yet, nothing had come back. The comms team were also preparing a press release, and pictures of Liam and Hannah had already been circulated on social media, asking anyone who'd seen either of them in recent days to come forward.

Emma had been focusing on the texts and calls between Hannah and Judith and she'd established that Hannah's call to Judith saying she was in Inverness had been made from Lichfield; in fact, they pinged off the same tower as Judith's phone so the call from Hannah's phone to Judith on the day she was murdered was made in the same vicinity. Emma assumed Liam had made the call and had been watching Judith, but at that point the link to Judith's murder was speculation and coincidental; there was still no hard evidence. Emma's team had also established the pool car had visited a road in Hammerwich several times, but it wasn't clear which address; it had been parked on the road in different places and officers were going door to door trying find out if any residents knew or had seen Liam or Hannah.

John called Emma again to let her know he'd spoken to the Officer in Charge in Birmingham City Police and they'd agreed to re-open Lucy's case with fresh eyes in light of the emerging events around Liam. Her apartment had remained empty for the past two weeks so City SOCO went back to dust for prints and fibres to try and find anything to disprove her death was suicide, and any evidence of Liam James in the apartment. Lucy had already been cremated so any evidence couldn't be found on her body. Emma put a call into Claire Wright whose name she'd seen on the forensics report to let her know they had Liam James' fingerprints.

She emailed them over just as her phone rang again, and it was Ian, Rachel's brother.

His voice kept cracking as he tried to tell Emma the condition of his sister. 'They said she's been very lucky,' he took a deep breath to calm himself, 'the impact of the rock didn't fracture her skull as they first suspected, but she does have a fractured cheekbone and a broken nose, so they're keeping her in for a few days for observation. She also has a severe concussion and they're managing her pain relief at the moment, so she's drugged up. Mom and dad are here, we're just waiting, hoping we can speak to her soon.'

The news from Rachel's brother was a relief; she was in a bad way but not as bad as they'd feared. Emma was desperate to see her friend, but the hospital had said close family only and Ian said he'd call her if anything changed.

When she called John, he said he'd spoken to the hospital as well and they should be able to see Rachel in the morning and try to interview her. She had come round, but doctors said she was too weak and incoherent because of the pain meds. Security had been stepped up at the hospital; they weren't taking any chances, they didn't know where Liam was, or what he was going to do next.

'I'm trying to find any evidence that links Judith to Liam and I know you've got City looking at Lucy's death but at the moment, even if we catch him, we don't have anything on him for those,' Emma said.

'If there is, I know you'll find it,' John replied confidently.

'How are you doing, John?' Emma asked gently.

John took a deep breath and sighed down the phone, 'You know.'

'Yeah, I know,' Emma replied. 'We can't let him get away with this.'

'At the moment we have nothing to find him, the Farrington's have confirmed their car's been stolen, but it hasn't been picked up by ANPR. How's the fingerprint match going?'

'We should have that back within an hour and DNA is being checked, that should come back late afternoon. I've already emailed the fingerprints we think are Liam's over to City forensics,' Emma answered. 'At least by this afternoon we should have confirmation that Hannah has been alive up to at least yesterday. SOCO said some of the blood appeared recent.'

'We've had some calls from the social media posts but as usual nothing solid, loads of speculation and the usual trolling that isn't helpful, just noise that distracts us,' John moaned. He hated social media – occasionally there would be the odd piece of information that came in that helped but it was always accompanied by a bunch of idiots who seemed to forget there were real people affected by the posts put out.

'It should be on the news within the next couple of hours, the boss is speaking to reporters shortly,' he said, referring to DCS Owen.

This would be beautiful,

If it wasn't so tragic.

Chapter 79

It was bright when Liam opened the boot. He leant in and Hannah recoiled, trying to push herself further into the well of the boot, expecting him to hit her again. Instead, he pulled her forward and lifted her; she complied and let him take her out.

Hannah tried to open her eyes fully and take stock of where she was. The sun glared low in the sky through the trees, and dappled light shone on the dewy grass around them as Liam carried her towards a grey stone barn. They were in the countryside, in the middle of nowhere, fields to the left and a wooded area ahead and to the right with a gravelled road behind them. Hannah's eyes followed the road past the barn; she could see the shape of a house within the woods. Liam put her on the grass to the side of the stone building; she was still bound in a foetal position as she lay on her side, watching him.

He pulled open the barn doors and drove the car in, shut the doors and returned to her. He picked her up as though she was his new wife and he was about to carry her over the threshold. He walked towards the woods and the house ahead about fifty feet away. Hannah could feel him getting weaker as he struggled to carry her; she was tiny anyway but without proper food she was a bag of bones. Even so Liam needed to stop and put her down three times. He'd been driving all night and he hadn't slept much; this could be her opportunity – he was tired, exhausted, and he could make a mistake.

The house came into view and Hannah could see it was a beautiful grey stone cottage; it looked immaculate and picture-perfect. A brook ran to the side of it, and it was the sort of place she'd have booked for a romantic weekend away. He put her down again at the side of the porch and took his phone out, checked it and typed a code into a key safe which popped open. He opened the door, picked her back up and carried her in through a small hallway and into a cosy cottage snug with a wood burner, two small sofas and a coffee table. He put her carefully on the floor and untied her arms and feet, removed the tape from her mouth and Hannah unravelled her body, pain searing through every joint and muscle as they unstiffened. For a moment she just lay there in silence, then Liam leant down and lifted her onto the sofa.

'Don't move,' he said quietly.

Hannah could see he was exhausted; she kept her head down and didn't dare look at him or move. She didn't know where she was. Should she run now before he tied her up again? Her body hurt in every joint and she doubted she could even stand let alone run; it would be futile. So, she remained obedient; her chance would have to come later.

She looked around the room. Immediately in front of her was a bottle of wine on the coffee table and a basket of fruit with a handwritten note. She could make out the word 'Welcome' and nothing else. To the left of the fruit was a navy padded book with 'Our Guests' embossed in gold on the front and a selection of leaflets of no doubt, lovely places to go. She could make out the words 'Abersoch' on one.

We must be in Wales.

Liam looked around the room and stuck his head through an internal door at the back to what she assumed was the kitchen and returned to her, making sure he could see Hannah at all times.

'Get up,' he said.

She tried to stand and frustrated he pulled her up and carried her into the kitchen; it had a slate floor and pale-blue Shaker kitchen units. He sat her on a chair at a glass topped table and bound her body and legs with thick black tape, round and round. It was tight, and she was held solidly on the chair.

'Water,' she managed to say as she looked up at him.

It took him by surprise, and he stood solid, thought for a moment, and then went to the sink returning with a full glass. He held it to her lips, most of it missing but, thankfully, Hannah was able to drink some. He held it back as she swallowed and then let her drink again until the glass was empty. Liam closed the curtains and then went back to the front room.

'I need to think,' he said as he left.

Chapter 80

Adam Sturges knocked on the red front door; it was the sixth house he'd been to in Hammerwich. A young woman opened the door; blonde, blue eyes, athletic and attractive. He was quite taken aback, but remained professional.

'Hello, madam, er, miss,' he stumbled, 'we're making enquiries in the area; do you know a Liam James, or a Hannah James?' Adam showed the woman the photographs on his tablet.

'No, sorry,' she replied and she pushed the door closed before he had time to say anything else.

He walked to the next address and knocked. He could hear a muffled sound and a thud, but no one answered, and as he knocked again a man's voice loudly shouted, 'Sorry, sorry, I'm not as fast as I used to be.'

The door opened, and a frail old man stood leaning on a walking stick for support.

'Oh dear, oh, I'm sorry!' The man was startled seeing a police officer in front of him.

'Nothing to worry about, sir, we're just doing some house-to-house enquiries,' Adam said to calm the gentleman. Adam asked about Liam and Hannah, showed him the photographs, and left; he hadn't seen anything.

He'd been going door to door with his colleagues, and although it didn't take long, it was hot and his uniform and PPE were heavy, weighing him down in the sun. There weren't many houses, and they were scattered around the village. The house to house hadn't brought any new information forward and the lead officer reported back to his superior at the station. Two officers remained in the village in an unmarked car in case Liam returned, or was in one of the houses, the other officers left.

Chapter 81

'Hey,' Emma said quietly, 'how you doing?' She smiled gently to her friend and carefully brushed the back Rachels left hand with her fingers.

Rachel slowly blinked to acknowledge Emma and opened her hand. Emma wrapped hers gently around it.

'Oh, Rach.' Emma was shocked by the state her friend was in, bloodied and bruised, lying helplessly in bed.

Rachel had two black eyes, and her nose was crooked and swollen with a cut across the bridge. Her forehead above her left eye was puffy with most of the damage covered by a gauze dressing, her left eye was blood red and her cheek bone swollen; she was unrecognisable as the Rachel she knew.

'Don't speak,' Emma said gently, 'I'll just sit here with you.'

Rachel squeezed her hand a little and closed her eyes. Emma watched Rachel drift off to sleep and her hand loosened. She checked her phone for any texts or calls she may have missed. There were two missed calls and a text from Ravi, her senior technician.

ring me ASAP, new developments Liam James

Emma gently pulled her hand from Rachel's and left the room to ring Ravi back.

'Hi, Emma, right, so, three things, we had a report by a railway worker late yesterday, he was strimming grass on the railway embankment and hit a scaffolding clamp, kicked it out of the way, it rolls over and get this – blood and hair on it. Thankfully, he had his wits about him, calls it in. I saw it first thing, it must have been protected somehow. The evidence is perfect; nice big fingerprint on there in the dried blood, matched to none other than Liam James. Blood is with the DNA lab already but we're expecting it to be Judith's, as the clamp was found next to the alley opposite her office.' Ravi reeled off the first of her news.

'Oh, thank god for that, that's great news. We've got him!' Emma said.

'Sorry, I forgot to ask about Rachel,' Ravi said.

'Yeah, she's not great now but they've said she'll make a full recovery. Her face is a mess, though. She was interviewed this morning briefly, just to confirm it was Liam.'

'That brings me nicely onto my next thing,' Ravi replied. 'So, Liam's CCTV was switched off but his neighbour's house at the top of the T-junction has a great shot facing straight down the road. Lovely lady there, Mrs Lees, was more than helpful. It's got Liam leaving the house, running out of the alley to his car. Luna nearly got him, she was literally a split second away from him. I want to hang him just for that. She's beautiful, I remember her being trained as a puppy. A real superstar in dog land. John must be distraught.'

'He is, poor Luna, but she's going to be okay.' Emma paused, reflecting on the past day's events. 'But great news on the CCTV, we should get a DNA match too from Rachel's attack, our girl put up a good fight. What's next?' Emma asked.

'So, DNA from the Farrington's house on Hartwell Lane, is finally back from the lab, confirmed it's Hannah's blood matched to a hair from a hairbrush and we've also got the clothes she was wearing when she went missing – sweat matches too. So, she was definitely there, and his fingerprints and just about every other piece of evidence is putting Liam James slam dunk in the middle of it. They just need to catch him now and he's done,' Ravi delivered her last piece.

'That's great news, and great work Ravi, thank you. Can you brief the team now? I'm still at the hospital and I want to talk to Ian, Rachel's brother before I leave.'

'Sure thing, consider it done,' Ravi said.

'Thank you, I should be back in about an hour. Oh, and I've briefed the team about Hammerwich. The pool car was going there regularly so they're checking Liam's mobile activity, bank accounts etc to try and find out why. Door to door didn't turn anything up though.'

Emma ended the call and returned to Rachel. She sat next to her bed and gently picked up her hand. Rachel opened her eyes.

'We've got the evidence we needed, Rach,' she said softly, 'we think Hannah's alive and everyone's looking for her, and we've got the evidence we need to confirm Liam killed Judith.'

Rachel squeezed her hand and closed her eyes as a tear trickled down her cheek.

'Also,' Emma paused as Rachel open her eyes. 'Jay called me last night, he was really upset and wants to see you. Is that OK?' Emma asked.

Rachel let out a long breath…relief. She closed her eyes again, as more tears fell, 'Yes,' she whispered.

'OK.' Emma nodded, 'I'll give him a call.'

Emma looked up as Ian walked in.

'Hey,' she said quietly. He smiled as she stood up.

'Hey,' Ian said. He hugged her and as his warm comforting arms wrapped round her Emma finally allowed herself to cry as she sobbed into Ian's shoulder.

'I thought we'd lost her,' she said.

'I know,' he replied, 'but we haven't.'

Chapter 82

After speaking to Ian, Emma went back into Rachel's room. She went to kiss her forehead but everywhere was bruised and she was scared of hurting her, so she kissed her own fingers and touched the back of Rachel's hand. 'I'll see you soon, Rach, love you loads.'

Rachel tried to smile but her swelling didn't allow it, so she just blinked slowly again. Emma left the hospital, and her phone rang.

'Hi, Emma, how was Rach?' asked John, 'did she tell you anything else?'

'She opened her eyes briefly, but she's exhausted and drugged up to her eyeballs. I've let her know that we've got the proof we need to nail the bastard. It just didn't look like her though. I was shocked to be honest, John.'

'I know, I was the same. Prison's too good for Liam James, but first we need to catch him and find Hannah, so this is where we're at. Obviously, you know the update from Ravi, so in addition, the car he was in wasn't showing up anywhere on CCTV then young superstar Ashley spots the same make and model driving through Mere Green, just down the road from the house; the plates were for a different car. Tracked it back through CCTV and the pub at the top of the road catches the car full on, Liam James driving it, no sight of Hannah though. We've tracked the car on ANPR as far as the Welsh border, but it hasn't turned up on anything there yet, so our Welsh colleagues are searching there too.'

Emma listened as John continued.

'We've also made a link to the Hammerwich address. Liam's bank showed a monthly payment to a letting agent and they've confirmed an address in Hammerwich. The occupant, a woman called Sarah Jackson, was interviewed in the door to door but said she didn't know anything. Our young Sturges who spoke to her says she's the spit of Hannah James. I'm just pulling up there now to speak to her, so I'll ring you later.'

Emma got into her car and thought back to her conversation with John after Judith was killed; she'd gone to his office as requested.

'Shut the door,' he said, and Emma complied.

'OK, so,' he started tentatively, 'I'm worried about Rachel,' he paused, 'and I know you two are close, so I'm telling you this in confidence with Rachel's best interests at heart.'

Emma nodded and listened.

'This guy's clever, and I think Rachel is onto something, but she's getting too close to it and this Liam James seems to be taking an interest in her. At the moment we haven't got any solid evidence or links, just hunches and speculation and if I take all this to Owen without anything concrete, he'll laugh me out of his office.'

Emma stayed quiet. She felt uncomfortable about what he might say next, and if he was asking her to bend the rules and break the law, she didn't know how she would handle it. Was a senior officer, someone she trusted, had known for years, and worked with on really complex cases about to put her in an untenable position? What should she say? She would have to stand fast and tell him that she would never break the law and she'd report him if he did.

'I just want you to keep an eye on her, make sure she's on the straight and narrow and doesn't do anything stupid to jeopardise the case, or her career,' John finished.

'Oh, OK,' Emma had answered, relieved.

As she thought back to that day, Emma thought if bending the rules had meant her friend had stayed out of harm's way and wasn't lying in a hospital bed today, it was justified. Emma had always been the one sticking to the rules, telling others to do the same. It was fundamental to her job to do just that and without it, her job was pointless. Today, though, the enormity hit her that sometimes sticking to the rules gets people killed or injured. If she'd been more flexible instead of giving her friend a hard time about bending the rules would Rachel be where she was now, lying helpless? Emma was angry, angry at the situation, angry at Liam James and angry with herself. She wanted to nail him, and John was right, prison was too good for him. He should be six feet under, and he needed to suffer before he got there. She remembered seeing the search that Hannah had done on her laptop about a peanut allergy and had crossed referenced Liam's medical record.

That would be a good way to make him suffer, she thought to herself.

Chapter 83

Sarah Jackson opened the door, just slightly, and peered through the gap.

'Sarah Jackson, we have a warrant to search these premises and I'd like to ask you a few questions,' John said as he and his officers piled into the house in Hammerwich.

At first she looked startled and went to protest, but then sighed deeply and stood aside.

John interviewed her whilst his officers searched the house to quickly establish that neither Liam nor Hannah were there and the story of her affair with Liam came to light.

Sarah was twenty-three and was a client of Liam's. As Adam had said, she was the spit of Hannah James.

'How did you first meet Liam?' John asked.

'We met at a seminar in January; it was the first time I'd represented my company and I felt a little out of my depth to be honest. Liam was there and he came over, said we were one of his clients and not worry, that I was doing a great job,' Sarah explained. 'He was really lovely, and helpful.'

'And when did you start an affair with him?' John asked and waited. Sarah looked uncomfortable.

'Erm, not that evening, if that's what you think. I'm not like that,' she answered.

'I wasn't implying that, Miss Jackson, I'm just trying to get some background,' John said.

'OK, well I'd finished packing up the stand and Liam helped me put everything in my car, he was a real gentleman, he didn't try it on or anything. We were both stopping over, a few people were to be honest and we all had an evening meal at the hotel and I ended up chatting with Liam until the early hours.'

John nodded and waited for her to continue.

'He told me he and his wife were in the final stages of divorce, that she had some mental health issues and although he'd done his best they'd agreed they needed to split up. Apparently, she could be quite violent and would have outbursts. He showed me a scar on his arm where she'd attacked him with scissors once and said she'd had one episode recently which was the final straw. He said he'd told her he wanted a divorce or he'd report her to the police, so she agreed to the divorce.' Sarah's face flushed, her voice cracked as she spoke. 'The following week he sent me an email and asked me out on a date, so I said yes.'

'OK, and when did you move into this house?' John asked.

'At the end of March. Liam's had this house for a few years and had rented it out, so he gave the previous tenants notice and I moved in. He couldn't stop here too often because he said Hannah was trying to use his absence against him to claim Liam's other house.'

John knew Liam only rented the house, and had done so since March. He'd clearly spun a web of lies to Sarah, if she was telling the truth, and he believed she was, she knew nothing of what had happened to Hannah.

'And can I ask why you lied to my officer when he asked you if you knew Liam,' John asked directly.

'I'm sorry, I do regret that. Liam told me she'd gone missing on purpose, she often stormed out trying to create drama, and her parents had reported her missing, but if I'm honest, I wanted to give him the benefit of the doubt.' She started to cry. 'He said he was coming back here and he hasn't, I've called him, text, I've been worried sick but then I saw his face on the news, I feel so stupid.' She put her head in her hands and sobbed.

'Miss Jackson, don't feel stupid.' John felt sorry for her, she'd been manipulated by Liam as well, she was young and naïve, and he'd taken advantage of her, in the same way he did with Hannah.

'But I can't believe I fell for it, he was so kind and loving, I was hoping it was all a mix up. I just wanted to give him a chance to explain.' She sighed.

'Is there anywhere you can think he could be?' John asked.

'I have no idea, I obviously didn't know him as well as I thought I did' she answered.

'Are there any places you've been together, or anywhere he's talked about?' John asked.

'I don't know if this may help but he asked me to look at cottages for us to take a break in Wales. It was supposed to be our first proper weekend away together, but we never went; after Hannah went missing he seemed to forget he'd even asked me to look and when I asked about it, he just said we'd do it another time.'

'Do you have the details?' John asked.

'Yes, I can find the emails I sent him, there were four or five that I really liked. I can't believe this is happening, I thought I'd finally met someone real,' Sarah said as she rubbed her teary eyes.

John went through each of the emails and forwarded them to himself, then to Emma and his other investigators to do some digging. They were getting close but every second mattered.

Chapter 84

'So, what have we got?' John asked Bob Moore. As much as John didn't want Bob Moore involved, he had no choice. Bob was lead on Judith's murder and by default, with Rachel in the hospital, he was now the Officer in Charge of Hannah's case as well.

'So far, we've managed to contact the owners of three of the cottages and ruled them out. All three are owner-managed and we've spoken to the occupants. Wales police are following up to confirm in person, they have pictures of Liam and Hannah. The last two we've not been able to get hold of the owners. We're still trying, and Wales police are also going to the properties to conduct surveillance before they go in. There's one in particular that looks promising, out in the sticks. If I were a betting man, I'd say they're there.'

John listened and asked for the details of their Wales contact. It turned out to be an old colleague who'd joined Wales from Staffordshire to move up the ranks.

'Hi, John, long time no speak,' DCC Tony Tweats answered the phone and got right onto business. 'Right, we've just confirmed we can rule out another one so we're down to one property. It's pretty remote, in a quiet wooded area which is great, plenty of cover for us. We've got a couple of drones up and we're just waiting for armed response to be approved before we move in.'

'Can I patch through to your gold command?' John asked, and within a minute he was able to view on his tablet both the drone and body cam footage.

John watched intently and his phone pinged; it was a text from Emma. He'd have to check it later, as he was still talking to Tweatsy and the image was live from the cottage. He didn't want to miss a thing.

The grainy image showed a cottage with drawn curtains and the lights on, but it wasn't showing anything inside the cottage; it was dark and the visibility poor. The drones moved upstairs where net curtains covered the windows, but they still couldn't make out anything; the rooms were dark and trying to get a good view inside them was impossible.

'OK, Armed Response confirmed, go go go!' John heard the order.

273

He watched the drones and body cam footage as officers circled and neared the cottage, everyone low, firearms at shoulder height, moving with precision and purpose. They were just about to go in when the front door opened, and a man stood there blocking the light.

Suicide is a choice.
Thinking about could I.
Thinking about how I'd do it.

Now I'm ready.
Thinking about when.

That is the choice I make.

Chapter 85

Hannah sat and waited for what felt like hours on the kitchen chair. She could hear Liam occasionally snoring in the next room, the TV on low. When he woke, he came in as it started to get dusky, cut the tape that bound her, helped her upstairs to the toilet, then sat her on the bed and closed the curtains. He didn't speak, and although he'd been asleep in the next room, she could tell he was still tired; his face was grey, and he'd aged in the days since she'd first tried to leave.

He gave her a cheese sandwich and a bottle of water, but she was too weak to even hold the sandwich, let alone the water; Liam tore a mouthful from the sandwich and fed it to her. It made her gag, but he gave her more until she managed to eat half. He held the water bottle to her lips, and she took small sips. She was weak and in pain and felt her life ebbing away as her will to live diminished; her situation, she felt was now hopeless. Hannah didn't know how she could escape and even if she could get outside, she was so weak she knew she wouldn't get very far. They were surrounded, it seemed, by woods, and she had no idea how far away the main road was to alert any passing drivers, or if there were any houses nearby.

She just wanted this to stop, she was ready for it to stop, the pain, the sadness, and the grief she felt. He bound her hands and feet again, put the tape across her mouth, leaving her on her side on the bed, and left the room; she felt the room darken as the sun went down outside.

As she lay there, she thought about her life, how she'd got to be where she was now and wished she'd taken the chance earlier to leave Liam when the first signs were there, years before; leaving then would have been possible, leaving now was impossible. She knew this would be the place she would die, if not by starvation, or Liam's hand, she would, when she could take her own life. She'd thought about it so many times in the past five years, first thinking about if she could do it, to how she could do it and now, unable to move, when she could do it. When she got the opportunity, she would take it; she was done, she was ready and had accepted it. This was how it had to be.

Lying in the dark she noticed a flicker of light through the window. It flashed briefly, and then again. She watched intently; there it was again. Then she heard movement outside. Was it the wind rustling in the trees?

Crack.

No, that was a branch.

Crack.

Her sense of hearing in the dark the past few weeks had sharpened, warning her that Liam was nearby. Maybe it was Liam, but she hadn't heard him go outside.

The light disappeared and she distinctly heard the rhythm of footsteps crunching gravel and snapping twigs, approaching the house. The light flashed across the window again – someone was there, someone was going to rescue her. She tried to scream and shout, but nothing came out, her throat was so dry and sore. She tried to move to the side of the bed, to roll off and make a noise. As she neared the edge, she heard the front door open and a man's deep voice echoed through the house, but she couldn't make it out. She froze and then forced herself to roll off the bed, hitting the floor with an almighty bang, her head bashing the corner of a cabinet on the way down, and she felt the impact of the floor thud solidly against her body.

Dazed, she could hear Liam and the other man, their voices getting louder. There was banging below her; it sounded like furniture being knocked over. The voices had stopped but she could hear the banging – they must be fighting. She tried to scream again but a hoarse, indistinguishable noise came from her. The banging continued and then it stopped; there was silence from below.

Hannah froze, held her breath and heard heavy footsteps walking across the wooden floor below her. Then she heard thumps over and over again and what sounded like screaming, an animal in pain; sickening tortured screams.

Stillness again.

Lying there, Hannah tried harder to hear and tune into the silence.

Footsteps boomed fast up the stairs, but she was on the floor behind the bed, the bedroom door out of sight. She heard it open, and someone rushed into the room, stopped, walked around the bed. She looked up.

Liam stood over her, covered in blood.

Chapter 86

'Seriously, I've got kids in here, mate. Sorry, doesn't cut it, can you please be quiet? They're in bed.' The cottage occupant continued to rant as the officers withdrew.

John realised it wasn't Liam as soon the door opened; the body cam was poor quality, but it definitely wasn't him. His heart sank and he felt nauseous.

'Look, we'll keep on it, John, there are other leads, and we know he's here somewhere, it's just a matter of time,' Tony Tweats reassured him.

John called Emma to update her. She'd sent him a text but he hadn't read it.

call me urgently

'It wasn't him, we're back to square one,' he said.

'Maybe not, where are you?' Emma asked.

'At the station, why?' he answered.

'Can you pop down to my office, I want to show you something.'

Five minutes later and John was leaning over Emma's shoulder, looking at her screen.

'Ok, so you got me thinking when you emailed me the holiday cottages. I remember seeing a few searches on the laptop Hannah used, they were for places in Scotland and Wales. In all she'd looked at about fifty places,' Emma explained.

'Fifty?' John said, disappointedly, 'but that's— '

'Hold on, so Ravi and Derek have spent the last two hours looking at this and found Hannah also had a bank account; we'd found the bank on the search history but couldn't link it to her. Genius Ravi realised the password we found in the cafe for another website was also for her online banking; she guessed her memorable information, it was just her birthday, and we got into her account. She'd been making cash deposits into it for nearly two years, but activity had stopped two days before she left. Two days ago, a payment was made to a cottage letting provider.'

'Bloody hell,' John's eyes widened, 'and?'

'And, I've got an address.' As she said this Emma clicked a link on her laptop and an image of a cottage appeared.

'Good work, send me the details and DCC Tweats, and the team here,' John said as he hurriedly left the office.

'Where are you going?' she shouted, but he'd gone.

John's pace quickened as he headed towards his car. He got in, put his siren on, and sped out of the station towards the M6 toll.

'John,' Tony Tweats said as he answered his phone.

'Tony, have you had an email arrive from—' John started.

'Yep, got it, from an Emma Whitlock.'

'That's it,' John said, and he explained to Tony how Emma had found the cottage.

'OK,' Tony said, 'that's North Wales. I'll contact them now and get this moving, where are you?' he asked.

'I'm on my way to Abersoch,' John answered. It was 11:30pm. Abersoch was over three hours away and even with his siren on it would still take him well over two and a half hours.

He rang his team back in Lichfield and got them up to speed. 'DCC Tweats has got your details, and he'll let us know when he's spoken to an ACC Langley in North Wales. This is going to move fast. I'm on my way there now to lead the interview when they arrest him. This is definitely the place and I want the files compiled sent to me and Langley so we can co-ordinate an interview plan. I'm not letting anything slip.'

'OK,' Bob Moore answered.

John put his foot down further and sped towards the M54 turn off; it was dark, not much traffic on the road, and he was soon on the A5 heading towards North Wales.

Chapter 87

Liam leant down to Hannah and roughly bundled her back onto the bed; her head was bleeding, and she could feel the warm trickle filling her left eye so she couldn't see out of it. He stood there for a moment, stationary, looking at her, thinking.

'You need to show me more respect, you are my wife,' he snarled at her. Then he picked her up and carried her down the stairs; he was limping and grunted with pain as he carried her.

They passed the open door to the lounge, and she could see the mess with furniture toppled over, ornaments broken, and a large man crumpled on the floor – blood everywhere. She only saw him briefly, but she couldn't believe anyone could still be alive looking like that.

Outside it was dark, warm, and humid as Liam carried her down to the barn. He dropped her on the floor hard, knocking the wind out of her and refreshing the pain all over her body. He opened the barn doors and the car, picked her up and bundled her back into the boot; Hannah immediately became claustrophobic again and her breathing became faster as the fear overwhelmed her. Liam slammed the boot and she felt herself going into a full panic attack.

Breathe, breathe, breathe, she kept telling herself, *breathe*, as she tried to calm her heart rate.

Chapter 88

John got a call an hour into his journey from ACC Caroline Langley.

'We've had a call from an Anne Jones. Her husband Wayne is missing and he's the caretaker for the cottage you believe Liam James is in. Mr Jones looks after three in all, but he's been reported as missing after going out on his rounds to welcome the guests,' she explained. 'I've received the files from your guys, but I need a quick update – what are we dealing with here?'

John filled Langley in on the events to date and what they knew, and they agreed they needed to treat it as a hostage situation; they couldn't just go straight in.

'I'll get the infrared sorted, we use it a lot for search and rescue around here,' Langley said, 'we need to see how many people we have in the cottage, and where they are. My officers are waiting at the property entrance now, out of sight, just in case they leave, but we need a clear arrest plan on this. The cottage is remote; it has a lot of woods around it and lots of ways in and out. Liam James, from what you've said, seems very unpredictable. I'd rather get a negotiator on this too, we can't just pile in.'

John agreed, but part of him wanted Liam to resist and be shot dead; being negotiated out was the right option but not necessarily the best outcome.

'OK, I've just had confirmation,' Langley said, 'Mr Jones's Land Rover is parked just outside the property boundary, so we need to assume he's in there and is a hostage. It's 12:30am so there's no way he's just chatting. How far away are you?' she asked.

'Sat nav says 2am, roads are deserted so maybe about an hour or so. I've got the blues on and tanking it,' John answered.

'OK, just be careful if you're not used to the roads round here,' Langley warned.

John carried on driving and Langley was right, the roads were unpredictable. He was having to reduce his speed a lot; he ploughed on through, trying not to kill himself as he drove.

Chapter 89

Liam sat in the driver's seat of the car, his bloodied hands on the wheel. The barn doors were closed and his engine was off; he couldn't think straight. Having to move Hannah so quickly had meant he couldn't plan properly, and he was injured after fighting with the man who'd turned up at his door.

When he'd knocked on the door, Liam had answered calmly and smiled. The man introduced himself as Wayne the caretaker, asked if he'd settled in, if everything was OK. But then his face changed, and Liam realised he must have recognised him from the press releases. Then, as soon as Hannah made a racket, the other man looked upwards toward the bedrooms and recoiled as he turned to run. Liam managed to lunge forward and grab him by his waist and they both fell to the floor; they scuffled on the ground outside the cottage. As Wayne got to his knees and Liam to his feet, Wayne launched upwards throwing Liam back into the house. Liam had never fought a man before and Wayne was a big and a competent fighter; trained, army maybe. Wayne knocked Liam backwards onto the stairs and landed punch after punch into his head and side; Liam held his arms in a guard and his legs curled up to try and defend himself and block the blows. He was taken back momentarily to his childhood; his stepdad. Anger burned inside him, growing; he would not lose.

Wayne took a step back and Liam rolled onto his front on the stairs, his back to Wayne. He threw himself backwards with all his weight hitting him with a full body blow and they both fell into the lounge. They both looked around for weapons as they scuffled, landing blow after blow into each other. Liam managed to bring his foot up straight into Wayne's groin with full force and he dropped to the floor. Liam stood over him as Wayne curled up in pain and he spotted a fire iron on the hearth. He brought his foot back and swung it hard, kicking Wayne in the head, he was motionless for a moment, then groaned. Liam calmly walked over to the fireplace, picked up the fire iron, held it across both his hands to feel the weight, walked calmly back to Wayne and pounded it over and over into his head. Liam screamed with rage with every single blow as he pummelled his long-held anger into Wayne's head; killing the man, he now imagined as stepdad there.

Unadulterated rage came with every blow. Blood splattered everywhere and Wayne's face disintegrated; unrecognisable. When he finished, he stood back and looked at the devastation. He didn't feel the same as when he'd killed Judith or Lucy, that had given him enjoyment and made him feel powerful. Now he felt different, he felt proud and smug standing over Wayne; he was invincible.

He turned and ran up the stairs to the bedroom he'd left Hannah in, picked her up and put her on the bed. He thought for a moment as he looked at the pathetic excuse for a woman lying on the bed. She was a mess, she'd let herself go, she should be ashamed of herself. He had two choices: kill her now or take her with him. He wasn't ready to kill her yet – she hadn't learnt her lesson.

'You need to show me more respect, you are my wife,' he'd said.

Now, sitting in the car, he tried to calm his thinking; he was covered in blood, how was he going to get anywhere like this? He needed to clean up first. He'd go back to the cottage, shower and change and try and book another cottage with Hannah's bank account. He had three days' provisions he'd picked up at a village shop on their way there, and he needed to get out of the area.

He looked at his watch. It was 10pm. He couldn't hang around, he needed to move in the dark and get out of the area as soon as he could. He went back to the cottage and thirty minutes later he was locking up and making his way back to the barn. He'd found a cottage in Keswick in Cumbria; it was four hours on the motorway, or six hours if he avoided them which he needed to do. He couldn't get in until 2pm but it was in a remote area that he knew well having hiked there many times. He knew where there were car parks in the remotest of areas, so he'd travel in the dark, park up, and move to the cottage when he could at 2pm. It was the only option he could think of; it was risky, but he had no choice.

He looked around the barn, there were various tools; he picked up a shovel and a fork, and put them on the back seat.

He opened the boot. Hannah was motionless, when he prodded her with his hand, she groaned. It was 10:35pm when he left the cottage, and he passed what must have been the caretaker's Land Rover. Liam smiled to himself. As he drove towards Keswick, he relaxed into the drive along the dark, deserted coastal path.

Chapter 90

It was just coming up to 1:30am and Langley called John.

'We're in position, but we don't think they're here. Infrared is showing the faintest of heat signatures and only one. So, we're going in,' Langley said.

'OK, I'll keep this line open,' John answered. Were they too late?

'OK, standby.'

John could hear the background noise of the gold command room and Langley instructing her team at the scene. He carried on driving but slowed his pace; there was nothing he could do to help; he waited patiently until Langley came back on the line.

'I'm sorry, John, we were too late. They've definitely been here. We've got one body we're assuming is Mr Jones,' Langley started.

'Oh no,' said John.

Langley continued, 'He's wearing the clothes described by his wife, but we'll need to do dental on him; his face is a mess. There's no sign of Liam or Hannah James. There's blood everywhere downstairs, in the bathroom and a small amount in one of the bedrooms. We need to proceed on the assumption that, without a body, Hannah is still alive. How long before you're here?' she asked.

'OK, thanks, I reckon thirty minutes. I'll go straight to the scene, I need to see it,' John said. As he spoke a call came in from Emma. 'Sorry, I need to take a call from my forensics, I'll call you back.'

'Emma,' John said as he answered his phone.

'Hi, are you at the cottage yet?' Emma asked.

'No, they've just gone in and they're not there, but the bastard's killed the caretaker,' John answered.

'Oh god, that's awful,' Emma replied, paused, and got back to business. 'So, I've been monitoring Hannah's bank account and an amount has just cleared for £408, and this time it's a straightforward payment for a cottage in Keswick,' Emma explained.

'OK, I'm pulling over, give me a second.' John pulled into a lay-by. 'OK, what's the postcode?'

Emma reeled off the postcode and John typed it into his Sat nav. 'Shit, that's hours away. Can you see what time it was booked?' he asked.

'Given the time the transaction cleared I'd say between 10 and 10:30pm.'

'OK, so assuming he left, let's say earliest from the cottage 10pm,' John thought for a moment, 'I can't work it out,' he complained.

'It's OK, I'm checking it now,' Emma interjected. 'Right, there's two main routes, one that takes six hours the other four-ish. The shorter ones on motorways.'

'OK, we haven't had an ANPR hit on the car there, and my guess is he'd want to stay off the main roads, but I'll get response units on there as well just in case.' John paused. 'Assuming he's still using the same car, but he may not be. Erm, OK, so if he left at 10pm where would that put him roughly?' John asked.

'Give me a minute,' John could hear Emma typing into her laptop. 'OK, let's say at varying speeds it puts him travelling maybe three and a half to four hours, I'd say between Wigan and Preston if he's taken the longer route, and between Lancaster and Keswick if he's taken the shorter route, but he could be there already to be honest.'

'Shit, you're probably closer than I am, whichever route I take,' John exclaimed.

'Where are you?' she asked.

'Nearly at Abersoch.' He thought for a moment. 'I'll go straight to Keswick, I need to ring the team, and sort patrols on both routes in, and around the cottage. Keep me informed of anything else,' he asked.

'OK, but I want to lead the SOCO team on the ground when he's picked up. I don't want anything compromised,' Emma answered.

'OK, right, got it, your scene. Erm, I'll instruct Bob Moore to get up to Keswick to take Liam back to Staffs for interview assuming we get him there. Jump in with Bob, I'll ring him now to tee him up with details.' John knew Emma was angry at Bob for not listening to her or Rachel but at least she could keep an eye on him.

'OK, be careful, you've done a lot of miles and you've been up hours,' Emma said.

'Nothing I'm not used to, though,' John answered.

I'm ready,
Just let me die,
Please...
Just let me go.

Chapter 91

Hannah lay in the dark, feeling every rut in the road and every turn of the car. She just wanted to die now, to drift off; she willed herself to go. *Just die, there's nothing left.* She felt the life leaving her body as Liam continued along the road. How had they got there? Why didn't she run at the first sign? She should have run; she should have made the choice years before at the first signs and at each sign after that.

She imagined people at her funeral thinking the same, 'Why didn't she run?' they'd say. 'Why didn't she just ask for help?' But Hannah thought back, and she remembered the times when people could have intervened, but they didn't; keeping quiet, turning a blind eye, not wanting to get involved. You're the reason I'm here, she thought to herself. They'd chosen to ignore what was right in front of them, not wanting it to stain their perfect lives, not wanting to take notice, or make the effort.

If she'd listened to Carl and hadn't shut him out, could he have talked her out of the relationship? If she'd met Judith earlier would things be different now? If she'd been given the confidence to trust her instincts and not let him drain away her self-esteem, her ambition, and her soul, until there was nothing left; just skin and bones tied up in a car, waiting to die.

Please just die. She willed herself to go; she didn't want to give Liam the final satisfaction of doing it himself, she didn't want him to pull over, open the boot and kill her and bury her. She wanted it to be her choice now, the only choice she had left.

'Just die,' she said, quietly in the dark.

Chapter 92

'OK, boss, yes, Cumbria have already done a reccy of the cottage and they've set up a perimeter and surveillance; he's not getting in there without them spotting him. They've also got unmarked cars out looking for him round here, and all routes in,' Bob Moore updated John.

'Thanks, Bob. We think the earliest he could get there is 2am, so he could be there already, but he could still be on the road. I'm sure he'd have taken the longer route and stayed away from the cameras. I'm miles away, it's going to be nearly 6am before I get there,' John said. 'Is Emma with you?' he asked.

'Yes, she's in the back and I've got a PC with me too, Adam Sturges,' Bob answered.

'OK, good, I'll see you there once we know his location.'

It was 3am and John had been up nearly twenty hours; he was used to long days, but he could feel himself struggling to keep his eyes open; he knew the right thing to do was pull over. He opened the window and let the cool morning air drift into the car, but his head dropped forward as tiredness took over; the sharp jolt woke him and he drifted onto the gravelled curb.

'Fuck.' He turned the wheel hard, scraping along the gravel verge. He got himself back onto the road and straightened up. He put his air con on full blast, widened his eyes and rubbed his face.

The next thing he knew, he woke as his headlights hit the hedgerow; light glaring back at him against the leaves. He slammed on his brakes and steered hard right, but it was too late as he skidded sideways off the road, through the hedge and came to a halt in a ditch at the edge of a field.

'Fuck,' he shouted. 'Fuck, fuck, fuck!' slamming his hands on the wheel.

Chapter 93

Emma continued to work whilst Bob drove, avoiding as much conversation as possible; he made light work of the journey, speeding along the deserted M6. Emma had hardly slept in the preceding thirty-six hours; nodding off briefly here and there, but now she was alert and fully awake. They'd reached Keswick just after 5am and were now driving around the area listening to the police radio, waiting for intel to come in. She'd heard John had crashed his car, but he was OK, and North Wales had sent a car to pick him up and take him the rest of the way to Keswick; he'd be at least another hour if not more. There had been five police forces in total working to find Liam James and, so far, he'd evaded capture.

'Bob, can you pull over please? I need your expertise,' Emma asked politely, pandering to Bob's ego. He complied, pulling into a National Trust car park.

'OK, so when Liam booked the cottage, he used a mobile phone, and that phone has hit three towers in this area; he's here somewhere,' Emma explained.

'Can you get the ordnance map up?' Bob asked.

'Yes, give me a second.' Emma tapped her tablet, 'Here.' She handed it to him.

'OK, so this is the road he would have come in on,' Bob's finger followed the road. 'Where was his phone signal picked up?' he asked.

Emma leant over and pointed. 'Here, here and here,' she paused, 'he's passed them, so it confirms he's travelling along this road.'

'Where's the next one?' Bob asked.

'Here,' Emma pointed further up the map.

'OK, so can we assume he's between these two points?' Bob stated.

'I guess so, but not for sure,' Emma answered, 'if he's switched his phone off, we wouldn't know,' she added.

'Where's the cottage?' Adam asked.

'Here.' Emma pointed to the left of the last point. 'OK, let's think this through,' Emma started. 'He's not at the cottage, we know that he's passed these points but not that one.' Her finger followed the line of the road again.

'He's probably in one of these car parks.' Bob pointed to three places.

'There's police everywhere, though, and they're watching the car parks. They'd have found him by now,' Emma stated.

'OK, Miss Marple,' Bob shot back sarcastically.

'Fuck off, Bob, if you'd have listened to Rachel in the first place we wouldn't fucking be up here.' Emma's anger spilt over.

Bob started his retaliation at what Emma assumed he thought was her insubordination, even though she out-ranked him in terms of seniority. But in his eyes was just a civilian worker and not a proper officer.

'There,' Adam interrupted loudly pointing at the map. 'That's where I'd go,' he said defiantly.

Bob shot Emma a dirty look then turned his attention to where Adam was pointing at the map and nodded. 'Yep, I was just about to say that, well done, Adam, good to see you're learning from me,' he said, trying to take back control, and no doubt credit when Liam was found. 'OK, we need to get out and walk, that's two miles that way. It's dark now but give it twenty minutes and the sun will start to come up.'

'No, we should wait here and let the rest of the team know,' Emma protested.

'Look, Emma, I'm the officer in charge here and what I say goes. You're staying here and Adam's coming with me,' Bob ordered as he got out of the car.

'You're kidding, right?' Emma opened her car door but didn't get out. 'You know full well you need to let the team know. I'm ringing John.'

Adam was still sitting in the car.

'Adam, with me now!' Bob shouted. He looked back at Emma. 'You stay out of my way. I'll let you know when you can sweep up the evidence after I've arrested him.'

Adam was half out of the car. 'Boss, I think Emma's right,' he said quietly.

'Are you for real? Get the fuck out of the car now or you can kiss your policing career goodbye. You do not ignore a senior officer's instruction. With me now,' Bob scowled as he reprimanded Adam.

'Stop thinking about your arrest record, Bob, and do the right thing,' Emma snapped as she dialled John. By the time John answered Bob was already walking off towards the woods.

Adam followed and looked back at Emma and mouthed, 'Sorry.'

'Any news?' John asked as he answered the phone.

Emma filled him in.

'That little shit,' John said. 'OK, I'll alert the rest of the team, we need armed response there asap; I don't want that idiot fucking this up. How confident are you that he's there?' he asked.

'Honestly, I don't know. His phone was definitely in the vicinity when the signal was picked up and Adam's spotted a timber yard that looks promising. I just don't know. I haven't seen anyone up here patrolling and we're about two miles from the cottage,' Emma answered.

'It's a big search area, Em, they'll have stuck to the main arterial roads and car parks, but this will narrow the search down between where you are and the cottage. Great work. You stay put, stay in the car, doors locked and keep down; that twat should never have left you alone. I'll call all this in and let the team know and make sure someone's sent over to you asap.' He paused, 'and I'll try to ring Bob, bloody idiot.'

Chapter 94

The terrain wasn't too bad, and it was an easy walk along a footpath that was maintained for walkers. Adam thought about Emma back at the car, still torn about whether to follow orders or go back. He now understood why some of the other officers moaned about Bob Moore and how he'd got his nickname Knobby; he started to think Teflon would be more appropriate. He'd heard about two bungled operations he'd led but it was clear nothing ever stuck to him, and he always scapegoated someone else. It was Adam's first day out of uniform since he'd started his degree apprenticeship – he didn't want it to be his last.

It was still dark but getting lighter and within ten minutes Bob abandoned his torch. The dew had started to settle and as the sun rose there was a warm mist hovering about a foot off the ground, swirling around them as they walked. Bob checked the map on his phone to make sure they were still headed to the right place. The path they were on would come out exactly where they thought Liam would be.

'Boss, should we turn off before we get there and walk through here?' Adam pointed, suggesting they walked the last few minutes through the undergrowth and trees. 'We don't want to just walk out in front of him.'

Bob shot him a dirty look. 'I know where I'm going, Adam, I don't need a fucking navigator,' he said.

'Sir,' Adam nodded. *Twat,* he thought.

They carried on walking in silence as the birds came to life and their song filled the air around them. About a hundred feet before the end of the path Bob turned off. Adam thought they should have turned off earlier and Bob probably wouldn't have turned off at all if Adam hadn't suggested it. They trampled through the undergrowth, coming out onto rough road that curved off to the left ahead, towards the logger's yard Adam had spotted on the map. Along the sides of the road sawn tree trunks were stacked high ready for transport, and two large trailers stood empty, no doubt waiting for their next load.

Bob took out a small set of binoculars and looked up towards the yard.

'I can't see him or the car,' he whispered as he scanned around the area and back down the road. 'I can't see round the bend. We need to walk up; stay in the edge, though,' he quietly instructed Adam.

Adam nodded and they tentatively edged up along the side of the road, stopping every few feet so Bob could take a better look through his binoculars.

About fifty feet in: 'Stop.' Bob held his hand up and Adam nearly fell into him. 'I can see a car, right make and model. It must be him,' Bob said excitedly. 'I can't see if he's in the car though, the sun's shining on the windscreen. No sign of Hannah either.'

'Shall I call for back up, sir?' Adam asked, knowing that Bob had already ignored a call from John.

'No.' His answer was short and sharp. 'You really seem to be struggling with who's in charge here. I'm quite capable of taking this dickhead, I don't want the locals messing up my arrest.'

Adam knew Bob wanted the glory and if anything went wrong no doubt that would be squarely placed on Adam's shoulders. 'Yes, sir,' he answered.

'Right, I want you to walk past the car as though you're just a hiker going out on a morning walk, so you can take a closer look,' Bob ordered.

'Erm, but he knows me, because of interviewing him, sir,' Adam answered, relieved that even Bob couldn't dispute that.

Bob huffed. 'Ok, I'll walk up past the car to see if he's there and turn back through woods and come back down to you. Stay here.'

Bob stepped out into the road and walked up towards the car; to Liam he'd just be any other hiker setting out on an early morning walk. He kept a steady pace walking up toward the car and disappeared from Adam's view.

Adam stood watching, his heart racing. This was without doubt the most stupid plan Bob could have come up with – they were completely exposed. If he called John Weaver, he'd be going over Bob's head; Adam could see his career going down the pan but at that moment he was more worried about Bob getting injured, or worse.

He rang Emma; at least he couldn't be accused of breaking the chain of command.

'Are you OK?' she asked.

294

'Yes, yes, I'm fine. We believe we've found the car, it's about fifty feet from where I am. We can't see if Liam or Hannah are there so the boss has walked up to look on his own. I can't see him, he's been gone about five minutes now,' Adam said, wishing he'd called John anyway.

'OK, stay where you are. I've already called John so there's help on the way,' Emma said.

Just as she spoke, Adam heard twigs cracking behind him, and he turned around expecting to see Bob.

Liam was running towards him at speed, with a garden fork held high in the air.

Chapter 95

Liam had been watching the two officers in the woods. He'd parked up in the logger's yard, remembering it from walking there the previous year; he'd wait there as long as he could and then make his way to the cottage. He'd booked it for nine days, the maximum slot available and he'd then need to find somewhere else to go; but for now, it was all he could get. He'd been injured; his face in particular was cut and bruised and his nose broken. In nine days, he needed to find a much better plan to hide and survive – and he needed to get rid of Hannah.

When he arrived at the logger's yard, he'd opened the boot to look at her; she appeared lifeless. He prodded her – no movement – then shut the boot. He'd decided it was time to ditch her, he needed to get away and she was now a liability; he had to put himself first for a change instead of pandering to her needs. He'd done everything for her, and she'd let him down; she'd betrayed him. She meant nothing to him now, the love he had was gone, replaced by resentment and disgust.

He started walking into the woods to find a spot to dispose of her body. The area was protected, and no one should be walking there if they stayed to the paths, so she should be well hidden for a while at least; long enough for him to find his new life somewhere. He'd brought the garden fork he'd found in the barn with him to start digging when he found the right place. Liam moved off the path and walked through in the half-light as the sun came up. He stabbed the ground with the fork as he walked deeper into the woods. The ground was quite hard in places, cooked over the last few weeks by the intense sun, but the deeper in he went, under the canopy of the trees, the softer the ground became; he found a place and started clearing an area ready to dig. Just as he was about to push the fork into the ground, he stopped dead. He heard a very slight sound of people talking. He dropped down and hid behind a stump. He couldn't see them, so he edged closer, keeping low, moving towards the sound, hiding behind the trees as he neared them.

Two men came into view, hiking through the woods; he needed to stay quiet whilst they passed. It was early and he wasn't expecting to see anyone. He'd also need to go further into the woods; he didn't realise the path was so close. He stayed still and silent, watching the men as they neared. When they were a few feet away from him, one of them turned to talk to the other and Liam immediately recognised him – the child PC.

Shit, he thought as he dropped down further, panicking, his heart racing, his hands shaking, and thinking about Hannah in the car; he needed to do something before they found her. They knew he was there; why else would they come? They must have been looking for the car. How on earth did they know which car I'm in, he thought; he'd changed the plates.

He watched them as they walked, stopped, and turned right into the woods. Into the opposite side to where he was hiding. If he sneaked up behind them, could he take them both? Unlikely; he was injured and slower than usual. He thought back to his fight with the caretaker in Wales – he got lucky then. *One at a time, but not both.*

Liam headed back to the car as fast as he could. He held back in the woods, watching the car briefly, trying to look down the road to see if they were approaching. He was just about to get into the car and drive it further along the road into the woods when he heard footsteps on the gravel road, nearing the car. He sank back into the woods, into the shadows and watched the older man walk past the car without breaking speed. This was his opportunity. He checked right to see if the younger officer was behind him, he wasn't there.

Liam ran up behind the man, bringing the fork up in the air and smashing it down hard onto the back of his head. He fell forward like an upright plank and hit the floor. He didn't move and Liam could see blood in his hair. He kicked him; he didn't move. He needed to be quick and deal with the other one. Then he could drag their bodies into the undergrowth and drive somewhere else.

He turned back into the woods and ran down the path to where he'd seen them cut across. He followed the trampled path through the undergrowth and could see the young officer standing looking out into the road up towards the car. He ran towards him just as the officer turned and Liam realised he was on the phone, but it was too late; he was already committed and carried on running. As he brought the fork

297

up and tried to hit him with it, the officer turned away and the fork came down across his back and they both fell into the road.

Chapter 96

Adam hit the floor hard on his front and immediately Liam came down on top of him, his dead weight knocking the wind out of Adam. Liam lost his grip of the fork and it flew forward, landing in front of them just out of reach, the prongs facing towards them. Adam, struggling to breath, tried to reach forward to get it but he couldn't move with the weight of Liam heavy on top of him.

Liam reached forward, scrambling over his body and Adam could see Liam's hands grasping and touching the prongs. Adam struggled beneath him, Liam's weight holding him down. As Liam lifted himself and leant further forward Adam rolled from underneath him and got to his feet.

Liam was on his knees leaning forward, one hand on the floor, the other on the fork. Adam thought about running but instead turned towards him, brought his foot back and kicked him as hard as he could in the stomach.

Liam grunted and dropped forward but his hand moved further up the fork and he got a better hold of it. He rolled onto his back and swung the fork round, and the wooden handle skimmed Adam's shins as he jumped back. Adam toppled backwards and fell again, but quickly turned onto all fours, and sprung forward and upwards.

He shouted, 'Bob, he's here,' but there was no response. Adam had no weapon or protection, he decided to run to where Bob should be; at least there would be two of them to take Liam down. Running towards the car and hopefully towards Bob, he could hear Liam on the gravel behind him swearing and shouting, 'Come here you fucking wanker.'

He spotted Bob up ahead lying face down, motionless. 'Oh god,' he said with despair, 'Bob!' He called out to him, but he didn't move.

He turned and Liam limped towards him. Adam needed to get something between him and Liam and give himself some time until support arrived. He moved towards the stacked tree trunks and ran behind them just as Liam reached the other end and they stood there, momentarily staring at each other. Liam started to limp towards him.

Adam turned, looking for something, anything to defend himself, but his back foot slipped down the embankment, and he tumbled a few feet down. He looked up towards Liam and could see him making his way down and across the embankment towards him, holding onto the trees and shrub branches to stop himself falling, using the fork for support. Panicking, Adam started to climb back up to the top away from Liam. It was only a few feet but as he looked at Liam limping and struggling, he changed his mind and descended further.

'Come here, you fucking little shit!' Liam shouted as he neared him. They were about thirty feet down and Liam was nearly upon him. Adam quickly turned and started climbing back up the embankment to try and get some space between him and Liam; Adam could see his speed was impeded by his injuries. Liam turned towards him and swung the fork, letting it go. It hurtled towards Adam, just missing his body, landing to his side.

Adam fell forward onto his front, banging his forehead on something hard. He was dazed for a moment but managed to push himself up and forward a little, his left hand reaching out to the side and grasping at the fork. His fingers touched the prongs, *just a bit further, nearly there*. He managed to get his fingers around one of the prongs but Liam was now right below him grabbing at his ankles. He pulled him backward down the embankment by his left ankle, thorns and branches scraping against his skin; the fork slipping out of reach. Liam pulled at Adam's ankles, dragging him further down the embankment, he fell forward landing on Adam's legs.

Both men scrambling for the fork to get the advantage, Liam climbed over Adam and got to it first. Within a split-second Liam stood up, straddled Adam and slammed the fork down towards his lower back just as Adam rolled over, throwing Liam off balance, the fork catching the side of Adam's waist as Liam fell backward down the embankment. Adam felt the thud of the fork against his skin; it felt like a punch, he'd missed.

Adrenalin spurred him on and he quickly got back to the top of the embankment, scrambling up, grabbing anything that helped him get back up onto level ground. He looked down and could see Liam climbing back up towards him; he was about fifteen feet below him, fork in one hand. Adam could see Bob up ahead, lying still on the floor. He desperately looked around for something to use as a weapon, there was nothing; branches too small logs too big.

He ran over to Bob – he was alive, but groggy. 'Bob, are you OK? We need to move. Can you stand?'

Bob looked at him; he was concussed and staring blankly. Adam grabbed his jacket by the scruff pulling Bob forward to a sitting position. 'Bob, look at me, we need to move.'

'Adam, are you OK?' he heard Emma shout.

He turned towards her. 'Behind you,' he shouted, but it was too late – Liam's arm came round her from behind and, in a swift motion, he brought the fork up to her throat.

Chapter 97

'Got you, you stupid bitch,' Liam snarled into her ear, his arm wrapped round her chest, trapping her arms; she could feel something hard and cold pressing against her neck. She froze, unable to move, her heart pounding, her eyes darting around, taking stock of anything to help her get away from him.

Adam stood facing her about twenty feet in front. She could see Bob on the floor behind him and the car they'd been looking for to the left of her, a few feet away. She couldn't see Hannah anywhere. *Is she in the car?* she thought. The faint sound of a helicopter was getting closer. *Thank god*, as the thud thud thud of the rotas got louder. She couldn't look up but she knew it was now directly above them, over the small clearing they were stood in, the sound thudding in her ears and the vertical draft swirling the dirt and dust up around them, grit hitting her eyes.

'Liam, stay calm,' Adam said firmly, shouting over the sound of the helicopter. 'Don't make this any worse.'

'You fucking ruined everything, why are you interfering, this is nothing to do with you,' Liam shouted, tightening his grip of Emma; his arm slid up round her neck, choking her and pulling her backwards.

The police helicopter thundered above them.

Liam shouted, 'Get rid of them or I'll fucking kill her.'

'Liam, just stay calm, we can talk this though, just let her go and we can talk,' Adam shouted as he calmly took a step closer to Liam. Emma knew Adam didn't have any hostage negotiation training, but he was doing his best.

'Fuck off, get back,' Liam shouted at him. Adam took a step back. Liam's arm was still around her neck, but he'd released what she now realised was a garden fork. He was holding it at the hilt, waving around and gesturing towards Adam.

'Get rid of it,' Liam shouted.

'OK, OK.' Adam waved his arms in the air towards the helicopter instructing them to move back; the pilot complied and the sound of the rotors dissipated into the distance.

Emma could see a growing red wet stain on Adam's white shirt beneath his jacket as he lifted his arms, blood seeping down to his jeans. He swayed.

Shit he's injured.

'Just us now, Liam, we can just talk, it's OK, let's just talk. How can I help?' Adam said, unsteady on his feet. Emma could see he was losing blood; he swayed again and she could see him trying to keep steady on his feet.

Liam was breathing heavily and jarring Emma as he looked around erratically. He moved towards the car, dragging her backwards, his arms now round her shoulders and chest again, her feet stumbling as he pulled her. 'Get back,' he shouted at Adam who complied a couple of steps.

At the car he stood with his back to it, his arm still around Emma, the fork in his other hand; he couldn't use either hand to open the door, so he dragged Emma away from the car. 'Open it,' he shouted at Adam, indicating for him to go to the car. Adam moved quickly as instructed.

'It's locked,' he shouted back.

'Fuck.' Emma heard Liam in her ear. He moved further backwards away from the car, he paused. Emma could hear and feel the heaviness in his breathing. 'Get back over there,' he ordered; Adam complied.

Liam dragged Emma back to the car. 'Put your hands in my left pocket and get the key,' he ordered Emma, still with his arm around her neck. She did as she was told, her hand scrambling around in his pocket. 'Don't try anything or I'll break your neck.'

Emma found the bunch of keys. She thought about grabbing his balls or stabbing his leg with the keys; his grip tightened on her neck, she pulled the keys out.

'Unlock it,' Liam ordered.

Emma pressed the alarm fob a few times, unable to see what she was doing, and she heard a click and the boot rose up.

'Idiot,' Liam snarled in her ear.

Chapter 98

Adam watched the boot open; Emma had opened it by accident.

'Shut it!' Liam shouted at him, indicating to the boot with his head.

Adam walked as quickly as he could to the car, keeping Liam in his sight. He felt faint and stumbled. He could feel the dampness of his top against his skin and realised Liam must have caught him with the fork. He put his hand down and touched the blood, he looked at his hand, it was soaked.

'Fucking hurry up!' Liam shouted.

He reached the boot and relief hit him; Hannah was curled up inside. His heart lurched – she was motionless. Is she dead? he thought. Before he had a chance to speak, he heard Liam. 'Shut the fucking boot, now.'

He looked back down at Hannah. 'Hannah, the police are here,' he said quietly, as he gently closed the boot.

'Get back over there,' Liam ordered.

Just as he said it, Adam heard, 'Oi!'

Bob had shouted, trying to get to his feet. Liam looked towards Bob, turning and loosening his grip on Emma momentarily. Now was his chance. Adam leapt forward, into Emma and Liam, and they all fell to the ground in a heap.

Adam scrambled on top of Liam, giving Emma enough time to get away, but instead of running she held onto Liam's left arm whilst Adam tried to turn him over onto his front so he could get his arms behind his back.

'Oi,' Bob shouted again, but stayed where he was.

The three of them struggled, Liam on his back, his legs kicking out, Adam straddling him and Emma lay her body over Liam's left arm, pinning it down.

The helicopter was back, the thunder of the rotors filling the air, hovering above them. Liam kicked and struggled under Adam and brought his free hand up, punching Adam's wound and throwing him off sideways into the car. He tried to reach back out to grab Liam, but he'd overcome Emma, dragging her up, back to her feet away from him, holding the fork to her throat again.

'Stay down or I'll fucking kill her,' Liam shouted.

'Mr James, Mr James,' Bob shouted, 'don't do anything rash.'

Adam slumped on the floor looked over at him. He hadn't even tried to help, but now the helicopter was there he was putting on a show.

Liam looked back and forth to Bob and Adam, the fork at Emma's neck.

'Stay there,' Liam shouted, his voice desperate.

'Liam, let her go,' Adam said calmly, 'you're surrounded.' He could feel himself getting weaker. 'Please just let her go,' he pleaded.

'Fucking idiots,' Liam shouted, and he pulled the fork back ready to slam it into Emma's neck.

Crack.

Adam watched as a bullet hit Liam's upper arm, the impact forcing it backwards, he let go of the fork and it fell to the ground. He loosened his grip on Emma and she fell forwards. Liam stumbled into the edge of the woods, he fell backwards with a thud and a look of surprise crossed his face as a root impaled him, through his lower back and protruded out of his stomach. His breathing heavy and laboured and then he was still.

Adam shouted to Emma, 'Hannah,' he said, 'she's in the boot.'

Chapter 99

Emma was aware of armed officers filling the space around them, the sound of sirens getting louder as police descended on the area. She lay Adam down and ordered one of the officers to keep pressure on his wound and another to check Liam. She looked around her and saw the keys on the floor, grabbed them and opened the boot. Hannah was lying motionless, facing upwards, her arms bound in front of her across her chest and her legs tied at the ankles bent up behind her. Bob appeared by her side.

'Oh shit, we're too late,' he said.

'Hannah.' Emma gently touched Hannah's shoulder. 'Hannah, can you hear me?' she said quietly.

Hannah groaned and opened her eyes slightly, looking at Emma.

'Oh, thank god,' Emma said. 'Hannah, you're going to be OK. He can't get you now, you're OK, he can't get you,' she reassured her.

Hannah exhaled as though she'd been holding her breath for a lifetime, the sounds of relief flooding out of her. 'Thank you,' she sobbed.

Within minutes police cars, paramedic bikes, ambulances, cordons, and an array of people waiting and watching gathered in the yard; John arrived within a few minutes and Emma filled him in.

'How's Hannah doing?' he asked.

'They're still working on her, it's touch and go,' she answered. 'She's over there, she's awake, and they're just getting her ready to go, the air ambulance has landed further up in a bigger clearing,' she answered. 'Adam's lost a lot of blood, but they've said he's going to be OK. He saved my life, John.'

John nodded. 'I heard. Where's Bob Moore?' he asked.

'He's over there,' she pointed to where a paramedic was tending to his head.

'OK, I'll deal with him later,' he answered.

They walked towards where the paramedics were working on Hannah. She was surrounded and Emma heard, 'OK, Hannah, you're doing really well, my love, the drugs should be kicking in any second now and the pain will subside.' Hannah came into view and Emma could see her straightened out, lying on a stretcher on the floor. One of the paramedics was holding up a bag of fluid and a drip inserted into her wrist, another was adjusting an oxygen mask on her face and the others were grabbing the gear getting ready to go. She was packed into the stretcher unable to move, ready for the journey to hospital. Emma peered over at Hannah and their eyes met. Hannah held her gaze for a moment as she drifted into a pain-free abyss.

To the side of them paramedics were trying to work out how to move Liam. He was unconscious and still breathing but he was held solidly in place by the branch. John and Emma stood looking at him, this man who'd caused so much pain.

'I hope he dies there,' John said.

'Me too,' said Emma, 'he'll just waste taxpayers' money in prison.'

'Have you been checked out?' John asked.

'Yes, yes, I'm fine, just a few scratches and bruises. I need to get back to my scene now, local SOCO are not as good as my team,' she smiled.

Chapter 100

As she sat in the hospital cafe she wondered how Liam ended up here, having done the most despicable things. Although, deep down she knew, she still asked herself why had he turned out so rotten and sour? At what point in his life did he become so evil, could she have done something to make a difference? She'd seen him earlier in his hospital room, he was awake, cuffed to the bed, waiting to be discharged and taken into custody; likely in a few days. The branch had missed every vital organ and the doctor had said how lucky he'd been. *Lucky?* It angered her to hear the doctor say that. She felt sick to her stomach that he'd survived when so many had perished at his hands. She thought back to Mabel James's diaries, when she'd learnt of the horrors she'd endured; is that where it had started? Years before when a poison had entered the James family bloodstream. She knew what she had to do.

As she passed the nurses' station, Liam came into view through the window of his room; an officer stood outside and she nodded to him as she walked in. Liam wasn't allowed any visitors, except her, she was an exception, and this was her second visit today. He'd tried to talk her round, make her see sense; it wasn't his fault he said, he was in a bad place, he'd been manipulated, they were telling lies about him. She asked him about the people he'd murdered, and he'd dismissed them, tried to change the subject. He felt no remorse, he didn't even acknowledge them, it all felt too familiar. How could he have treated Hannah so badly? She was always a kind soul and he'd taken so much from her. Putting Hannah through a court case was bad enough, he'd already said he'd plead not guilty, but for her to know that that one day, even if it was years later, he may get out, knowing that feeling herself from years before, knowing the pain she'd suffered for years. Well, Hannah would never be able to move on, would she?

She sat down in the hospital chair, she felt calm. She no longer felt any attachment to this man, who was still talking, telling her they were wrong, he hadn't done it, it was a mix up, they were lying, it was a conspiracy. She sat beside him not saying a word, and after a few minutes she stood.

'I'm going now,' she said, knowing this would be the last time she'd see him.

She leant down, kissed him on the lips and stood back. Within a few seconds Liam stared at her in horror when he realised what she'd done and his lips started to swell. The coronation chicken sandwich she'd just eaten said contains peanuts; she knew it would take seconds. She looked at him as his airway closed, the panic on his face, his free hand grasping at his neck, he couldn't call out for help, *no one would come and save him.* She looked at him one last time, without feeling for him, only sadness for everyone he'd hurt.

'Goodbye, Son,' she said, and Edith left the room.

The warmth of freedom fills my heart.
No need to hide.
No need to fear.
No longer a shadow of myself.

No longer feeling like an inconvenience.

And I think to myself.

What a wonderful world.

Chapter 101

Sitting outside the stone-built cottage in Salcombe, North Sands, Devon, Hannah looked down the lane towards the water. She could hear the waves gently lapping against the sea walls and families laughing and chatting in the distance. Seagulls squawked, no doubt eyeing up their targets of left-over BBQ king prawns served at the local restaurant, the Winking Prawn.

The sky was pure azure blue, and the sun was hot and warm on her skin with a gentle breeze brushing over her bare shoulders. She lay back in the sun lounger and watched a grey-haired man slowly walking his dog past the cottage, up a gravelly lane disappearing into woodland.

As she lay there, her feet ached and throbbed from the day's events. She'd got up late, about 9:30am and lazed about the cottage; she'd arrived quite late the evening before in the dark and hadn't had time to explore. When she peered out of the bedroom window in the morning, she realised how close the shoreline was; just a short two-minute walk and she could be dipping her toes in the icy water. She didn't rush though, she had plenty of time for the day's endeavours; no clock to watch, no alarms to set, no rules to follow.

She had a couple of coffees and some cereal, showered, and got dressed for her day; in denim shorts, a black t-shirt and trainers. Hannah walked just under a mile up a steep road to Overbeck, a National Trust house. Her muscles burned just from the short walk, and she wondered how other people less fit and able than her managed to get there. Overbeck was a small manor house set in beautiful grounds overlooking the bays of Salcombe. She meandered through the tropical gardens and took in the gentle scent of flowers and the moisture of the undergrowth. She sat on a bench on her own for a while.

She didn't think about the past.

She didn't think about the future.

She just sat and breathed in the aromas and the view, looking over the treetops to the sea watching it gently undulate. She listened to the birds singing, and watched bees going about their busy day. She could hear the rustle of the tall bamboos; they whispered as the wind brushed against their leaves.

After a short tour of the manor house, she walked down to the beach cafe she'd passed on the way up and had a chicken and bacon sandwich with lots of mayo, a bag of cheese and onion crisps, and an Americano coffee with milk. She savoured every mouthful and watched the land ferry preparing to start a new trip across the bay. She finished eating and without looking at her watch she wandered over, paid, and took her place in line. A family waiting with her had a fluffy and very friendly black Sproodle that she petted whilst she chatted to the dog's owner. Sandra who was there with her mother Jean, daughter Emily, granddaughter baby Leah and Frankie the dog; a girl's holiday, she said.

Hannah stepped onto the ferry taking a seat near the front. As it departed North Sands, she took photos of the beach and the lane up to the little cottage she was staying in. It was such a still and perfect day as the ferry gently bobbed along its route to Salcombe; the water spray occasionally splashing her face. She took in the soothing sea air and let the breeze wash over her as she settled into her new adventure.

Once she'd disembarked at Salcombe, she wandered through the lanes, looking in the shops and galleries. She bought some vanilla fudge for later and had a honeycomb ice cream with a flake and chocolate-dipped cone, which melted quickly in her hand. She sat on a bench eating her ice cream by the wall looking out to the sea, watching the boats bob around; some tied up and some sailing in and out of the bay.

She looked across the estuary to the houses on the other side with beautiful settings and private beaches. Hannah thought about the people living in the expensive houses, with their private beaches and no doubt wealth, but Hannah didn't feel any jealousy; she had everything she needed. She smiled as she watched families ambling along the lanes, of all ages, each with their own rich tapestries of their lives.

When Hannah had finished her ice cream she continued along the narrow lanes as they twisted and turned through the shops; the sun had brought everyone out and Salcombe was busy, but it was a gentle busy. No one was rushing, no one was arguing or shouting, no one was impolite as they stepped aside for each other. She could hear chatter and laughter and she watched proud mothers and fathers tending to their babies and children. She watched older couples, young families, groups of girls and boys and individuals like her, meandering along as she did. She chatted to the owners of the shops and galleries, finding out a bit more about the area. In one of the gift shops, she found a cute ornament of a sheep. She just liked it – no particular reason – so she bought it.

She looked at a few of the menus in the restaurants and pubs; either for tonight or later in the week. One of them, The Ferry Inn had a garden looking over the estuary. It looked nice, so she ordered herself a pink gin and tonic which arrived adorned with mint, lime and juniper berries. She sat in the garden at a large wooden table and drank it slowly, savouring every sip and watched life go by. Kayakers, paddle boarders and boaters; maybe she'd try one of those tomorrow.

She finished her drink and as she wandered around, she passed a Co-op, so she bought a few bits and pieces; not too much and nothing too heavy. It was a trek back to the cottage, so just enough to carry and see her through for a day or two. She walked back along the coastal road, past the Winking Prawn and back to her cottage where she now lay on a lounger reading a book in the sun; her feet throbbing, over 14,000 steps already today, and she didn't know if she was staying in tonight or going out yet.

She didn't need to make any decisions, and she didn't need to wait to be told what to do. She just sat in her lounger and enjoyed the peacefulness, the calm, and the relaxation. The events of the past year, although forever etched in her psyche, were a long way from where she was now. She'd received a lot of therapy and she'd had some very dark times, with what felt like a continuous stream of nightmares and panic attacks, but now she was in a good place; she felt in control, she felt calm, she felt happy. She'd reconnected with her parents and family and even her dad, who never showed any emotion, cried when he visited her in hospital, and her mum called her nearly every day over the past twelve months.

Hannah had inherited quite a bit when Liam died; he hadn't made a will, but as next of kin it all went to Hannah, and he had a lot more than she thought. At first, she didn't want any of it, but Rachel, Emma and even Liam's mother Edith, had convinced her. She'd met Rachel and Emma when she'd been transferred after a week in Cumbria to a hospital nearer to home so her parents could visit, and Emma and Rachel had also come to see her a few times. They'd told her about Liam attacking Rachel, and how Adam's heroic efforts had saved Emma and earnt him a commendation.

Apparently, the officer who was with Emma when she opened the boot of the car Hannah was in had been reported to professional standards and had been demoted a couple of ranks. Rachel said, 'It was for being a complete and utter twat and I'm looking forward to the day he is on my team reporting into me.'

They also let her know who the man was in Wales that Liam had killed. Hannah told them she would never forget the image of him lying there covered in blood. Hannah had also clarified to police that Liam had bragged about killing Lucy and Judith. The police had then found half a fingerprint on Lucy's suicide note, matching Liam's; Lucy's parents were informed, bringing them closure that Lucy hadn't killed herself.

After Hannah left hospital, she met Rachel and Emma for coffee in Lichfield, and they soon became firm friends. They all cried together with John at Judith's memorial, and they helped her laugh again when Rachel invited her to BBQs and movie nights at her house, and they'd hit the town on her first girl's night out in years.

Hannah knew Emma had been there and opened the boot and saved her, but they'd never talked about it, they didn't need to. She'd never forget the kindness in her voice and the caring in her eyes. She'd also met Adam at one of Rachel's BBQs and he hugged her when they met, a knowing, lingering hug; he was kind of cute, she'd thought. She knew about Rachel's relentlessness to find her, and she would be grateful to them all forever. Without all three of them, she wouldn't be alive, and without Judith she'd never be sitting where she was now. She missed Judith and wished she could spend just a few more minutes with her, to thank her, to hug her. But she always felt Judith's strength within her.

Liam had taken so much from her, and Rachel and Emma had said why shouldn't she take the money? It took some convincing but once she'd made the decision, she knew she would put it to good use. Her cottage holiday was just the start, and her trip was research for her new adventure; she was now working with the charity Judith had set up and she wanted to provide free holidays for abused men, women, and children. She was in Salcombe looking for somewhere she could buy. She wasn't sure yet where to buy or what, and she'd given herself permission to enjoy a few weeks travelling round to different areas to find the perfect place.

Although Salcombe was clearly an area where the wealthy holidayed, she thought it was starting to look pretty good for her holiday retreat to be set up. Why shouldn't those who use the charity benefit from such a beautiful place?

Hannah started to nod off in her lounger; maybe she'd just stay in tonight and relax. She'd never felt such peace. It was an unfamiliar feeling, freedom. It was hers, that's all she needed, and she was never letting it go again.

Milton Keynes UK
Ingram Content Group UK Ltd.
UKHW010646080724
445166UK00004B/134

9 781068 667909